Kentucky Cowboy

by Marlene Worrall

- **ISBN-10:** 1979554757
- **ISBN-13:** 978-1979554756

DEDICATION

This book was inspired by the late Steve Worrall, horse
enthusiast and polo player.

ACKNOWLEDGEMENTS

Thank-you to the kind staff at Palm Desert Library for their valuable assistance with technical issues.

.

Chapter 1

Dana's cell chirped just as she was settling into her office and sipping her morning coffee. A number she didn't recognize flashed on her screen. *I bet it's a call on my new listing...Sugarbush Stables. The sign just went up but I know it's a hot listing.* A caller was on her cell. "Dana Lockhart, Lockhart Realty." She put a smile into her voice as she spoke.

"Graham Van Rensellier. I'm calling about Sugarbush Stables. Ah was drivin' around and just spotted the new sign." The man's voice was husky, his accent Southern. The timbre of his voice held power. Whoever he was, she would bet he was a force to be reckoned with.

"Ah'd like to view the property at your earliest convenience." His voice seemed to waiver somehow, making him sound almost vulnerable.

Dana played by the rules. Ever since an acquaintance of hers had been murdered at a showing on a remote ranch, she'd been cautious. Roger, her sometime partner, usually accompanied her on showings, but when he was out-of-town, as he was now, she usually went solo but always left a phone number, location and the time she expected to return to her office. She shook her head. Lame. If something ever did go wrong, tracking her down after the fact would be a useless exercise. It would probably be too late. Still, none of life came with a guarantee; that was a certainty. And she needed to sell property for her financial survival.

Since giving her heart to the Lord a few years back, she prayed every morning for wisdom, leading, guidance and protection. *"In all your ways acknowledge him, and he shall direct your paths."* She was proud to say that she lived by that adage.

"Please come into my office if you would, Mr. Van Rensellier." She glanced swiftly through her appointment book. "Should we say 3:00 this afternoon?"

Silence. Soon the rich, powerful voice was back on the line. "That works, Ms. Lockhart. If there are any other fine horse farms in your area, perhaps we could view those as well."

"How soon do you need to get in?" Dana was a born closer. She never lost an opportunity to inch closer to a sale.

Silence again. When he finally spoke, his voice seemed sad. Distant. "I...I guess as soon as possible, because mah boys need to get settled into a local school before September."

Bingo. This guy's a serious buyer. Time will be of the essence for him. But what about his wife? There had been no mention of her. Women's intuition told her not to go there.

Dana walked out of her office and into the receptionist area. Georgia was poised on her chair, her long legs crossed in front of her. She wore a short skirt as usual. She was filing her long, fake red nails and alternately admiring them. A clever girl, she was, however, overly fixated on her nails and hair. The dye jobs changed frequently. Currently the hair was bouffant with red and blond streaks. Still, she was by far the best assistant Dana had ever had.

"Georgia, Hon... would you pull the file on Pale Horse Ranch? You know...that new exclusive out on Langley Road..."

"Will do..." She swirled in her chair and reached into the file drawer.

"That eccentric owner is always changing his mind...but one of these days I'm going to bring him an offer he can't resist and finally collect the commission." Dana stood next to Georgia, waiting for her to pull the file.

"I'm surprised you put up with him." Georgia shook her head, as she pulled the file from a nearby cabinet.

"Well, Georgia, we both know how difficult it is to get good listings. Everybody wants to buy...nobody wants to sell ranch land right now... and when they do, they want outrageous prices..."

Georgia handed Dana a copy of the exclusive listing. She took it back to her office, studied it and called for an appointment to show the properties. She would plan to show Sugarbush at 3:00 and Pale Horse Ranch around 4:30 to 5:00. She always left ample time between appointments when showing ranch properties; between the time needed for viewing and driving. She was often late even at that.

Dana and Georgia munched corn-beef sandwiches at their desk. A few other realtors stopped into the office, milled around in the Bull Pen, worked on the computer and checked the blackboard for new listings. A few realtors were on the phone. They would soon roar off in their fancy cars. Dana only has twenty-two realtors. Still, her company had quickly risen in the ranks and was the number one successful company in the area, based on the number of realtors and sales per year. This was due in no small part by the fact that Dana Lockhart was known and highly respected in the horsey circles.

Betty's Burgers across the street made delicious soups and tasty sandwiches. Georgia fetched and Dana often picked up the tab. Dana thrived selling ranches in horse country. It was second only to being active as a jumped. She was glad she'd taken the extra classes and earned her Broker's license. Being in control was her "go-to" mode of operation. *Too bad she wasn't in control of her love life. That was some fiasco, after that last beau.*

Dana took care of some personal business on the phone and then settled down with her sandwich and coffee to review the details on both ranch listings in preparation for the meeting and showings with the new client.

Dana glanced out her office window. A late model or brand new white Jeep was swinging into the parking lot in front of the office. A sizeable man was at the wheel. It looked like two boys were in the back seat.

Dana glanced at her watch. 1:45. This must be her 2:00 appointment. Mr. Van Rensellier was fifteen minutes early. That was a good sign. *He's a serious buyer. I feel it in my gut.* She'd learned fast how to ferret out the "Looky-Lou's" from the "Real McCoys." Something told her Graham was definitely in the latter category.

The burly guy stayed in his car for a few minutes. He turned to the back seat, probably talking to the young lads. Soon, a pair of sassy-looking, tawny-haired boys jumped out of the back door of the jeep. In synchronicity. A tall, broad-shouldered man in a short sleeved floral sports shirt stepped out of the Jeep and herded his sons to walk like young gentleman, as they joined him.

What a hunk, Dana's mind raced. Her heart beat faster. Mr. Van Rensellier, assuming it was him, was a gorgeous hunk of a man. Looks like he'd brought his sons with him. The trio strode into the real estate office. Dana watched from her vantage point in her office through louvered blinds, undetected from the outside. She would wait in her office until Georgia announced her 2:00 PM appointment had arrived.

~

Graham was apprehensive about uprooting his sons; though he'd carefully thought through the plan to start a new life here in horse country. The only way he could emotionally move on and heal from the traumatic years of watching his beloved Myrna slowly ebb away; was to remove himself from everything and everyone that reminded him of her. If he threw himself into the work on the ranch, as well as raising his sons, he would get through it one day at a time. *"One day at a time, Sweet Jesus, that's all I'm asking from you."* The words of that old gospel song he'd heard as a child, rang in his heart and mind, encouraging him. *How does anyone get through this life without God?* If he could not lean on the Everlasting Arms, he wouldn't make it through another day; that much he knew. He drew all his strength from the Good Book.

He'd owned race horses in the past that had been kept on a ranch in Kentucky. His dream was to have a winning racehorse. He dreamed about winning the Kentucky Derby. He and Myrna had travelled every year to the Derby for ages. Now that she was gone, it seemed like all he had left on this earth was his passion for the equines, horse country and his beloved sons. It only made good sense to move here.

Two high-stakes winners to his credit were a start. He and Myrna had owned many thoroughbreds over the years. They had been farmed out here over the years. Currently, he just had one farmed out in the area. If he bought a horse farm, naturally that racehorse would move onto it.

Graham frequented the Stakes races in Keenland. A couple of years ago, he brought his sons to the races and they'd become bitten by the horse bug, also. Would they become ranchers? Would they eventually become involved in the stakes races at Keenland the way he had? There was just one way to find out. He had to give them exposure. Move them onto a ranch. He was burnt out as a commercial real estate investor and broker. It was time to move on.

Horses were in his blood and his sons inherited his passion. Yes, moving from Texas to Kentucky was the absolute right decision. It was late June. The weather was hot and sultry, just the way he liked it.

~

Georgia was usually bored with her reception duties. But today she was jolted into paying attention. The handsome gentleman standing in front of her desk stood well over six feet, his broad shoulders practically bursting out of the floral shirt he wore. The man wasn't wearing a wedding ring, but that didn't mean anything. A lot of men didn't. He sported a fine gold cross at his throat. His vivid blue eyes were intelligent and piercing. They were laced with humor and...maybe a tinge of sadness. The man was deeply tanned. She sensed that he was suffering terribly.

What a powerful presence the man had. When he walked into a room, he seemed to fill it. Georgia flashed a professional smile, after the impressions had flashed through her brain. "Graham Van Rensallier, right?" It was touch flirtatious. Georgia knew how Dana hated it when she did that; but Dana wasn't here. She was coyly waiting in her office to be notified that her client had arrived. *Relax, girl, there's doubtless a little woman somewhere. Guys like him are never single. Give your head a shake* ."Please have a seat, Mr. Van Rensallier. I'll let Ms. Lockhart know you're here." She smiled again at him, all quite unnecessary she knew. *The man looks out of place with those long legs stretched out in front of him. He was much too large for the club chair he sat in. He didn't look comfortable.*

His sons were obviously fascinated by the goldfish swimming gleefully around in the fish tank. They stood next to the glass case, riveted to it. "Wow, aren't they somethin', Jay?" Will was enthralled like his brother.

"Ya... I wish we had goldfish. Do you think Dad would let us get some?"

"Why not? As long as it keeps us out of mischief, right?" He grinned mischievously at his brother.

Georgia could spot expensive clothes a mile off, fashion diva that she was. The guys all wore Top-siders and the finest T-shirts and jeans out there. Big bucks. No doubt about it.

~

Dana Lockhart smiled confidently as she strode across the room, extending her hand in greeting to Graham Van Rensallier. "Dana Lockhart. So very nice to meet you," The greeting was routine; but what wasn't routine were the powerful emotions welling up inside her upon the impact of meeting this...incredibly sexy hunk of a man. The room seemed to sway. His presence had an intoxicating effect on her. The impact was startling...frightening, even.

Graham was by far the most appealing, striking man she had ever encountered. His vivid blue eyes seemed to look right through her. She caught a slight whiff of shaving lotion or some other fresh male scent. Maybe he had splashed on a tangy, masculine cologne. Whatever it was, it set her head to spinning.

The man downright jolted her. It was as though she'd just been aroused from a long, deep sleep. Like a bear in hibernation, maybe. His presence was just that powerful. *I hope I can concentrate on showing property and take my eyes off him!*

Twenty-nine wasn't old. But Dana wanted to be married like her best friend, Jan fields. She had dated a fair number of guys since breaking up with her college sweetheart, but she had never met one like this guy. She almost had to give her head a shake. *Oh right, he's here to do business. He's going to buy a ranch from me, I hope. And, of course his wife just can't be bothered looking at the ranch. I bet it's a second or third property anyway, by the looks of this guy.*

"Please, Mr. Van Rensallier, come into my office, won't you." She was almost shaking with the intensity of the impact the man had on her. Soon Graham was seated across from her in a leather chair in her spacious office. She sat at her desk and began her usual qualifying process. Buyers were looking for certain types of ranches and most had budgets and/or specific criteria. She didn't want to waste their time or hers. His sons stood protectively by their Dad. Well-behaved. Silent. They listened with interest. They seemed to digest her every word like a sponge soaking it up.

She had to focus on the task at hand and forget about the tremendous appeal of the man and the charm of his cute, young sons. She wouldn't be gauche enough to inquire about his status. That would come up soon enough.

It did.

Graham started talking to her as though he'd known her for ages. "Mah wife died...jest under a year ago...I want to start a new life here with mah sons...I want to raise them on a ranch and teach them to love horses...like ah do."

"Do you have a property to sell before you can buy?" Dana asked, determined to qualify the man, and not be deterred because of his charisma and good looks.

"No, Ma'am... I'll...I'll be...ah... keepin' the house in Houston."

"How soon do you want to get settled onto a ranch?" Dana's eyes travelled over him and she had to admit she *loved* what she saw. Was *he* looking at her with interest, too? Or was that just wishful thinking on her part? *Get a grip, Dana. The man has just lost his wife. He's grieving, no doubt.*

"As soon as possible. Ah want to get mah sons settled before school starts in September."

"Okay, so you need to be reasonably close to the elementary school. That would be Langley Road School. It's not too far from either of the ranches we'll be viewing today. I've gone ahead and set up the viewing appointments, but I did want to meet with you first. Incidentally, there's a new sports centre near the Langley school, as well. I'm sure that would be of interest to you and your sons."

Dana wasn't going to waste another minute qualifying him. He was the real deal. They didn't get any better than this guy. *Or was she missing something? Was it all too good to be true?* "The owners of both properties will be present, and that's a distinct advantage when it comes to ranches. Former ranchers have often given a hand to the new owners, and of course they are very knowledgeable about their ranch."

Sugarbush Stables was spread out over fifty-five acres of green, rolling hills. The property was mostly fenced, consisting of corals, a thirty stall horse barn and an old Southern mansion that needed some work. It was Colonial, and featured grand pillars at the entrance. The property came with several buildings, including a two-bedroom and den guest house.

Dana wheeled her white Mercedes SUV down the long road leading to the rambling old mansion. Graham and his sons followed in the Jeep.

Dana heard the muffled sound of a neighing horse in the barn. A pair of Shepherd dogs barked their greeting as she stepped out of her vehicle.

Graham and his sons joined her, minutes later.

Dana spotted a couple of Quarter horses milling around near the long, white fence. An Appaloosa grazed near them in a corral. Beyond the long white fence, which faded into the distance, were a dozen or more horses grazing lazily on the rolling, green hills of Bluegrass country. The sun cast it's sparkly, bright rays over the sprawling ranch, giving it a warm and inviting look.

Sidney Shaw, owner of Sugarbush Ranch was commiserating with one of his Thoroughbreds behind the fence as she drove up. Dana stepped out of her vehicle. "Good afternoon, Mr. Shaw, so nice to see you." She shook his hand, smiling.

"Likewise, Dana. You look mighty fine. Already bringin' me a buyer? You work fast. I'm mighty impressed."

A God-incident, no doubt. Dana didn't believe in coincidences. Everything existed from the hand of God. Every blessing was from the Almighty.

Graham had stopped his jeep behind her SUV. His precocious sons jumped out of the back of the vehicle in synchronicity again.

Seems like they have a sense of humor. Dana made the introductions.

"How about if I tag along on the showing, Dana? There's bound to be some questions. The ink is barely wet on the listing, after all. You haven't had much time to check out everything." Sid Shaw grinned, the creases around his pale blue eyes in his weathered, deeply tanned skin deepened.

"I was hoping you would say that, Sid. Nobody knows this ranch better than you do." Dana smiled at her new seller. He was already heading toward the sizeable barn. Dana and her new clients trailed him.

~

Well over an hour later, Graham and his sons had had the grand tour. "Thanks so much for all the information. I appreciate it," Graham shook hands with Sid, grinning.

"Wow, isn't this place amazing? It would be so cool to learn to ride those Thoroughbreds, Jay." Will grinned at his brother.

"They're not all thoroughbreds, you know," Jay was adamant about it. "Some of 'em are Quarter Horses and... I spotted an appaloosa."

"You don't know anything about horses." Jay kicked a cluster of small rocks on the ground to emphasize his point. "Anybody can spot an appaloosa, they're so..like...distinct... with that light... mottled coloring of grey and white..."

"How much you wanna bet I'll learn more about horses faster than you do?" Will challenged his brother.

"You're on Will." Jay smirked.

Sid Shaw snickered. "I think the young lads are smitten with the horses. The wife and I are gettin' a little old to work a farm of this size. We're goin' to retire to about five acres closer to the city. We probably should have sold years ago...that big house will come alive with the young lads..."

"How many ranch hands do you have? We only saw one." Graham peered around at the property as he followed Sid.

"Well, they come and go. We had two just last week. Phil was a drifter—a good man, but he never stays in one place very long. Yup, we git some real interestin' types out here on these ranches." He grinned, his eyes crinkling at the edges. The man had a real deep tan. You sure could tell he was an outdoors man.

"Thanks fer lookin' at the place, Graham. It's a real good farm. If you decide to put an offer and we can make a deal; I'd be real happy to give you a hand gettin' into the routine of ranchin'—since, as you say, you're new to this game."

"Well, I might just take you up on that. That's a mighty generous offer...and one ah won't rule out. And, by the way...since you're scaling down, will you be selling those quarter-horses? What about the thoroughbreds? How many of them are you thinking to bring with you?"

They were walking from the barn toward the house. Dana hadn't mentioned the horses, because Sid hadn't been clear on what he intended to do. Maybe it would depend on how much he liked the buyers. If he were to include the horses, or some of them, he'd want to make sure they would be well cared for by the new owners, and be clear on factoring in their value.

"After Dana tours you through the house and guest house... and if you decide to make an offer, maybe we can chat about the horses. They mean a lot to me and I would want to make sure they are well cared for. I get a good feelin' about you and your sons...maybe we can work somethin' out...because I won't be able to keep all of them at the new place I'm buyin'."

They had reached the mansion. "Dana knows the house real well. Maybe the wife and I will set on the back porch and she can give you the grand tour."

The boys were excited. "Wow, Dad...a real Southern mansion...like in *Gone With the Wind.*" Jay exclaimed. Jay and Will glanced around in awe. "Our grandparents live in a mansion, you know. But it's...contemporary...not antebellum like this one." Will enjoyed flaunting his knowledge.

Graham grinned. His sons were growing up. He loved them so much his heart ached. He wanted to be extra good to them because of the sorrow they'd had to endure with losing their Mom at such tender ages.

Dana loved houses, especially grand ones. Showing this Turn-of-century mansion was a real treat. Thrilling, actually. Properties like this one didn't come on the market very often. *I think Graham and his sons and this property is a match made in heaven.*

A couple times Graham had to restrain his sons. They wanted to run off and explore the old mansion on their own "We're all going to stay together, boys. It's a grand home and enormous. Dana will point out the features as we tour it..." Graham grinned. He was happy. He liked the place, and his sons seemed to be enthralled with it

Graham and Sid shook hands after the viewing. Sid waved as he strode back to the old mansion and Graham ambled over to his Jeep. He glanced around for his sons and discovered they were peering, fascinated at a couple of goats behind a coral. "Bah...Bah...Bah..." they cried.

"Time to go, sons" Graham stepped into the jeep.

The boys immediately obeyed their father and headed toward the Jeep, but they kept looking back in fascination at the goats.

~

Sid Shaw and Graham Rensallier definitely clicked, Dana decided. *That's a good start. I've known of more than one deal that went sour because the owners just didn't want the new buyer to live on their ranch. Folks get real emotionally involved when they spend years building a fine ranch like this one. Not to even mention the horses. I know all about it.*

"Okay— onward to Pale Horse Ranch. I'll lead the way." Dana slipped behind the wheel of her white Mercedes SUV.

Graham strode up to Dana's vehicle. He peered over at her, grinning. "Odd name... Pale Horse Ranch... wonder how that name came about?"

"There's a little story behind it..."

"Well?" His sons were still peering at the animals with fascination. Graham stood outside the window of the driver's seat of her SUV. "The former owner was part Indian. He bred and raised Palominos and Cremellos. Cremellos are champagne colored with blue eyes, as you may know." She glanced toward the two boys who stood protectively next to their dad and listened intently as Dana talked about the horses.

"We know how Palominos look," Will's tone was proud. "They're golden colored... with white tails and manes."

"That's absolutely right." Dana smiled. "The new owner continues to breed those pale-colored horses, so the name stuck."

"Makes sense. So, between both breeds, how many

horses does he have?" Graham gazed directly into her eyes. They were a vivid shade of green with some turquoise thrown in. He conceded that she was a gorgeous woman. He would have to be blind not to see it.

"Twenty-two." Dana was a touch nervous. Graham made her feel that way. "He has a twenty stall barn. The ranch is a little over sixty acres."

A unique goat nuzzled up to the fence, "Bah...bah..." It was brown with white blotches and had an odd, curly horn. He seemed to saying good-bye to his visitors.

Dana stopped her SUV in the driveway of Pale Horse Ranch. Graham parked his Jeep behind her vehicle. She glanced over at the vast, rolling green acreage, the white fenced fields and dozens of horses scattered throughout the acreage. She was glad she'd had her hair colored. It was a bright blond instead of the natural ash color growing in at the roots. *Lord, never in my life did I want to look as good as I want to look now. Graham caused her pulse to quicken whenever she was around him.*

"Good-afternoon, Mr. Connors," Dana shook Jake Connor's hand.

Jake was an enormously tall, rangy man—a Cherokee Indian. Long black hair and long-limbed, he wore cowboy boots, well-worn jeans and a red Western shirt. He was maybe around sixty...perhaps older. The house was a rambling rancher. It had been amateurishly updated. Dana knew it wasn't desirable in many respects. Of course a new owner could always build. The property was desirable.

Jake's wife, Lorna, was pleasant looking but very

thin and oddly silent. Too silent. Even when the listing had been signed, she'd served everyone coffee but had not uttered a word. Dana had tried to strike up a conversation with her on several occasions, but had failed. Lorna always wore the same colors Jake wore. She remained in the kitchen sipping coffee from a mug, while Dana toured Graham and his sons through the house. Jake appeared and disappeared during the showing as though nervous or apprehensive about the showing or something else.

Chapter Two

Graham sat opposite Dana in her office.

Dana could feel his wheels turning a mile a minute
It was fun doing business with Graham

"There's no comparison, Dana. Sugarbush with that great, old colonial mansion is far superior to Pale Horse ranch—though I certainly see your point about the beautiful property. Of course, I would have to build a new house and frankly, I'm not into that project at the moment. I wouldn't be happy living in the house; nor would mah sons."

"No, of course you wouldn't" She smiled and peered into his piercing eyes. *I knew he was rich and spoiled. That statement proves it.* Dana nodded.

"So...do you want to put an offer on Sugarbush?" Dana smiled, knowingly.

"Yes." Graham's face was sombre. "I'm just not sure how much I should offer." Dana guessed it was an emotional time for him, based on everything he'd told her.

"I can certainly help you there. In fact, I just

18

happen to have a file with comparable listings that have recently sold, with similar properties." The file was on her desk, ready to be perused by clients. She turned the file toward Graham. "The first property sold three months ago and it is probably the best comparison...as you likely know, a comparable consists of a similar property, similar in acreage, area, buildings and the main house. There is a separate file for the horses and the details of the breeds. That, of course, is the most complex aspect of the sale of a horse farm. And, of course, no two horse farms are identical. Just as no two horses are identical."

"However, you will see what the owner paid on Wild Horse Ranch which sold three months ago. Keep in mind the house was nowhere near as marvelous or as stately as the colonial on Sugarbush..."

Dana hadn't expected Graham to be so tough. She had expected that since he was new to the area and had never owned a horse farm, he would rely heavily on her judgement. She soon discovered how wrong she was.

"I'm not so sure the grand house at Sugarbush is a plus...I mean, generally, in the market. I admit it is for me, because I intend to have some staff...like an assistant, maybe a nanny and a cook. If I get involved with horses to the extent that I'd like to..."

"I won't tell you you're wrong. Graham. Most folks don't want or need a house that large...and one with a guest house. By the way, what do you plan to do with the guest house? Rent it out?"

"I guess so. Though I'm not sure how easy it would be to rent. What do you think?"

"There's a buyer for every property. And there's a renter for every rental. I'm just not sure how soon you would find a renter that would suit you..."

"I'll cross that bridge when I get to it." Graham grinned.

Dana's heart lurched. .

Graham studied the comparables. Dana studied him. *Gorgeous. The man is really gorgeous. An absolute hunk.*

~

Specializing in ranch properties, Dana had settled on her daily attire. Growing up on a ranch, she had been a professional horsewoman; both a jumper and trainer. But after her younger brother was killed doing a Show jump, she was traumatized. She stopped jumping overnight. She was never able to resume her passion for training horses, either. Something inside her died that day, along with her only sibling. She had loved him deeply. She'd quit the horse world and gotten into real estate then. That was four years ago. Restlessness was settling in. She wasn't in her right place in life. God had something better for her. She was sure of it. She longed to be back in the saddle again. Needed to live on a ranch, the way people needed air to breathe.

Her well-worn cowboy hat was a throw-back to the horsey activities she'd been involved with since her early teens. The hat had been expensive. She wore belted designer jeans that fit her like a glove. Riding and jumping had kept her fit and fabulous. She had great pride in her appearance and watched her diet carefully.

Okay, so she had about ten pairs of similar jeans in her closet. A girlfriend once asked her why she had so many pairs of identical or almost identical jeans. "Who would know whether you're wearing the same pair or another pair from your collection?" she'd asked. "*I* would know," Dana had replied, without skipping a beat. She'd grinned at her friend, Clara. Clara just shrugged. She didn't get it. That's okay.

Dana's cowboy boots had seen better days, but they were so comfortable, so she just kept right on wearing them. She stood about 5' 7." God had blessed her with a willowy figure. She had won a couple of beauty contests when she was a teenager. Still, she wondered if Graham was attracted to her. He'd given her no signal of his interest, thus far.

The pricey white linen shirt she wore was tucked into the belted jeans. That choice of clothing had become akin to a uniform. She'd worn a scarlet jacket and white breeches during her years as a Show Jumper. Now, specializing in the sale of horse farms, she'd devised the equivalent of a uniform; a closet stuffed with white linen shirts with a few pink linen ones thrown in for variety. That was her summer wardrobe. In winter she stayed with the same colors in sweaters. Shopping was not her thing, and this kept her life simple and organized, she never had to worry about coordinating clothing.

Chapter Three

Dana drove up to her rented cottage in town, made some iced tea and speed dialed her Mom's phone number on her ground line. They'd always been close. "Mom, you're not going to believe this, but this really great guy from Houston put an offer on Sugarbush. There's a guest house there and he suggested I rent it and move my horses onto the property. That would be heaven. But Mom, I've got a big crush on him...and sometimes his sons seem to resent me...like whenever he pays me too much attention, for instance. I told him I wouldn't consider it for professional reasons. People talk."

"Stop worrying about what people think. Have you prayed about this? Have you asked God what his take is?"

She felt foolish. She couldn't lie to her mom. "No..."

"Well, honey, that's the whole reason you don't have any peace about this. You won't until you settle it with God. Actually, it sounds like a fit of circumstances made in heaven." Danielle chuckled.

"Well, that's just it, Mom. It's too easy...and I don't like the idea of being in such close proximity with him either..."

"Why not? What are you afraid of? That you might fall in love? That he might do the same?"

"Mom, I honestly don't know what I'm afraid of. I guess, if the truth be known, I don't like the idea of being so available...by living in such close proximity. If the man ever becomes interested in me, he knows where to find me." Dana always felt better after she'd shared everything with her Mom.

"You know what I think?" Danielle knew her daughter.

"No, but I bet you're goinna tell me."

Danielle paused. "I think you're smitten with this guy and you're afraid that you might fall deeply in love with him..."

"Oh, Mother. Give it a rest. Besides...that would be a huge waste of time on my part...if I did become smitten with him... because he's already declared that he will never remarry. He has... this... incredible loyalty to Myrna, his deceased wife."

"Guys have been known to change their minds, despite earnest resolves, you know."

"Not this guy. I've never met a man as stubborn as he seems to be; nor as adamant about not getting involved with another woman or remarrying. He insists he's going to throw himself into the racehorses and raising his sons, to the exclusion of everything else... well, except God, I guess."

The minute the owner of Sugarbush had toured them through the guest house, Dana had been struck with a bizarre and unique idea. She might as well share it with her Mom. She'd find out anyway. "Mom, you know I've never felt settled in my rented cottage. You did the right thing selling the acreage after dad died; but..."

"Honey, let me guess...you miss training the horses...and jumping...I know you thought you could live without it. But Dana, it's like air to you. I...know how traumatic it was for you to lose your brother...not a day goes by without my thinking about him. But honey, horses are your life...you do need to get back to them...they're in your blood. Not having them is like...not breathing for you. Though, I must say, they haven't always brought us luck."

"Mom, I gave up the life of a trainer and show jumper...and yes, I yearn to be back on a ranch again. Riding *is* in my blood. I thought I could shake it off and move on. It's been almost three years since the accident. But...my passion for horses has not subsided...in fact... it's begun to dominate my mind. I need to live on a ranch again...but they're so darn expensive..."

"I don't know what the big deal is, Dana. The guy needs a renter...you want to live on a ranch. It's a no-brainer. Maybe...you could give riding lessons to his sons to sweeten the pot."

"I don't know, Mom. I might fall in love with him...and he's spelled out the fact that he's dedicated to his sons...and isn't ever going to remarry..."

"Don't listen to what he *says*. Watch what he *does*. Look, honey... why don't you tell him you'll try it for three months. Ask him to give you a month-to-month rental..."

~

Back at the office, Graham makes an offer on Sugarbush. "I would need to build I bought Pale Horse Ranch, and I'm just not into that project right now. I love the horse set-up...and the Palominos are beauties...but I need a traditional farm, Dana. And since I will be hiring a housekeeper/cook, the extra space will be useful. Also, my sister, Sybil comes to visit...and I like the idea that I have a potential revenue property on the farm, as well." Graham was relaxed as he drank a cup of coffee in Dana's office. He rattled on and was happy.

With the signed offer in hand, Dana drove back to the ranch and presented it to the owners that evening. Sid countered. Negotiations went on for three days. Finally an accepted offer was in place. Graham was in Dana's office when she learned his last counter-offer had been accepted.

"Congratulations, Graham. You bought yourself a fine ranch." She shook hands with him and gave him a copy of the accepted offer, as soon as the fax came through. "I must say, your timing was superb. Sugarbush would not have stayed on the market for long. I know at least two other buyers that have had their eye on that property for some time now. I would have called them if you hadn't moved so quickly on this. Real estate is all about timing, as I'm sure you know. Yours was superb." Dana smiled, sensing his eyes on her. He quickly averted them, when she met his eyes briefly.

"Or more accurately, God's timing," Graham grinned. "Truthfully, I felt led to travel here at this particular time. Aside from the fact that mah sons just got out of school for the summer; I just had a hunch that I should get on down here and look at horse farms without delay. I know how popular Bluegrass country is."

Graham's sons were restless. "Hey, Dad...we're hungry. Can we go somewhere and eat?" Will glanced at his dad, expectantly.

Graham grinned. "Sure we can." He paused for a moment, glancing in Dana's direction. "Dana, will you join us for lunch? A celebration is definitely in order. Are there any good restaurants near here...some place you would recommend?"

"Absolutely. There's a decent little Italian restaurant not far from here. I bet you and your sons would love the food. Real good home cookin.' The Romeros have had the place for ages."

"Do we need a reservation?" Graham's eyes met Dana's. The gaze held.

A thrill zapped through her. "Not really. But I'll make one, anyway." She punched in the numbers on the desk phone by memory. She could feel his eyes on her.

~

Graham's sons were stirring around, anxious to get out of the office. They milled around the reception area, brimming over with energy. They were hovering over the goldfish in the glass case as Graham and Dana entered the reception area.

Dana could see the boys were obviously well behaved. She sensed they were restraining themselves. They'd been taught good manners. Given their youth and energy, she was sure that they would thrive in the wide, open spaces of a horse farm.

The Italian restaurant was homey and delightful.

Dana glanced at the menu. Soon, one of the Romero sons stood by the table. "I recommend the Lasagna or the Veal Parmigiana...the specials." The pudgy young server glanced around the table at the group waiting for the orders.

"I'll have the lasagna, please," Dana set down the menu.

"Sounds good. I'll go with that. Boys?" Graham glanced over at his sons.

"Veal Parmigiana, please." Will grinned and set down the menu.

"Lasagna, please." Jay addressed the server and then set down his menu.

Lunch was served with home-made bread, pesto and a crisp salad. The Romero boy hovered over their table when everyone had finished. "Would y'all like to try the Key Lime Pie for dessert?"

Dana sensed the boys restraining their responses while they politely waited for her response. "Not for me, thanks." Dana smiled. "I stay away from sugar."

Graham grinned over at his sons. "Go for it, guys. It's my favorite... I won't even try to resist it."

As his boys finished their pie, Dana glanced over at Graham. "Would you like me to find a renter for the guest house?"

"Nah. I'll just leave it vacant. Some of my friends from Houston will probably come and visit at some point."

"You're sure you want to leave it vacant when it could be producing revenue?"

"For now, anyway."

Here goes. "Uh, well...I...I'm in the market for a rental on a ranch where I can bring my two thoroughbreds. There isn't much available at the moment. I could teach your sons how to ride as a bonus. You know I'm a professional equestrian...spent over twenty years as a trainer. I used to be a Show Jumper."

"Really? A show jumper? That's impressive. Why did you give it up?" Graham's interest was piqued.

"Sad story. I don't think this is the time. Maybe I'll share it with you sometime. The thing is...horses are in my blood... I grew up on a ranch...after Dad died and Mom sold the ranch, I farmed out my two thoroughbreds on a horse farm. Currently, I rent a cottage in town...but I miss having my horses near me...and the place I'm renting is going on the market..."

For a moment, Graham seemed to like the idea of her living on the ranch. He quickly vetoed it though. "Well, I guess if you really can't find anywhere else to rent where you could bring your horses...I guess you could probably live in the guest house...maybe temporarily until you find something." He was nervous. He turned to his sons. "How would you boys feel about having a professional equestrian around to teach you how to ride?"

The boys exchanged excited glances. "You used to be a Show Jumper? Like...that is *so* cool. Did you ever win?" Will's eyes were as big as saucers.

"Yes. I won first place Show Jumping at Keenland three years ago—and then quit the business."

Jay glanced at Will. "She must be an awesome rider."

"Yeah, I guess!" Will agreed. He turned to Dana. "So, why did you quit jumpin'?"

Here goes. "My...younger brother, Stefan...was a

show jumper, also. He was killed doing a show jump, a couple years ago. I quit the business after that." She turned her face from the boys. "I knew it would never be the same again. It was hard to get that...image of him...out of my mind."

Graham glanced over at Dana. "I'm sorry, Dana. What a tragedy...must have been very traumatic. I'll talk it over with the boys...about your renting the guest house. I'll get back to you in a couple of days."

"Sounds good. Actually, I was thinking maybe it could be a temporary thing, like you said. I'll be looking for five acres to buy. Hobby farms are real scarce right now, though."

"Well, I welcome you out on Sugarbush. After all, it was through you that I got this place. Maybe God wants me to bless you, also." Graham finished his slice of Key Lime Pie.

The boys were restless. They'd finished lunch and were raring to go. "Can we go outside and look for frogs, Dad?...like while y'all are finishing your coffee?"

"Go ahead boys. I know you're antsy. We'll head back to the hotel and maybe go for a swim." Graham grinned.

"When is your wife expected to arrive?" Dana hadn't meant to pry; the words had slipped out of her mouth involuntarily.

Without warning, the vivid blue eyes that reminded her of her favorite gemstone, Lapis Lazula, became still and sad. Instantly, she regretted firing the question at him. There was a long pause. Graham looked away from her and out the window. When he finally spoke, it was as though the words were being wrenched from him by some giant hand. "Mah...wife died... of cancer...

jest over a year ago..." He paused for a long moment. "I had to get away from Houston and all her family and friends...from everything there that reminds me of her...and of the life we shared."

Dana was engulfed with a sudden, unexpected impulse to comfort him. She had the urge to throw her arms around his neck. Oh how she wished she hadn't pressed him into talking. His sorrow was so profound it almost felt palpable."I'm sorry." But as the words she'd meant to be comforting, left her mouth, she knew they sounded trite. And, of course, they couldn't change his sorrow.

"Mah sons weren't keen to leave their friends behind. Jay just turned twelve and Will is ten. They didn't want to move here, but ah got them to promise they would try it for a year and if they hadn't settled in to their new life on a ranch here by then, we would sell and move back to Houston."

Dana noted his accent was more pronounced than before. He seemed to be in a kind of daze. Maybe he was reminiscing. She had a lot of questions she wanted to ask him, but she didn't want to bombard him at the moment. Maybe they would become good friends. But Dana already knew she wanted a whole lot more than that from him.

"Mah boys are in pretty bad shape emotionally and ah figured the only way we could survive was to start fresh...away from all the memories. I finally managed to get them somewhat excited about the adventure of it all." Graham seemed to settle down when he spoke about his sons. "Ah think the change will do us all a lot of good."

"I've never met a young boy who didn't want to

grow up on a ranch." Dana smiled, hoping to somehow encourage the broken-hearted man. Her heart went out to him. She knew what it was to lose a loved one.

Chapter Four

Dusk was fast approaching by the time
Dana unpacked her last box. Bliss to her was being
around her beloved thoroughbreds. It had to be God's
timing that Graham needed her to help him run the
ranch and care for the horses. The guest house was
ideal, particularly given that she could bring her two
beloved thoroughbreds onto the property. She had a
crush on Graham but she was determined to keep it a
professional arrangement. She crashed early, exhausted.

Dana jumped out of bed the moment the alarm
rang the next morning. It was 6:00 a.m. Time to start
the morning chores. She switched on the coffee maker,
jumped into the shower and then pulled on jeans and a
T shirt. It was going to be a hot one today—so the
weather report had claimed.

She smeared on pink lipstick and applied two thick
coats of black mascara and voila! She was ready for the
morning chores. She allowed herself a quick glance in
the full-length mirror and gestured her thumbs upward.
"I'm on my way." She turned her body this way and

that in a mock dance movement. *"Yes."* Riding was a great form of exercise. Her body was sinewy and supple. Not that it mattered where Graham was concerned. He was immovable in his resolve to go it alone. But a girl could dreamy, anyway.

When she reached the horse barn, she was surprised to discover that Graham had already placed the large buckets of water in each horse stall and was commiserating with one of his thoroughbreds. He had Will and Jay with him. They seemed in awe of it all.

"Mornin', Ma'am." Graham tipped his Stetson in a right Southerly manner and grinned.

A true Southern gentleman. Her heart raced. But she so wished he would stop referring to her as *Ma'am. She had a name, after all. Maybe that's the way he liked it. Impersonal.*

She felt anything but impersonal toward him. In fact, at the sight of his tousled, dark auburn hair, Dana's heart began to beat wildly. *Not again. No man she had ever met before had this effect on her. For a flashing instant, she wanted to grab him and bring him into her house, lock the door and throw the key away. Every fibre of her being cried out for him. She held herself in firm check, forcing herself to take deep breaths.* When Dana finally dared to speak after the quivering had subsided, she acknowledged his sons. "Your boys don't waste any time, do they?"

"Mah sons are rambunctious, no doubt about that. Ah'll need to supervise them. Looks like ah did the right thing bringin' them here," he drawled. "They have so much energy. And they just love the place."

"You did—and they do." Dana flashed him a big smile. *So much for playing it cool.*

"I see you managed to transport your horses here, Dana. I checked them out this morning...earlier. Wow—powerful, handsome thoroughbreds."

"I was fortunate to have my buddy, Tom, help me transport them and drive the horse trailer. Lightening and Prince Alexander are both finicky...but they're amazing thoroughbreds."

"So...Prince Alexander is a golden Arabian Stallion?"

"Right. Tom helped me unload the horses and then drove the trailer back to the Circle H where my horses were boarded."

"I want him!" Will excitedly pointed to Prince Alexander, spotting him for the first time. He jumped up and down with glee.

"I saw him first!" Jay shouted, moving toward his fine thoroughbred who stood regal and tall in his stall, surveying the boys.

Dana had just finished watering and feeding him. She hadn't expected such unabashed enthusiasm about the Prince Alexander.

Graham and Dana exchanged furtive glances.

"You have just singled out the most temperamental, difficult horse on the entire ranch." Dana sighed. "Prince is unpredictable and moody. Nobody gets to ride him but me." Her voice was laced with a serious edge as she spelled out the warning. "Prince is for the most advanced riders out there. Trust me."

"Listen up, boys. Dana is a seasoned equestrian. Nobody rides Lightening or Prince Alexander except her. Is that clear?"

"Yeah, okay... Dad. But it's not much fun. It would

be so exciting to ride him. Couldn't I go for just a short ride on him? Couldn't I, Dad?"

"No, means, no, Jay" and that goes for you, too, Will. The subject is closed. You want to ride... Dana will pick which horses you ride. And I want y'all to take some lessons from her, too. You're both still novice riders. A few weeks at a dude ranch hardly makes y'all expert riders. In fact, we all have a long way to go to become good riders. Respect the fact that Dana is a professional equestrian. None of us are." Graham's feisty sons needed the law laid down from time-to-time. This was one of those times.

Graham glanced lovingly at his sons who were making a show of feeding the horses. "Living on a ranch and having a riding instructor, you will soon become fine equestrians. Why don't we set a goal? If Dana says either one of you are ready to ride Prince Alexander, then so be it. Until then, I don't want to hear another word about it. You can saddle up and go for a ride once you've done your chores. Dana will select the horses you'll ride. You'll need to listen up to her instructions."

"Do we have to do chores *every day*, Dad?" Jay sulked, as he set out feed for one of the horses.

"Yeah. That's a big part of livin' on a ranch. The benefit you receive from your work is the joy and...thrill of riding. Also, I'm going to get Dana to show you how to groom the horses. The sooner you realize how much work it is to groom the horses and feed and water them, the sooner you will become a seasoned equestrian."

The boys were noticeably sulking. "Can't we afford a groom, Dad? I thought most horses would have their own groom...assigned to them."

Ah, the mind-set of the rich kid. Dana smirked. Graham had his hands full. He was going to need all the help he could get. It just so happened, she was up for it.

"You said you wanted to live on a ranch, so get with the program, boys. You'll hit your stride after a while and you'll enjoy taking care of the horses. Guaranteed."

Graham and Dana monitored the boys as they methodically did their chores. They weren't too pleased about doing it. They stalled and sulked, but nevertheless continued the chores.

"It's not so bad, is it?" Graham glanced over at Will. "And don't you feel you get a greater sense of connection with the horses when you care for them?"

"Yeah. I guess." Will conceded, as he watched one of the thoroughbreds gobble up water in his stall.

"You'll get used to it." Graham hovered over Will and Jay, overseeing the process. He fed and watered the horse in the middle paddock. One son was on each side. This way he could monitor both boys.

"I doubt it." Jay sulked, as he watched one of the horses gobble up the water.

"The lesson will begin at 10:00 a.m. sharp, tomorrow. You'll ride Toby, one of the thoroughbreds. I'll meet you at the barn at 9:30 and we'll get saddled up and ready to go, Will." Dana had stopped by to see how the boys were doing. She'd already figured out Will was much keener to ride than Jay.

"Yippie. I can't wait." Will jumped up and down enthusiastically.

"When is *my* lesson? I want to learn how to ride, too." Jay sulked. He called over from two stalls away where he watered one of the horses.

"How about right after Will's lesson? We'll meet you at the barn right after his lesson. That will be roughly 11:00. a.m."

"Okay. What horse will *I* ride?" Will glanced at the row of horses.

"You seem to have bonded with Black Diamond. That's the one we'll use."

Dana was at the barn saddling up one of the thoroughbreds by nine-thirty. It was a glorious, sun-filled day. She felt glad to be alive. God had provided an ideal place for her and her thoroughbreds to live.

Dana whispered a prayer: "Lord, thank-you for allowing me the joy of having my horses near me. I missed them so much! It wasn't the same as visiting the ranch and going for a ride whenever I had time. I realized then that I needed to be near them, needed them close to me like I need air..."

Graham stood next to Will. He was so handsome that he took her breath away. His blue T-shirt perfectly complimented his vivid blue eyes. The cowboy boots and Stetson he wore made him look like a real Southern gentleman farmer.

Summer is my favorite season of the year. I wish the weather could always be sunny and warm like this. I come alive this time of year. Maybe I should live in Florida where my friend Jan lives.

"Ah think it's gonna be a hot one today...it's already in the seventies..." Graham watched as Dana demonstrated the proper way of saddling a horse, while his sons listened. He was learning too.

Dana chatted to Jay to try to get him to relax. "So,

you've ridden a couple times before when your Dad...or your folks took you to a Dude Ranch...but that's it, right?"

"It was Spring break, Dana. We were here in Kentucky...at a dude ranch. That's when I knew I wanted to become a good rider!" Will grinned at her activating the dimples on his cheeks.

"Me, too. That's when I knew I wanted to get into riding..." Jay nodded in agreement.

Dana smiled. "So, you boys have been bitten by the horse bug. I know all about it."

~

Graham helped Will mount the horse. Once he was secured on it with his helmet fastened, Dana went through a few basics before they began the ride. Will took to the sport with ease.

They cantered down the trail, having spent considerable time reviewing the use of the reigns, the position in the saddle and all the basic, starting points of the sport. They hadn't gone far when suddenly Dana heard Will's horse whinny and then he reared up.

"Hold on. Stay calm, Will, he'll settle down." Dana's voice was even and calm as she cantered closer to Will and the horse he rode.

But the thoroughbred wasn't settling down, despite her soothing voice and seasoned professional savvy. He heaved Will onto the grass. It all happened in seconds.

"Stay." Dana commanded her horse. She quickly dismounted and hurried over to Will. "Are you okay?"

A long pause ensued before he spoke. "I...I think so..." He paused as he brushed dirt and grass from his jeans, a stunned expression playing over his features.

"You're in shock, Will. Take it easy. Do you have

any idea what triggered his rearing up?

"Maybe...maybe I was holding the reigns too tight. Do you think maybe he could tell that I was scared?"

Will looked so vulnerable, so young and sweet. "Horses get everything, Will. They're remarkable creatures. Try to relax and enjoy the ride. I'll help you back onto the horse. Don't let this incident put you off, or you may never get back on a horse again." Dana smiled confidently.

"Sometimes these feisty thoroughbreds just like to test us humans. *They* want to be in control rather than us controlling them." She brushed off more dirt from Will's jeans and shirt. "You're sure you're okay, Will?"

"Yeah, I'm sure...I just wanna go home."

"We can do that." Dana knew that no two riders were alike—and no two horses were identical, either. Personalities came into play. Will was just a kid, after all. And considering the trauma he'd been through with losing his Mom, he just wanted to go home. It was understandable.

Soon, Dana's frisky thoroughbred, tail swishing, was trotting back on the way to the barn, Will following close behind. Soon, Will caught up and cantered next to Dana, as she instructed him to do. This allowed her the freedom to instruct Will and observe how he handled himself and Toby. "Watch how I hold my reigns, Will." She nudged him just enough to assist him in developing good, correct habits.

"Every time we go out, you will feel stronger and more solid with your riding. Always connect with your horse. You're riding on their back; you're extra weight, think of them as a friend, a favorite friend you want to be good to...." Dana always infused her lessons with knowledge gleaned from decades of working with the graceful creatures. *Thank you, Lord, that Will was wearing a helmut when he fell.*

Dana dismounted. "Growing pains, Will. Everybody falls off a horse now and then. The sooner you get beyond the trauma of it, the better." She helped Will remount. Gradually Toby settled down and took a drink of water in the creek. A light rain was drizzling. It was growing cooler. The sky suddenly darkened.

"We're going back to the barn, Will. Toby is a high-spirited horse. Finiky...as well. We'll stay closer in, next time. And, we're going to try you with a different horse. Maybe one of the quarter horses...the older one." Dana usually got it right with horses. Not this time. *Will's fall never should have happened. She would have to face the music with Graham. Lord, what if something had happened to one of his sons?* She found herself actually shaking as they cantered back to the barn. This lesson had definitely not gone well.

In a short time, they were back in the barn. While Toby gobbled up water and hay, Will told his dad about his fall, in great, effusive, dramatic terms. "...and...the next thing I knew...I was on the ground...I was so scared...I've never fallen off a horse before, Dad..."

Graham glared at Dana. He'd been in the barn, waiting for Will to return. Dana had heard Will call his Dad on his cell. He lit into her. "Why did you let Will ride that feisty Thoroughbred? Why didn't you start him off on one of the other horses?" Graham glared at her.

Dana saw red. "Like the thoroughbred tripping was somehow *her* fault? "Suddenly you're an expert on teaching riding? You would have chosen a horse that didn't stumble." She was seething. "Let me explain something about horses, Graham. They're unpredictable. Riding is not, nor never has been 100% safe. There is *risk* involved. It's a sport for the privileged, as you well know. I grew up on a horse farm and started riding when I was five. Horses are in my blood..."

"I get that you're a good equestrian, Dana. I just wonder about your judgement. Will is just a kid."

"My judgement?" Dana saw red. She knew horses like a mother knew her child. *Her horses were like her children. She understood them, had cared for them, ridden them, loved them...how dare he question her judgement where horses were concerned?* "Excuse me, Graham. I'm going back to my house. When you get your Southern manners... and... gentlemanly charm back— do let me know. Meanwhile, I'm not available!" She glared at him, threw her long blond locks back over her shoulders and stomped off. Fuming. She glanced back for a fleeting moment.

Graham stood rooted to the spot. A stunned expression clouding his features.

Good, the man owes me an apology.

~

Dana wheeled her white Mercedes SUV into the lot at the real estate firm. She settled into her office, following up on some leads, but she was still upset. After an uneventful afternoon, she drove home. Minutes after she pulled her vehicle up to the guest house, she heard a knock on the door.

Graham stood there, grinning sheepishly. "Dana, please accept my apology. I was way off-base...my emotions have been in an upheaval...I over-reacted...of course you couldn't know the thoroughbred would stumble..."

The man looked so vulnerable and so incredibly handsome. She had to fight an urge to throw her arms around his neck and stay in the embrace for...a very long time. Instead, she said nothing.

"I'm going out for a ride. I need to relax. Any chance you would consider joining me?" Graham peered directly into her eyes.

His sincerity and vulnerability touched her. He was like a little boy. And he was so very sad. Again, she fought an urge to hug him and smother him with kisses. She had planned to relax in the tub and listen to some music... put on a CD of Beethoven or maybe an opera. Horseback riding with Graham was a much more interesting choice... though she wasn't going to give him the satisfaction of jumping at his invitation. "Looks like a storm kickin' up...I don't know if..." She started glancing out the window but was inexplicably drawn to the man's brooding, cobalt blue eyes.

He cut her off. "Please, Dana. I am really sorry. I...I just want to be friends with you...and let you know how much I appreciate your teaching my boys how to ride..."

The man looked so forlorn. Again, she fought the urge to throw her arms around his neck and smother him with her kisses. "Sure, okay. Come on in, I'll be ready to go in a few minutes..." *Was that her voice speaking? So much for playing hard-to-get.*

Graham and Dana mounted their thoroughbreds and cantered along the rolling, green hills. Soon they were galloping full out and heading toward an area she hadn't been to before. A vivid scarlet sky was blindingly bright.

"It's magnificent, isn't it Dana?" They galloped close to each other, passing scattered Oak trees lining the winding pathway. Vivid rays of sunlight bounced off the trees, alternating between being blindingly bright and diffused or blocked where the massive oak trees stood. It was a palette of crimsons, golden yellows and flaming orange tones. A lone sparrow flitted from one of the oak trees, startled by the infringement of privacy as they cantered along the trails.

"It really is."

It was much cooler by the time they returned to their respective homes. Graham gave Dana a peck on her forehead as he bade her good-night on her doorstep. He turned and walked rapidly away. Graham was clearly determined to keep his emotions intact. Would he succeed?

Dana was in love. Totally, absolutely smitten with the Texas hunk who had somewhat miraculously been plunked down into the middle of her life.

Chapter Five

Summer morphed into fall. Soon it was September. Graham enrolled his sons in Bluebird School. He requested a meeting with Dana. She suggested meeting at her Real Estate office, so that's what they did.

Graham had had two months to analyze the existing stock. He had developed a strategy for revamping and maximizing the usage of the ranch. "Here is how I envision the ranch operating..." he began.

Dana resisted rolling her eyes. The man was fresh out of the big city; a former resident of one of the poshest areas of stately homes in Houston. In minutes she'd figured that out when he gave his address and she checked it on the internet. Graham had told her he was a semi-retired businessman. He claimed to be a rookie rancher. But as she listened to him, she realized that he was adapting to the horse world with the speed of lightening and would doubtless soon have a thriving horse farm.

His plan for running the ranch was remarkably sound, particularly given the fact that he was new to the game. Graham had elaborated on his mandate to upgrade the existing horses and auction off inferior stock. "I welcome your expertise when it comes to buying new horses. I've penciled in a monthly budget and a daily schedule of duties and other details required to operate a thriving horse farm. I will need to hire a groom and other staff to make sure the farm runs efficiently. It won't be easy. But I'm committed to it.

Dana was struck anew by his fierce intelligence and mental discipline. He was focused on his goals. He'd told her he had a Masters in business. It showed. *Too bad he wasn't available.* He'd told her repeatedly that he would always go it alone. He had made a promise to Myrna, his wife, on her deathbed that he would never remarry after she went on to glory. Myrna had apparently begged him to move on with his life, but he was heartbroken and wouldn't hear of it.

Chapter Six

At her wit's end where her prospects for a
husband were concerned, Dana called her best friend,
Jan Fields who lived in Palm Beach. "Oh Jan, I'm so
frustrated. Every time I meet a guy I like, it turns out
he's not available. Graham was so traumatized by the
death of his wife that he has sealed off his emotions.
He's determined never to love again. Irrational—right?"

"O.K. He's fiercely loyal to his wife's memory.
How long since she passed on?" Jan really cared about
Dana's future. They'd been close since college.

"It's only been about a year." Dana sighed.

"Hey, give the guy a chance! He's barely beyond
the grieving period. He'll come around in due time.
Besides...you know the drill...if God wants the two of
you together, He'll bring it to pass." Jan was one of the
most positive people on the planet. "He might be
impulsive. Some guys pop the question when their
girlfriends least expect it. Watch for the signs. Maybe
he'll whisper it into your ear some night when you're
half-asleep watching a movie on TV with him." Jan

chuckled.

"Ya. right. Anyway, talking to you always makes me feel better." Dana was cheered up momentarily. Still, she felt sad and alone. She called her mom just to chat. Then she ran a tub and put in a CD with Maria Callas, the late opera diva. She identified with her. Dana's heart had been broken a few years back when the man she loved chose another woman to marry. Maria Callas had been famously dumped by Ari Onassis for Jackie Kennedy. She'd never recovered or found another man after losing him. *Please God, don't let that happen to me.* You promised that you would do a new thing. I want to love again. I *need* to love again.

It was a lazy Friday afternoon and Graham and his sons leaned over the corral fence. Dana could see them from the windows of her cottage. She ambled over to the three of them. "Hey...looks like y'all are dressed real nice and goin' somewhere." Dana smiled over at the three of them.

"I'm drivin' mah boys over to Bobby's, their new friend's ranch, not too far away." Graham glanced over at his sons. "I told you that you would probably make new friends if you attended Sunday school and...look at that...a new buddy after only two classes."

"Bobby said we could spend the afternoon at his ranch. And if we wanted, we could even stay for dinner... could we, Dad? Please!" Jay's vivid blue eyes lit with joy in anticipation of the new adventure.

"I don't see why not. Of course that means we'll want to have Bobby over here for dinner soon. We can barbecue something. Have fun, boys. Chow for now." Graham grinned, gesturing good-bye.

An hour later, there was a knock on the door at

Dana's cottage. Dana peaked through the peep hole, saw that it was Graham and opened the door.

Graham stood on her porch. He rarely knocked on her door. They usually met at the barn or his house. "Ah confess ah am at loose ends with the boys gone, ah don't suppose you would consider goin' for a ride with me? It's a glorious afternoon...too nice to stay inside."

Dana thought about it for a nanosecond. She was chomping at the bit to go riding with him. But she'd made up her mind she was going to play hard to get. Not that *any ploy* was likely to work on Graham. Still, she had to try. She smiled. "What a nice idea...it's a little late though... the sun will soon be setting... "

"Sunsets are a magnificent gift from God. He provides them for our enjoyment!" He grinned at her, his cobalt blue eyes peering through her and to her very soul. "It would be real nice to have company watchin' the sun go down..." He grinned. "it's awesome just to meditate on the glory of God as revealed in the sunsets."

He pulled at her heartstrings. She couldn't resist him if her life depended on it. Already her knees felt weak and wobbly as waves of excitement coursed through her body. "Yes, sunsets are glorious. Give me a few minutes and I'll meet you at the barn." Okay, so she was weak as mush. It wasn't her fault that God had made the man irresistible to her.

Graham grinned. His piercing blue eyes seemed to bore right through her and into her very soul. Her heart melted. *Darn him. The man was downright irresistible!*

They saddled up and cantered out onto the hilly bluegrass country. Dana was adventurous. She had discovered some meandering trails at the edge of

Graham's property. She'd been curious to see where they led. "Mind if I show you a beautiful spot...it's not too far away..."

"Sure." They galloped close to each other, the balmy weather warming their backs. It was a glorious, warm, cloudless day. God was smiling down from the heavens. She led the way to an area she'd recently discovered. It had a gurgling creek zigzagging through it. A large Blue Jay chirped, flitting through the lower branches of a lone Shumard oak tree as they cantered by. Vivid rays of sunshine streamed through the branches. The light caught on Graham's face. It shone brightly for a few minutes until they moved on.

The sunset was lit with a flaming orange fireball laced with magenta and shades of red. God was generous and magnificent. He apparently wanted all mankind to enjoy the majestic wonders he created. Focused on the blinding sunset, they did not see the Copperhead rattler slithering toward Black Prince.

Black Prince's ears flickered back and forth intensely, swiveling, Dana realized her thoroughbred was in a heightened state of anxiety. She spotted the Copperhead rattler too late. Spooked, Black Prince reared up, throwing Dana off his back. She hurtled almost thirty feet, finally hitting her head on a rock by the creek. She was knocked unconscious.

~

Graham dismounted in seconds. He'd seen the rattler and it had slithered away, *thank God. The accident had happened so fast.* He tried to force himself to be calm, but his hand shook as he punched in 911 on his cell. *I almost didn't bring my cell on the ride and at the last minute I decided to take it. Thank you, Lord. Why hadn't Dana worn a helmet? She'd always insisted his sons wear one?*

His heart was racing as he picked Dana up and cradled her in his arms, praying fervently that she would be okay. "Dana...darling, you're going to be fine...just fine." Still, his heart raced frenetically. He was overcome with emotion. He had not admitted how he felt to Dana, but God knew his heart. *"Lord, I've just found her...I can't lose her now...please God...let her be okay."*

He slapped the horses on their rears, commanding them to get back to the barn. The whirring of the emergency helicopter would spook them.

The horses, fortunately, were out of earshot by the time he heard the deafening sound of the helicopter whirring and spiraling toward them. He glanced up at it, waving his hands.

Graham phoned his oldest son, Jay. His sons would still be at Bobby's ranch. "Jay, you and Will need to come home right away. There's been an accident..." He briefed them about Dana's fall. "Ask Bobby's Dad to drive you home. See if he'll give you a hand with the horses. I sent them back to the barn. Hopefully, they'll make it. I'm on my way to the hospital by helicopter. I'll call you from there."

"Oh, no, Dad...I'll...we'll be prayin'" Jay tried to be brave like his dad had always taught him.

The distinct, thunderous whir of the helicopter spiraled toward them. In minutes, it had landed in the field. Graham and the emergency worker helped Dana into the helicopter. She was still unconscious as the helicopter spun into the air spiraling upward and flying to the hospital in Lexington.

Chapter Seven

Dana awakened in a sterile hospital room the next morning. She had no idea where she was or why she was there. Her head throbbed, and her body ached. *Strange people stood around her bed.*

Danielle smiled over at her daughter. "So, you've decided to rejoin the human race, Dana. How do you feel?"

Dana stared vacantly at her mom, her mind a total blank.

"How do you feel, Dana?" Graham's voice almost shook as he spoke. He felt like bawling. *Lord, give me strength. You are in control.* His eyes searched her face for any sign of recognition. He already saw the writing on the wall. *If she doesn't recognize her Mom, she won't recognize me.*

Dana stared blankly into Graham's eyes. Her brain felt fuzzy. Weird. Nothing made any sense. She had no recall. *Who is this handsome guy? Where was she? Why was she here? What had happened?*

A mature nurse appeared, as if on cue. "Ah...

you're awake. How do you feel, Dana?"

Dana stared blankly at the nurse. She did not respond.

"I'll let the doctor know you're awake, Dana." The older woman smiled. "I'll be right back."

A tall, distinguished gentleman with silver-flecked hair strode into the hospital room. A warm grin lit his kind face. "Good-afternoon, Dana. I'm Dr. Struthers. Glad you've decided to give the human race another try. How do you feel?" He grinned at Dana.

Dana touched her head, glancing over at him, confused and disoriented. She did not reply.

"Do you know who that lovely lady standing next to your bedside is?" The doctor grinned, encouragingly as he nodded to Danielle.

Dana glanced momentarily at her Mom and then over to Graham. A vacant look clouded her features.

"Do you know why you're here?" The doctor observed Dana closely.

Dana continued staring vacantly at the doctor and the visitors.

Graham and Danielle exchanged glances. They wore sombre expressions. Danielle fought tears threatening to overtake her. Graham tried to be stoic, despite feeling devastated.

The doctor leaned toward Dana. He poured her a glass of water from a small jug on a nearby stand. "Have some water, Dana." He handed her the glass. "You're going to be just fine. You've had a fall from your horse, you've hit your head... you've been traumatized, but never mind...you're young, you'll bounce back and your memory will soon return." The handsome, wise doctor was filled with a kind of easy confidence, borne from many years of dealing with a multitude of illnesses.

A faint smile played over Dana's lips. It was almost as though she both heard and understood him. *Did she?* Graham allowed himself a fleeting moment of hope as he flirted with that idea.

"We'll need to run some imaging scans and blood tests. You've had major trauma to the brain, but fortunately you were brought in right away to emergency. Once we determine the extent and details of the damage, I can give you a prognosis. Right now, there are a lot of unknowns." The doctor glanced from Danielle to Dana and then over to Graham.

Was Dana going to be alright? Was the doctor being positive? Or was her prognosis better than it appeared? Danielle stood stoically by, determined to remain strong. She fought the onrush of tears with every fibre of her being, plastering a shaky smile on her face.

The doctor glanced from Danielle to Graham. "There's nothing you can do right now but pray. If you'll follow me to my office, I can give you more information. The nurse will stay with her right now, because she's disoriented. I'll visit her again later, first chance I get."

~

Inside the doctor's office, he spoke from his vast wealth of knowledge and experience. "Dana's memory could be totally restored in a few hours or maybe up to 24 hours...worst case scenario, her memory could be severely impaired and it might take a significant amount of time for her to regain it. There are many unknowns at this time. I'll know more when the tests we take are analyzed. And...I just have to tell you...some patients never recover. I have your phone numbers. Either myself or one of the nurses will get it touch with both of you." Dr. Struthers shook his head. "There is just no sure way of knowing which way this could go. Right now, I'm sure we're all grateful to God that she's alive and in good hands."

Danielle glanced heavenward. *Thank-you, Lord.* Unbidden tears slid down her cheeks.

Graham was overcome with emotion. Then Danielle knew that he and Dana had fallen hard for each other, whether they wanted to admit it or not. Graham and Danielle walked together from the doctor's office, down the hallway. "I just want to go home and pray." Danielle glanced over at Graham. "God can restore her completely. I am believing that he will do that." She fought back tears.

"Life is full of challenges...and sorrows...I know that all too well..." Graham spoke from his own pain.

"She'll snap out this. Guaranteed. Dana is a survivor and a fighter. She learned a lot being a Show Jumper and God is not through with her yet." Danielle spoke with a confidence she was working hard to restore.

"Do you want to get a cup of coffee?" Graham glanced over at the Danielle and was struck by her remarkable resemblance to Dana. They looked more like sisters than Mother and daughter.

"Sounds good. There's a cafeteria downstairs." Danielle was shaking but she managed a weak smile.

The caffeine jolt helped him.

Danielle sipped her Mocha coffee. "My work is cut out for me." She was resigned to her fate. "This isn't the first horse trauma I've lived through." A flash of sadness soared through her. *First, my son Stefan died doing a Show jump and now Dana has amnesia. Lord, I cannot handle losing Dana. Surely you know that.* The words were a whisper in her spirit to the Almighty.

What exactly do you mean?" Graham asked.

"Prayer. I need to go to my prayer closet and pray unceasingly for Dana. I know she'll snap out of this, because I'm going to pray and stand on the promises of God *until* I see victory..." Tears sprung to Danielle's eyes. "You know, Graham, I'm not saying this is the case... but I believe that sometimes God allows suffering and setbacks in our lives to draw us close to him. With the busy schedules we all have, it's easy to leave God behind. It's humbling when something like this happens...we realize what little control we have over our lives...and how much control He has..." Danielle fought back a trickle of tears.

Graham glanced over at Danielle. The handsome, tanned woman wore her hair short cropped and platinum. Despite a few tiny wrinkles, she looked more like an older sister of Dana's than her Mom. He set down his mug of coffee. "That's true...so very true. I've been telling myself that Dana is just a friend, but the truth is that I care for her. I'll never get serious about another woman, though...Dana probably told you...I'm a widower and my goals are to raise my sons and focus on my racehorses..."

"Don't short-change yourself, Graham. I have a hunch it's already too late...with you and Dana, I mean. I get the feeling y'all have bonded. Seems like you have a camaraderie...a shared vision..."

Graham glanced over at Danielle. "You're a

handsome and wise woman—what about you? You're not going to remain alone for long."

Danielle smiled. "You're right about that. I'm just meditating on the Word, knowing that in His perfect timing, he'll bring the most...awesome man right on over to me..." She smiled. "We were never created to do life alone, Graham...don't even *try* to go against the laws of God and nature. Instead, meditate on the Word and in His perfect timing...you will be happy and fulfilled. I'll leave you with a scripture: *"Delight thyself also in the Lord and he shall give thee the desires of thine heart."* Check it out. It's *Ps. 37:4.*

"So you've never tried one of the dating sites?" Graham teased.

"No, I haven't even been tempted to. Though I must confess, I keep bugging Dana to try them. I must admit I'd like to see her married and settled." Danielle peered right into Graham's eyes.

Graham was uncomfortable and turned away.

"Maybe God allowed this...as a wake-up call...for you." Danielle sipped her iced Cafe Mocha.

"You speak as though you're a 100% sure she's going to fully recover." Graham sipped his Latte.

"That's exactly right, Graham. She *is* going to recover. *Mark 11:23 & 24* tells us that whatever we speak, believing, we shall receive. I guess most of us have learned that God's timing is not always our timing... but on the other hand *Jesus Never Fails.* So knowing that, I just rest in his promises." Danielle managed a weak smile.

"Considering this crisis, Danielle...you're remarkably relaxed." Graham signaled for the bill. It was time to go.

Danielle drove Graham home from the hospital since he had arrived there by helicopter. Graham tried to be strong for Danielle. He worked at staying positive. "I'll be real interested to see what the doctor's prognosis is, once he's analyzed the tests. Then, we should have some idea of what's goin' on." Graham glanced over at Danielle.

Her eyes were on the road. She prayed silently while she drove. God was in control and she believed in miraculous healings. Dana would snap back. God would see to it. She drove onto the long driveway leading up to Sugarbush Stables, stopping her car in the roundabout in front of the mansion.

Roamer and Rover barked their greeting, bounding toward the vehicle.

Jay and Will bounded down the stairs from the veranda, racing toward the car. "Hey, Dad," Jay hurried over to him, Will right next to him. "How is she?" They spoke in unison.

"Dana has amnesia. We'll know more when the doctor calls with a detailed prognosis." Graham's tone was sombre. He put his arms around his sons, one on each side as they ascended the stairs together.

"We got the horses back in their stalls.... Bobby's dad helped us...and...we didn't go riding...'cause you said not to...we did the chores like you showed us... and then just hung out." Will blubbered.

"You're good sons," Graham grinned, messing up Will's hair, which was auburn like his. It was thick and wavy.

"Amnesia..." Will was alarmed. "How do they know when...or if she'll...ever snap out of it?"

"That's just it, boys... they don't know. The doctor

will have a better idea of her prognosis, once he's done a series of tests and analyzed the outcome. He'll call me...and of course Danielle, also... once he's done that. We just have to trust God and believe that she'll snap out of it sooner rather than later. Come on, boys... let's go check on the horses. And then, I'll rustle up something for dinner."

"I might drive back to the hospital tonight. Maybe I'll sit at her bedside and pray for awhile. I'm real impressed that y'all got the horses settled into their stalls. I'd better hire a ranch hand right away. You just never know what can happen..." Graham strode in the direction of the barn, his sons hurrying to catch up with him.

The next morning, Graham got the call. "Dr. Struthers here...regarding Dana.... I wanted you to know that the brain damage appears to be limited, but we have no idea when or even if she will snap out of amnesia. There is no way of knowing...just pray for her and visit as often as you can...patients often have a sense of the people visiting them...they seem to perceive it on some visceral level, despite their temporary memory loss."

"Thanks, Doctor. I appreciate the call."

The doctor signed off.

Graham called his sons. It was time to do the morning chores. Normally, he was in the barn no later than 7:00 starting the chores, but today he'd stayed home in his room. He'd been praying fervently for Dana, surprised at the intensity of his feelings. He'd been on his knees in his bedroom asking God to heal Dana...asking for a miracle...no...pleading with God for a miracle for her. He finally admitted to himself that he was crazy about the woman. *And that took a lot.* They weren't just friends; it was much, much more than that. Still, it wasn't going to go anywhere. There would never be anyone for him other than his childhood sweetheart, Myrna. He was a one-woman man, and he'd had the most wonderful woman in the world. He didn't mind being friends with Dana; but that's where it would end.

He phoned Danielle after his prayer session. He sat at the kitchen table, a mug of coffee in his hands. "Well, seems like the bottom line is that the doctor doesn't know when or *if* Dana will snap out of amnesia; though most people do recover. So that's promising."

"Yes, that's pretty much what he told me, too. I'm going to visit her this afternoon...probably around 2:00. Meanwhile, I'll just keep praying for a miracle...you know, it just makes me realize how helpless we are...it's so easy to move on with our lives and catch up to God when we have time...barely comprehending how little control we actually have over our lives..." Danielle felt comfortable to share her thoughts with Graham. She sensed he was a man of great compassion and understanding. And despite Graham claiming the contrary, Danielle knew that he was crazy about her daughter. She rather liked that idea, although sometimes she felt a wave of jealousy about their budding romance. She despised living alone.

Chapter Eight

Graham slept restlessly. Hospitals. He despised them. He reflected on the last conversations he'd had with Myrna at the hospital, just before she descended into the blurred, medicated state prior to her final days. She'd pleaded with him. "You must go on, darling. You have a life in front of you. God always has a new door. There must be a reason why I must go to eternity and you must remain on earth...there must be a new love for you, my darling... a love...maybe even greater than the one we had...greater...because you will have a new... depth of understanding...a new... level of love... borne... from your sorrow..." as Myrna haltingly whispered those last words, her voice weak, shaky and barely audible, her hand suddenly went limp and she breathed her last earthly breath.

Graham had leaned over and kissed his beloved Myrna on each cheek. Tears had trickled down his cheeks. He couldn't stop them. He'd never cried before...well, almost never. But he'd been overcome with emotion and sorrow. "Good bye... my darling.

Good bye...love of my life...my precious, precious sweetheart." Tears had streamed down his cheeks then. "I shall always love you." Overcome with unspeakable sorrow, he somehow managed to ring the bell to alert the nurse of her death.

The nurse had arrived swiftly. Graham knew she had been waiting patiently nearby. Once she entered the room, he turned and walked sorrowfully out of the room and the hospital, heading to his car. He recalled his profound sorrow that day and the tears that followed. Those final moments were etched indelibly on his mind.

The next morning Graham arose earlier than usual. A glance at his bedside clock told him it was only 5:00. a.m. He headed into the kitchen and put on a pot of coffee before opening his Bible to the book of Psalms. That book had always been his favorite. He read for some time and then returned to his bedroom where he kneeled and prayed. "Lord, thank-you that Dana is alive. Thank you for the joy and privilege of knowing her. You have all power and all authority, Father, please cause her to quickly snap out of amnesia."

By 7:00 his sons were up. "I've made oatmeal for breakfast, boys." Graham served it, setting it on the kitchen table and topping it with blackberries.

"Hey, Dad? Can we go pick some more blackberries today?" Jay was eating them before the cereal.

"I wish you would, Jay. They don't last long around here." Graham grinned at Jay.

After breakfast, Graham and his sons headed to the barn to do the chores.

"Morning, Lightening. I know Dana misses

you...but never mind...God is healing her, her memory is coming back..." Graham was overcome with emotion as he commiserated with Dana's horse, Lightening. He whispered, making sure his sons couldn't hear him. "I'm in love with that girl. How could this have happened to me so fast? I was so sure I'd never love again...I promised Myrna..."

At that moment, Lightening reared up. He whinnied, unsettled and remained in that agitated state for a while. *Could Dana's thoroughbred actually know I'm talking about her? Lord, as outrageous as that is, could it be possible?* Graham commiserated with Lightening as he fed and watered him. The thoroughbred finally settled down. He was certain the horse understood Dana had been badly hurt from the fall. No doubt, he missed her loving presence.

Is Dana fiery like her beloved Lightening? Uncontrollable, the way he is? Is that why they've bonded? Why couldn't he stop thinking about her?

After the watering, feeding and chores were finished, Graham decided to go on another ride. His sons were restless and had asked if they could join him. "Okay guys, we'll go on a little ride. I'm going to pick which horses you'll ride, and we're not going for long...but you boys have been awfully good, so this is a little treat — for all of us. No galloping. We're just going on a nice easy trot. And put your helmets on and make sure you have your cell phones. Keep your wits about you. Horses can be unpredictable, as you know." Graham laid down the law. Dana's fall had rattled him.

Graham couldn't stop thinking about Dana. *What was happening to him? He wasn't supposed to love again. He'd fought the idea...and now, this woman he couldn't get off his mind had amnesia. Lord, help me!*

"What about Rover and Roamer? Should we feed them when we get back?" Will pulled his helmet from a wall hook, putting it on. Jay and Graham did the same.

"I've already fed the Shepherds, boys. Stay awake." *He adored teasing his sons. They usually retorted with practical jokes. Graham wouldn't trade them for the world. They kept him young.* "Or your old man will get ahead of you."

"Yeah, yeah, okay Dad," Will grinned. "It's way more fun livin' on a ranch than livin' in a city, anyway...you're right about that."

"I love it, too," Jay sulked. " 'Cept I miss my favorite library in Houston. "

"When the fall comes, we'll make regular visits to the main library in Kentucky, Jay. I've heard it is excellent." Graham strapped his helmet on. As he cantered out of the barn, the thoroughbred he rode was chomping at the bit to get moving. Graham controlled him, realizing the power and strength of the animal he rode.

"I wish I had my very own thoroughbred, Dad." Will led the designated Quarter horse out of the barn, following his dad.

"That's a good goal, Will. Once you prove you're a strong, consistent rider, we'll select a horse that's right for you. That goes for both of you, of course." Graham grinned over at Jay, who was perched happily atop the other Quarter horse.

"Wow. That's cool, Dad. Thanks." Will was suddenly sombre. "I've been prayin' for Dana every day. I sure hope she gets better...and comes home soon..."

They cantered next to each other while they conversed.

Graham knew Will was deeply upset and sad about Dana having amnesia. They all were, but Will had always been more sensitive than Jay. Jay cared deeply, but he took the misfortune in his stride. Will actually burst out in tears from time-to-time when he spoke about Dana. *The world could be a cruel place.* Graham knew how Will still grieved the death of his mom, but he also knew that he was genuinely fond of Dana and had thrived on the attention she'd given him, as well as the riding lessons.

Chapter Nine

Will lounged in the family room watching sports on TV. Jay was nowhere around. *He's probably in the den gobbling up yet another book. He'll likely become a writer.* The young lad was a voracious reader. He had an insatiable appetite for the written word. He'd been like that for years. He read everything in sight and was irrepressibly inquisitive. *The apple doesn't fall far from the tree.* Graham thanked God for his sons once again.

Graham drove to the hospital praying most of the way. Would Dana show signs of recovery? He slipped a tape into the deck as he drove. Old gospel songs. Simple. Beautiful. Powerful. He wanted to be mellow and strong for the visit with Dana. She needed him, whether she realized it or not. Danielle meant well, but he felt he knew and understood Dana far better than she did.

Dana was sitting up in her bed, the same vacant express clouding her face. She glanced over at Graham as he entered the room.

Danielle occupied a chair by Dana's bedside. She smiled shakily, acknowledging his arrival.

Graham had prayed fervently for strength and wisdom. It's a good thing he had, because seeing Dana in this strange state upset him terribly, despite the strong front he fought to maintain. *She had to get well. She looks beautiful even when she's sick.* Graham held her hand and gazed into those incredible sea-green eyes. He could lose himself in her eyes. He wanted to do that. He glanced at his watch. It had been a half hour. The doctor should be here soon. And his imagination was running away with him.

Dr. Struthers strode into the hospital room as if on cue. His smile was warm, compassion emanating from his persona. He glanced over at Dana and grinned, then turned to Danielle. "Danielle, now that we have conducted all the necessary tests... and we have your daughter on a medicine program it is time for us to release her from the hospital. I hope I will be able to release her into your care." He grinned from Danielle to Dana. Then his eyes rested on Graham. He held a chart, glancing at it intermittently.

"Absolutely," Danielle nodded. "She can come and stay with me."

The horses will be crucial to her recovery, in my opinion." The doctor glanced over at Graham. "She should spend as much time as possible with them. This will speed and trigger her recovery. Animals have a remarkable healing effect on people, and much more so when someone has devoted so much of their life to them. Also, being around...*Lightening*...the horse she was riding when the accident occurred is imperative, because seeing him could trigger a return of the events and thus a return of her memory."

Graham jumped into the conversation swiftly. "Well, I suggest Danielle and Dana both stay in the guest house at Sugarbush...there's plenty of space...it's two and a den, doctor...if the proximity to the horses is crucial to her healing, that's...maybe the best choice."

"I was hoping you would suggest that, Graham, having shared that possibility with me previously." The doctor nodded his approval.

"Right, Doctor. And I'm happy to...ah...make this a priority. All that matters is... that Dana snaps out of this. And I know she will." Graham realized he was falling all over himself.

Danielle turned to Graham and the doctor. "I'll need the rest of the day to make some arrangements; perhaps I can pick Dana up first thing in the morning."

"Good." Dr. Struthers nodded his approval.

Graham peered at the doctor and then glanced at Danielle. "I want you both to know that Dana will be my priority. I'll be hiring a ranch hand as soon as I can find a good one...and a groom...and I'll do everything I can to help Dana recover." Graham's voice held resolve. "Yes, Dr. Struthers. Horses are her life and I just know that they will be instrumental in her snapping back."

"We just don't know how it will play out and that's the challenge...the peculiarity of having amnesia...no two people are alike and no two cases are identical. She is in God's hands. We'll see you tomorrow then." Dr. Struthers shook their hands, took a last glance at Dana and left the room. Minutes later, a nurse, her hair red and frizzy like it had just been zapped from some kind of electric current, stepped into the room. "I'll take it from here." The redheaded nurse announced.

Graham and his sons enjoyed an early dinner on the veranda; barbecued fish and corn-n-the cob. Soon, they were all settled in the family room, watching the Sports channel. Will spoke up after the tennis game was concluded. "Dad...well... do you really think... Dana *will* get her memory back?"

Graham didn't hesitate. "Absolutely. Personally, I think it's just a matter of claiming God's promises. *"With God, nothing shall be impossible."*

"What do you mean by claiming God's promises, exactly?" Jay was puzzled.

"By that I mean that we have to stand on God's promises. Keep speaking the scriptures aloud and meditating on them. Keep calling things that are not as though they are... Jay, get your Bible and bring it here, please. Open it to *Mark 11:23* and read aloud verse 23 and 24. Will, get yours, too."

"Okay, Dad. If you think it will help." Will scooted off to the library trailing his older brother. With their Bibles in hand, they scooted back to the family room. Jay opened his Bible to the book of Mark, flipping the pages until he found the scripture he was searching for. Will copied him. Jay read the verses aloud. *"For verily I say unto you, that whosoever shall say unto this mountain, Be thou removed, and be thou cast into the sea; and shall not doubt in his heart, but shall believe that those things which he saith shall come to pass; he shall have whatsoever he saith. Therefore I say unto you, What things soever ye desire when ye pray, believe that ye receive them, and ye shall have them."*

Jay set his Bible down and studied his dad's face. "Wow. That's amazing. I think I'll memorize that scripture. I'll claim that promise over Dana...and Prince Alexander...I wish I could ride him and have him for my very own."

"You don't have a chance of owning that horse, Jay. You would be lucky if Dana ever let you ride it...I mean...if she gets well and everything." Will sulked. "Besides, I saw him first."

Jay's nose remained in the Bible. He'd always been an impressive student. "Dad...help me out here—is this scripture true or not? It says I can have whatever I *say*. So...like... either that's true... or it's...a lie. But if it's in the Bible, it must be true, right?" Jay peered at his dad, searching for answers.

Graham grinned. "It's true, Jay. And because of your faith and the fact that you are willing to press in to what God has for you; you will be rewarded. Don't listen to the hecklers..." He glanced over at Will. "I'm just teasing, Will. But there's a lesson here and one that will stand you in good stead, if you heed it."

"So when does Dana and her Mom move onto the ranch?" Will glanced up at his dad.

"First thing tomorrow morning, Will. I thought I would hire a catering company to come out to the house and prepare a festive, celebratory lunch for us all. We're going to celebrate Dana and her recovery before it happens. You can even put up some streamers, if you have a mind to. You know, a sort of Welcome Home theme." Graham grinned, faking a confidence he was trying hard to feel. *With God, nothing shall be impossible,* kept ringing in his mind and heart.

Chapter Ten

The next morning, shortly after 9:00, Danielle cruised her Mercedes onto Sugarbush Farm, stopping at the roundabout in front of the mansion. A balmy breeze caressed them, blowing Dana's long tresses about as she stepped out of the car. She looked lovely in a pale pink linen shirt and white jeans. Danielle looked sharp in her lime green top and pants.

Graham had been listening for the sound of a car, heard it and met them at the door. The two attractive women stepped out of Danielle's Mercedes.

Will and Jay followed their dad. "Hey, Dana...and Danielle...come on in! Nice to see y'all." Graham grinned, ushering the Mother and daughter team into the house. He didn't expect Dana to respond. Still, she would soon have her memory back and he was determined to act as though Dana had already recovered from amnesia.

Dana peered at Graham, her expression vacant.

Danielle smiled confidently as she settled onto the

large, comfortable candy-striped, canvas sofa in the family room.

"I made a fresh pot of coffee." Graham grinned, determined to be upbeat for everyone.

Danielle acted cheerful; as though nothing was wrong.

"Y'all have had breakfast, I'm sure..." Graham glanced from mother to daughter.

"We have." Danielle smiled, a bit shakily.

Graham plopped onto the matching wingback chair. "I have the caterers coming around noon. They're bringing a buffet lunch and there will be plenty left over for dinner... and probably food for tomorrow as well."

Danielle took the mugs from Graham and set them down on the coffee table. "Thanks for the coffee, Graham." Danielle smiled. "You know, Graham, I had a private chat with the doctor. He doesn't agree with me, but I'm going to try to obtain guardianship for Dana...since I'll be looking after her, anyway. And the first thing I'm going to do is sell her thoroughbreds and get her moved into the city. She needs a new life. Horses were responsible for the death of my only son, Stefan...and now my only daughter has amnesia. I think it's time that Dana got a new life...away from the world of horses."

Dana stood up. "You'll do no such thing, Mother! And you can please leave right now!" Dana was furious. "How dare you think such a thing, Mother?"

Graham and Danielle stared at each other and then at Dana. *Dana's mind had snapped back! She no longer had amnesia! Just like that.*

"Dr. Struthers said it would be the horses that would likely be instrumental in bringing her around.

And he's right! He just didn't know how quickly it would happen. Dana must have perceived this idea of her leaving horses and the ranch on some...deep, visceral level. How is it possible that Dana would understand...suddenly...what you planned to do?" Graham was dumbfounded.

Graham had shared Dr. Struthers diagnosis and recommendations with his sons. He'd advised them to treat her as though she already had her memory restored. He knew it would be. His sons shared his profound faith. They'd grown up with it. He was overjoyed. Overcome with emotion, he pulled Dana into his arms. "Come on, Dana...let's go see the horses..."

Danielle was fuming. "Well! I guess nobody needs *me* anymore. I know when I'm not wanted. I have a date anyway...I'll just be on my way...I'll hand the reigns over to you, Graham. It seems you know it all." *If only she could meet a man like Graham.* Sure, she had the odd date. But they never amounted to anything. She kept herself in great shape. In fact, most folks thought she and Dana were sisters. *But, oh no, it was always Dana that the men flipped for. It was always Dana, Dana...Dana...Dana. Darn her anyway. And just when she thought she had a chance with Graham, Dana had to spring back to life! Well, at least she wasn't saddled with being a caregiver.*

She was sorry she'd walked away from the church after Stefan had been killed in the jumping accident. Why had God allowed it? She'd managed to put on a good act for Graham, pretending to be a prayer warrior...it seemed to add to her mystique and intrigue him. But now her wicked heart was exposed. Yes, she'd wanted Graham all along. She'd bonded with him and flirted with him; and he'd flirted right back. After all, a lot of men liked mature woman, if they were in great shape like she was. And thanks to the gym and indoor swimming pool, which she frequented, she didn't have an ounce of fat on her. Fit and fabulous! That was her motto. And with her masters in business, she was ideally suited to run the ranch. Much more qualified than Dana, who only knew horses and had never taken business management. She'd been too busy as a Show Jumper and Trainer.

if Dana never fully regained her mind, it would just be a matter of time until Graham lost all interest in her. She would have to live in a group home or institution of some kind. Then Danielle would become lady of the manor. She was always good at organizing and running things. The Ladies' boutique she owned and operated in the city was highly successful, and so was the hair salon she operated. But becoming a lady of a manor would be far more intriguing and stimulating. She would sell the other businesses. Yes, with Graham as Master of the Manor it promised to be very, very intriguing. She hated competing with her own daughter. But Dana was young, if she fully recovered, she would find someone to love. It was harder for her, because she was fifty-three to Dana's twenty nine.

She had been the mastermind of Dana's equestrian career. She'd been the catalyst pushing her sister, Eve, to sponsor Dana's pursuit. After all, she could well afford it. Considering everything she had sacrificed for Dana, pushing her sister and her hubby to mentor her equestrian career and give her the thoroughbreds...along with countless lessons and all the other costs associated with an equestrian career as a Show Jumper and Trainer. It was all her doing. She was the brains behind Dana's career at Keeneland. Now it was her turn to have a life. She was a young, vivacious widow, after all, and keen to live life on a much grander scale than her current life.

Graham deliberately steered the conversation to the topic of horses. Maybe something he said would trigger her memory. But it was the *sound* of a horse neighing that caught Dana's attention. She stood up. Her ears seemed to be straining in the direction of the sound.

"Let's go out to the barn." Graham turned toward Dana and Danielle and glanced at his sons.

"Yeah, Dad. Let's go see the horses!" Will was excited. He rushed ahead, bounding down the stairs.

The troupe headed to the barn and made a beeline for the horses. Dana went directly to *Lightening*. She stood there gazing at him. He reared up slightly, neighing. "Woah, Boy, easy," Dana gradually got him settled.

Graham was stunned. Thrilled. Speechless. A glance at Danielle told him she was elated, too. He held his breath. Would there be more? *Dana had recognized Lightening!*

The boys cooed and petted some of the other horses in their stalls, stealing secretive glances toward Dana.

Danielle held her breath not daring to speak and break the magic of the moment. But some part of her didn't want Dana to recover. The dream of attracting Graham would vanish instantly once Dana had fully recovered.

Dana stayed with Lightening. She was silently

commiserating with him.

Graham and Danielle stayed close by Dana—one on either side of her.

It was well over an hour when Dana finally seemed somewhat restless. She glanced at Danielle.

"Ready to go, honey? We're going to have a marvellous lunch." She smiled and took Dana's hand, leading her out of the barn and back to the mansion.

Graham fell in step with them. He chatted with both of them as though he expected Dana to join the conversation. *Soon. She's going to come around soon. Lord, help me to be patient and trust you with a whole heart and lean not on my own understanding.*

The caterers served a splendid lunch. It was buffet style. Dana held a plate, silently glancing over the vast array of delectable food.

Danielle traded glances with Graham. *Dana would be hungry. The doctor said her appetite would likely be unaffected. She would have lots of food selections and it would be interesting to see if she would hesitate on choosing certain food; or if she would be decisive and choose foods she favored.*

Graham wondered about the thought process regarding Dana's selection of food.

Will and Jay were ecstatic with the vast array of food. They walked by the table, peering at the smorgasbord.

Soon, Graham prompted Danielle and Dana to start the line-up for the buffet. Will and Jay followed them with Graham at the end.

The caterers had set the formal dining room exquisitely with a centrepiece of fresh flowers. A few tasteful party decorations completed the scene.

"I think you've gone a little overboard, Graham." Danielle smiled over at him. "But I must say, everything looks wonderful. Maybe I should have an accident myself...if it means I would get the star treatment like this..." Danielle shot Graham a flirtatious glance.

It's not my imagination. The woman is flirting with me. He would ignore it. "I would like to give thanks for the food set before us. Let's bow our heads while I pray. "Father, we give thanks for the sumptuous meal set before us. Bless it to our use. Amen."

Everyone began eating. "I'm believing for nothing less than a miraculous healing. I trust the Lord with all my heart. He will bring it to pass."

They were all seated at the table. Graham occupied the host's seat at the head of the table and Danielle sat to his right. He'd thought about designating the honor seat to Dana, but it didn't feel right. Somehow, he and Danielle were in this together. They shared a common goal mingled with a common sorrow. And she was the mother of the woman he...cared deeply about. Yes, the place of honor belonged to her. But after Danielle was seated, Graham knew he'd made a mistake. Something about the way she looked at him was off base.

Danielle didn't see it as their common sorrow, she interpreted the seating arrangements as subtle interest sparked from Graham. He *did* like her. This just proved it. It would be sad if Dana never recovered...but if that occurred, maybe the two of them could take care of her. Danielle smiled inwardly. *Forgive me, Lord, for thinking this way. But Dana is not married to the man. If I can capture his interest...well, so be it. Dana is younger than I am. She has many more years to find a man than I do. Look what I've given up for her. Yes, it was her turn.*

Chapter Eleven

A gentle breeze tempered the late afternoon sun. "Summer is just about over guys. We need to enjoy this good weather as long as we have it. *"Lord, thank-you for this food; bless it to our use. Amen."*

"This food is amazing," Jay demolished his heaping plate of food with gusto.

"Awesome," Will dug into his vast array of delectable food with gusto.

"I've got a ranch hand coming tomorrow. We need some help with the horses...especially since Dana's not in the equation at the moment. Also, the agency is sending over a woman who is interested in permanent employment. She's a housekeeper/cook. If I decide to hire her, I want you boys to meet her, of course."

"Cool, Dad." Jay grinned. "Does that mean we don't have to make our beds and vacuum anymore?"

"Dream on, guys. You'll still be doing your daily chores, but she'll keep the place looking good. The cleaning service Dana organized has been working just fine— but before the school term starts this fall, I need to get some staff settled in. Barbecues are great for summer, but when fall sets in, we're going to want soups and roast beef and that sort of thing..." Graham had a teary moment. *Myrna had been a fine cook. He'd been spoiled rotten. Now it was his turn to spoil his sons. He wanted to be good to them, the way she'd been good to him.*

"Yeah. Things went a lot smoother when Dana was hangin' out here....I mean, before she had the accident and amnesia... I don't think we realized all the stuff she was doin'..." Jay took the last bite of his cheesecake.

What exactly had Dana been doing? She's a lousy cook. Danielle was a fine cook but Dana was useless in the kitchen.

"That's true, Jay. The cleaning service she organized has worked out well; but given the size of the house, I need someone to seriously maintain it... plus take care of shopping and cooking... once fall sets in." Graham was contemplative. He glanced from one son to the other. *Thank-you, Lord, for blessing me with these wonderful boys.*

~

"Okay, boys, dinner is done, you can hang out here or play with Roamer and Rover, if you want. I'll just put on some music and marvel at the sunset. Maybe y'all will join me once you get tired of playing Fetch or whatever...with the Shepherds." Graham cleared off the table and set the dishes in the dishwasher.

"Dana found us those Shepherds, too...don't forget." Jay stroked Roamer. He stooped down and picked up some balls from a wicker basket in a corner of the veranda, racing down the steps, Roamer and

Rover hot on his heels.

Graham watched his sons play *Fetch* with the dogs. *Thank God for animals.* Still, his heart broke for his sons as he glanced from one vulnerable, tender, young lad to the other. They were much too young to have to live with the sorrow of losing their Mom. A tear trickled down his cheek. *Maybe they aren't ready to seriously get into riding, either. Maybe he'd been pushing them too hard.*

After his sons were done playing with the Shepherds, Graham called them back to the table. "Got a surprise for y'all... I've got an extra Key Lime Pie. Bought it from the caterers."

"Yeah! I love Key Lime Pie, Dad!" Will grinned.

"I saw it in the fridge, Dad. I was just waitin' to see if you were going to serve it to *us* or give it to Dana and her Mom." Jay glanced over at his dad.

"You don't miss much, do you, Jay?" Graham had a twinkle in his eye.

"Try not to, Dad. Learned it all from you." Jay smirked.

Graham reached over and touselled Jay's hair. "Anyway, just so you know, I sent enough cooked food with Danielle to last them a few days. And they've got four slices of Key Lime Pie. We need to keep praying that Dana will snap back...and the fact that she recognized *Lightening* and commiserated with him, is huge."

The boys lost no time. They plopped back onto their wicker chairs. A couple minutes later, Graham set down large pieces of the Key Lime Pie. The boys dug in and so did Graham. Momentarily, he turned to Will. "That last lesson you had with Dana...what caused

Toby to stumble?"

"We told you, Dad. Toby stumbled on a rock and I flew off. It was scary and everything...but I was okay. She said most novice riders had a few falls before they settled into becoming good riders."

"She said that, did she? Graham was introspective. "I wonder why she took you down by the creek?" Graham set down his fork and waited for the answer.

"I told her I wasn't a...novice rider—but I said I knew I had a lot to learn... I suppose there was no reason not to ride down by the creek..." Jay shrugged.

"No...I suppose not." Graham was introspective.

"Dana was quite upset after you yelled at her, Dad. I think you really hurt her feelings." Will demolished the last bite of his Key Lime pie.

"I apologized to her, boys. We went riding...that's...when she had the fall."

Will realized he'd touched a sore spot. "Dana's gonna get better, Dad. I just know it." Will's eyes grew larger. They sparkled with youthful optimism. His faith could move mountains.

~

Dana awakened early. It wasn't daylight yet. She glanced over at her Mom sleeping soundly in the next bed. *"Lightening.* I must go and feed *Lightening..."* Suddenly her mind was crystal clear. "Mother...wake up...I...have to feed *Lightening...*and I remember what happened...the fall..."

Danielle was awake in seconds. She sat up in bed, disoriented. "Dana!" She leapt out of bed and hugged her daughter. "Dana, I'm thrilled to pieces! Tell me what you remember..."

"Mother, I...I fell off *Lightening* and hit my head.

I...I remember vaguely driving here with you...but most of all, I remember *Lightening* and...*Black Prince!* And Graham...and Jay and Will...and of course, you, Mom!"

Danielle was jolted totally awake. She leapt out of bed, grabbed a robe from the closet and tied it on. "Come on, Dana, I'll make some coffee and we'll go out to the horses."

Daylight filtered in at Sugarbush farm as Dana and Danielle strode to the barn.

Graham was already there when they arrived. It was almost as though he knew. God had awakened him early and in his spirit he'd felt elated. *He just knew Dana's mind had sprung back. It was as if the Lord had tapped him on the shoulder with the good news he had so fervently sought.*

Dana saw Graham milling around like he was waiting for her. She smiled, drinking him in. "Good morning, Graham." Her smile broadened as she strode over to *Lightening's* stall and began stroking his neck and whispering to him.

"How do you feel?" Graham moved toward her, elated. He felt like clicking his heels and shouting with joy to the Lord. He restrained himself. Instead, he peered into Dana's eyes. "You look...absolutely...wonderful." He was filled with male appreciation and overjoyed that Dana had snapped back.

"You don't look too shabby yourself." Dana smirked.

Danielle felt left out and was about to sulk, when Will and Jay showed up. "Guess what, boys? Your riding teacher has miraculously recovered." She flashed them a big smile. *But even while she was happy for her daughter, some part of her longed to steal Graham away from her, and keep him for herself. But now that Dana was well, she had lost that window of opportunity.* "I'm sorry, Lord." Her prayer was a silent whisper. "If I hadn't given up so much for her, maybe I wouldn't be resentful of her budding relationship with Graham." Tears clouded her eyes. Tears of sorrow and regret.

"God heard our prayers!" Jay was over the moon. "I knew it would be the horses that would bring her back. We should have twigged when she recognized *Lightening*...we should have realized there would be more..."

Graham and Dana remained transfixed to each other.

Danielle turned, gave a little wave and headed back to their house.

Danielle felt ashamed. *I'm sorry, Lord. I don't know what I was thinking. Maybe...maybe Graham is just too darn good looking and wonderful for any woman to resist.* Dana was fine. Her presence here was redundant. She phoned the doctor and left a message about Dana's recovery. Then she drove off. She would pick up her stuff later.

~

After feeding and watering the horses and leading them out to pasture, Graham threw out an invite to Dana. "Come on over for breakfast. You can help me select some staff if you like." Graham drank her in, feeling more alive than he had in ages.

"We're going berry picking, Dad." Jay and Will carried plastic containers for the berries. They jumped on their bikes and rode away.

Graham and Dana held hands as they walked together back to the mansion. "What time are your appointments, Graham?"

Graham put his arms around Dana and held her close. He was overwhelmed with gratitude to God. He hadn't dared entertain the thought that it might be years before she recovered, or maybe never. He nuzzled her neck. His breathing became ragged. "Dana, oh...oh...oh...I stayed awake many nights praying for you...I knew only God could restore you, and I believed...with all my heart...that you would get your memory back. To Will and Jay's credit, they prayed, also." He kissed her then. A fiery passion arose within him. A passion that Dana, not Myrna had ignited. *Lord, are you trying to tell me that I need to love again?* The passionate kiss and embrace lasted interminably.

Dana was engulfed with a fiery passion she didn't know she possessed. She had never felt like this before. Never wanted a man like she wanted Graham. Every fibre of her being danced with new and joyful vibrancy and...a longing for him that so deep, it was inexpressible. *So this was love. This was what the songs were written about. What men and woman fought for, killed for, betrayed for... Lord, thank you for the incredible gift of love!*

Her eyes were filled with tears when they finally pulled apart. "Oh Graham, thank you for your prayers...I could feel them...even when I was completely out of it...I knew someone was praying for me. Praise God for you and your wonderful sons."

After breakfast, they sipped coffee on the veranda. The vintage white wicker sofas with the large turquoise and green floral cushions was comfy and relaxing. A balmy breeze tempered the sultry heat. A smattering of sizeable tropicals—mostly Palm tree fronds, were interspersed throughout the rambling veranda. They swayed in the breeze. Everything was right with the world. *"For I know the plans I have for you, saith the Lord, plans to prosper you and not to harm you."* The scripture muscled its way into Dana's mind and heart. *Thanks for that word of encouragement Lord. I needed that.*

Graham remained conflicted. Now that the crises was over and he felt vulnerable to loving again, he dug his heels in, allowing himself to return to his original mandate of never loving anyone but Myrna. That was his "Go to" mode. He closed off his heart and sealed off his emotions. *He couldn't live through the deep sorrow he'd experienced, ever again. He couldn't open himself up to being vulnerable. He wouldn't love again. He couldn't love again.* Dana's mind had snapped back. They would be good friends. Nothing more. He would need to set boundaries. He didn't want to lead her on.

Dana sensed the turmoil and conflict rising up in him. It was almost palpable. *Thanks a lot Graham. You're teasing me. Just when I think there's hope, I see that look in your eyes and I have to give my head a shake. You're off bounds.* And as frustrating as it was, she would just have to live with it—for now, at least.

Dana had a will of steel. It's why she was a good equestrian, an ace horse trainer, why she knew and understood horses so well. Equines possessed a mind of their own, as well. Graham had met his match. He just didn't know it yet. *Maybe I have to teach him how to let go and let God. Is that what this is about, Lord?*

Suddenly, unexplainably, his arms encircled her again. He held her so close she could barely breathe. His lips came down on hers. The pent up passion he'd hidden from her raged in the kiss and soared through his being. It was a fire out of control. His breathing got faster, heavier.

He stopped suddenly.

He held her away from him for a moment, gazing at her with love-struck eyes. "Dana, I'm crazy about you!" He blurted out the words that had been engraved in his mind and heart for weeks. *In fact, if he were to be totally honest, he'd flipped for her the moment he'd laid eyes on her.*

~

She refused to edit the words that sprung unbidden from her lips. "I'm...wild about you, too!"

He seemed to snap to his senses then. And he stopped. Cold. He pulled away from her, shaking his head. "I'm sorry...I don't know what I was thinking..." He turned away.

Dana hid her disappointment in favor of trying to understand his volatile emotions. "You've been through a major ordeal with losing your wife... and then moving here....why don't we just agree to be friends...for now? I want to be someone you can count on to help you through the deep valley... you've been stoically walking through alone..."

"Never alone, Dana. God has been with me every step of the way. I must tell you...I didn't really want you to move onto the property—but when I prayed, seeking God, I knew it was destiny...I knew you were *supposed* to move onto the ranch. So...here we all are."

"Okay. I'm going home to take a nap and relax.

Knowing Danielle, she probably already left. The woman is a mover and shaker; but I guess you've already figured that out."

Graham chuckled. "Yeah. I sort of have. She moves fast. Has she always been like that?"

"Always, Graham. For as long as I can remember."

Join us for dinner tonight, Dana?" Graham was on the phone. "I...uh...want to know how much salmon to buy. We're having salmon steaks."

"Can you imagine me turning that down?" She paused. "I'll bring the salad and veggies. Danielle left a lot of that stuff in the fridge."

"Okay, Dana. You're on. I'm thinking dinner for 6:00. Is that okay?"

"Sounds good." She put down the receiver and smirked. *Lord...I really wish you would tell me what's going on. Is there hope for us? It sure seems that way.*

She wasn't expecting an answer, but she got one. *"For I know that plans I have for you, saith the Lord, plans to prosper you and not to harm you. Plans to give you a hope and a future."* Her heart soared. Whatever and whomever was in her future, it was was positive and wonderful. *Thank-you, Lord.*

Will and Jay dawdled with their barbecued salmon. It wasn't long before the curious, young lads began asking a lot of questions. "So...why would someone want to steal a retired racehorse, anyway? " Will's eyes shifted from Dana over to his dad.

"Simple, guys...stud fees. Wealthy horse owners get rich by breeding horses with good pedigrees. These breeders own a lot of good mares and produce as many foals with top pedigreed horses as they possibly can." Graham savored the salmon.

"So...like... is that why you bought him, Dad? " Will was contemplative.

Graham chuckled. "Actually, no. I happen to love and respect the beauty...and...majesty of the horse...to turn them into a money-making machine...by having mares line up for...sex with a stud, is not something I want to do. I believe in letting nature take its course..."

"In polite, horsey circles, Graham...just so you know. It's called *covering* the mares. And it's often a public spectacle, which I find offensive. I'm saddened that these pedigreed thoroughbreds are turned into cash horses, forcing them to operate like a machine with little regard for the psyche of the animal."

Jay spoke up. "Well, Dad. You said we live in a free enterprise society. Isn't that just...like an easy way of making money? And since horses can't talk, how do we know how they feel about it?"

Dana spoke up. "Horses *can* talk, guys. They talk when rear up, they talk when they whinney, they talk when they buck a rider off or run away with them...they talk in so many ways...they just don't use the English language as we know it." Dana glanced over at Graham.

His broad shoulders were practically bursting out of his tropical shirt—and...big surprise...he wore a pair of cotton crème-colored Bermuda shorts with Top-Siders. A fresh, masculine-scented cologne wafted her way. "A man with principles...I rather like that." She glanced his way and their eyes met and held. She smiled at him. *What was it about this man that...excited her, charmed her, fascinated her...more than any man she'd ever met in her life. If only he were available.*

~

Dana couldn't sleep. She tried reading the Bible she kept on her night table. Still, she was restless. . She couldn't stop thinking about Graham and his sons. His sons had gotten under her skin. She adored them. They were a joy to be around. Sure, there were times when one or the other became melancholy. And other times when they got snarky and wanted Graham exclusively. She empathized with their plight. But they were good boys and well-mannered—easy to love.

She finally drifted off after claiming a scripture. *"He gives his beloved sleep."* Something awakened her, startling her. It was a noise outside. She sat bolt upright. Moving out of her comfortable bed, she padded over to the bank of windows at the front of her house, peering outside. She could hardly believe her eyes. A young guy...a kid really...maybe eighteen or so, was poised to mount *Rising Sun*, Graham's best thoroughbred...the retired racehorse! The porch light illuminated him.

Acting purely on instinct, Dana grabbed a robe, tied it on and picked up her rifle. She always kept it right next to her bed. She raced outside, cell phone in one hand, rifle in the other.

The kid had mounted the racehorse. He spotted Dana, turned the thoroughbred and dug his heels into his belly. The kid was riding bareback.

"Freeze!" Dana's voice bellowed in the night. She cocked the gun, ready to shoot. She'd call the sheriff once she got things under control.

Rising Sun reared up slightly. The kid jumped off, raising his hands. "Ma'am, I'm so sorry...I...my Mom and I don't have enough to eat...and...we don't have the rent...I had to do somethin'..." He was a gangly kid and didn't look well cared for or well fed. Maybe he was telling the truth.

"I'll have to call the owner...Graham...and see what he wants to do." Dana stood next to *Rising Sun*, calming him down as she speed dialed Graham's number. She rang several times but there was no answer. *"It's 4:00 in the morning, Graham!. Where are you?"* Dana suddenly got a pit in her stomach. Was something else wrong? Was the kid with other hoodlums? Had they broken into Graham's house? She fired a shot in the air, then another. Maybe it would wake Graham. Instead, Roamer and Rover raced toward them, barking frantically. The Shepherds circled the kid and the racehorse. *Why hadn't they heard the kid stealing the horse?*

The kid sprinted off on foot, moving with lightening speed. He was soon out of sight.

Should she mount *Rising Sun* and chase the kid? Call the sheriff? Pound on Graham's door? *Why wasn't he answering?* She couldn't outrun the kid, particularly while holding the shotgun. The dogs began chasing him. She felt sorry for the punk. She called off the dogs. They turned and ran back to Dana. She stood next to *Rising Sun* waiting for Graham.

Graham hurried down the front staircase of his house. He touted a rifle. He'd taken the time to pull on a pair of jeans and a sweater. "What's goin' on, Dana?"

She held the reigns of *Rising Sun.* "Thank God, you're okay." Dana managed a weak smile.

"What happened? Did you just manage to stop a robbery-in-progress?" Graham's expression was somewhere between incredulity and sheer amazement.

Dana was suddenly very aware of the flimsy robe she wore. She realized she must look incongruous in her lavender silk robe, masses of thick, mussed-up hair and touting a rifle. She was starting to feel chilly and a little shy about Graham seeing her like this.

"I guess you got a description of this guy, did you?" Graham was clearly unnerved.

"Yeah, I did. The kid is around 5' 11" He's gangly, has brown hair, longish, unkempt...and he has enormous brown eyes. He looked terrified. I managed to snap a photo of him on my cell. He told me that he and his mom were starving. Guess he was hoping to steal the racehorse and turn it into a money-making machine." Dana sighed.

"The kid must know horses. And he must have known the retired racehorse was in the barn." Graham sighed, and began mindlessly walking Dana back to her house. The question is, how did he get into the barn? And how did he know we had a retired racehorse in there? Did one of the boys forget to lock the barn?"

"A lot of ranchers don't lock their barns, in case there is a fire, it makes it easier to access." Dana's mind was racing. "Maybe the boys didn't lock it. Regardless, horse thefts do happen, occasionally."

"I know Will can't bear to lock the barn in case of a fire. Maybe he was the last one in there." Graham peered at Dana with male appreciation despite everything that was going on.

"The barn door was unlocked." Dana shrugged. "You may want to look into a security gate with a code at the entrance to Sugarbush. Although this kid apparently came on foot, which leads me to believe he lives in the area. Maybe he works as a groom at nearby farms. I had a sense that he was real comfortable with horses." Dana led the retired racehorse toward the barn.

Graham accompanied her.

"Most likely. I don't buy his story...but I guess you never know. If it's true, If he and his mom are really in dire straights... maybe...I'll give an anonymous gift to his Mom...maybe see if I can meet with the kid and help him...looks like he's lost his way...easy to happen when you have little or no parental authority. No Dad to guide you." Graham was introspective. "The kid isn't much older than my sons."

"I didn't realize you had so much empathy for teenagers... I suppose I might have guessed, given your proclivity for philanthrophy...and the fact that you have two boys." They had arrived at the barn.

Graham inspected the lock. "No sign of forced entry. The door was unlocked. The kid just walked right in. We need to check every stall. Make sure nothing else was disturbed."

Dana settled the thoroughbred back into his stall. Then, she did her own investigation to make sure nothing else was stolen. She checked the Tack room. No saddles were missing. She moved toward Graham who was taking a close look at all the horses and checking that their gates were closed.

"Doesn't look like anything else is missing." Graham turned to Dana. "Maybe you want to get dressed and put on the coffee. I don't think either of us will be able to go back to sleep. Let's go to my place. I'll...wait while you get dressed, then maybe I'll brew some coffee. Given the weird stuff going on, I don't want you to stay at your place alone tonight. I don't know if I'll *ever* be comfortable with you staying there, now."

Dana thought her heart would springboard out of

her chest. *The man was irresistibly gorgeous. In fact, he was downright thrilling. She actually liked him bossing her around. Weird. Really weird. She loved the fact that he took control.* She grinned. Was there anything she *didn't* like about him?

Dana was beginning to feel at home in Graham's kitchen. She found the gourmet coffee, made a pot of it and served it in the rambling, country kitchen. She glanced around the comfortable room. She had added some touches to warm it up. A couple of tropical plants. Some designer kitchen towels and a few carefully chosen knick knacks.

"Do you think there is more than one horse thief involved?" Graham poured coffee into two large mugs, handing Dana one and keeping one for himself.

"Well, given the two incidents happened in the same week, my best guess is that it's the same kid. But you just never know." Dana sipped the coffee.

"I'll head over to the sheriff's office as soon as daylight breaks. I need to have a chat with Will and Jay, also. We need that barn door locked every night. My heart goes out to this kid...if he's telling the truth. Teenagers that grow up without a dad...or maybe have a violent one, tend to run amuck. Maybe he believes the end justifies the means...maybe he loves his Mom and wants to take care of her...he just doesn't know how." Graham took a long sip of the coffee. His mind was racing. "Maybe we can get this kid to come to church where he'll meet some teenagers that are grounded. I'll help this kid if the sheriff assures us that the kid doesn't have a long record, and we find out he's telling the truth about his Mom."

Graham walked Dana back to her house as soon as

daylight broke. They reached her door. "What if he's a phoney? A street kid, maybe...or a druggy? What if he's mixed up in a gang?" Dana continued to have serious reservations about getting involved with the kid. She felt that the sheriff should track him down and charge him with the theft.

"Obviously we don't know how it's going to play out; but I promise you I'll get to the bottom of it. Nobody wakes up my girlfriend in the middle of the night...and terrifies her to the point that she runs outside in...a robe...touting a rifle..."

"Girlfriend? Did she hear him right? Graham just referred to her as his girlfriend. Wow! This was huge. Maybe there is hope, after all.

As though Graham could read her mind and her reaction, he suddenly realized what words had slipped out of his mouth. He had to correct that. She was *not* his girlfriend. *What had he been thinking?* He needed to set the record straight. Fast. "Ah... Dana. Just so know...when I referred to you as "girlfriend" I didn't mean it literally. After all, all female friends are "girl*"* friends, if you see what I mean."

Dana saw red. And she was dog tired. Not in the mood for pedantic nonsense. Hadn't she just defended his retired racehorse? Risked her life by confronting the would-be horse thief alone, in the middle of the night? She was just starting to feel good about herself and Graham...dreaming that they might have a future together...dreaming that he and his sons might someday become her family. She didn't need him throwing cold water on everything.

Didn't God promise to give us the desires of our hearts, if we delight in him? He promised life abundantly. Well, Graham wasn't the only man on the planet, and she knew for sure she was attractive. Aside from her mirror confirming this, she got second glances from more than her share of males. Even Danielle, her mom, was a knockout at fifty-three. Some folks thought they were sisters. But she wasn't good enough for Graham. Your loss, buddy. I'll move on. "Graham, I'm tired. It's been a taxing night. I need to get back to sleep so I can function properly today. Oh, and don't worry about me thinking I'm your girlfriend. God says *"I will do a new thing..."* Don't you know that after we sorrow, God desires that we get on with our lives? Life was meant to *lived*, not just walked through. This is not a dress rehearsal. We have to get it right now. God took Myrna to be with him in Glory, but you're still here, Graham. And you're a red-blooded male, as far as I can tell...God didn't create you to go through life solo. Sure, your sons fill the void right now...up to a point, anyway. But guess what? They're going to grow up and go to college and you'll be alone. Do you really like your own company so much that you don't want to share your life with a special someone?"

Graham took her in his arms then and kissed her with fervor, shushing her up. When they pulled apart, he spoke from some private, deep place inside him. "I needed to hear that, Dana. For some...crazy reason...I have all this loyalty to Myrna...and I promised her on her deathbed that I would never remarry. She was my one and only love. Yet...*she* encouraged me to go on with my life, to live it to the fullest..."

Dana put up one finger over his mouth, shushing him. "I know, darling. I know."

He kissed her again, more passionately and with

total abandon. He wanted this woman. Really wanted her.

She sensed he had the urge to pick her up and carry her to his bedroom. She wanted that too. But Dana lived by the Bible and because of it, she knew that somehow she would come out a winner...she didn't know how or when...but it would happen, of that she was certain. Someday... she was sure... God would see to it that she would marry a fine and wonderful man. *Could it be Graham? Could there be a chance they could share a wonderful life together?*

Chapter Twelve

The kid had been telling the truth. The sheriff had paid the kid and his Mom a visit and had been stunned by the deplorable conditions they lived in. Home was a run-down apartment in a seedy neighborhood. Mom was depressed, unemployed and living off welfare. She told the sheriff that because of some pressing dental issues she had to deal with, there wasn't any money for food.

When the report came back to Graham, he stopped by Dana's house to share the news. "I'm going to send an anonymous monthly check to them...but first, I want to meet with them and learn the best way of helping them long-term. After all, *There but for the grace of God go I.*"

Dana made a jug of iced tea and they sat outside on her patio sipping it. A Big Leaf Magnolia tree shaded them. Next to it stood an Ashe Magnolia. The fragrance from the flowers on the trees wafted toward them, enhanced by the balmy breeze rustling the leaves. It was early afternoon. Intense heat beat down upon them, despite being tempered by the wind.

"So you're going to reward his failed thievery with cash for him and his Mom? That's a really great way to spread the news of your philanthropy to young hoodlums...and great motivation for them to get into horse thievery..." Dana peered over at Graham, realizing she'd come down too hard on him.

It was too late.

Graham rose from the wicker chair he'd been lounging on. "What happened to...love and compassion, Dana? *Love thy neighbor as thyself* and all that. His face reflected his disappointment in her lack of compassion.

Even if he were available, she would never do. "And I will take your heart of stone..." What was that scripture again? It came to him. It was *Ez. 36:26. A new heart also will I give you, and a new spirit will I put within you, and I will take away the stony heart out of your flesh and I will give you an heart of flesh."*

As the scripture flashed into his mind, he realized he was acting impulsively. "Dana, we're all on a spiritual journey. Look up *Ez. 36:26.* We're to have a heart of flesh. We can change the world one person at a time. I can't turn my back on someone I can help. I don't live in fear; and you shouldn't either. If I have to hire a night guard to monitor the place, I will. Nothing in this world is safe and sure; we just do the best we can, and help those that God has thrust in our path. None of us has to do it all. You know the drill...one sows and another reaps. So let's just do what we can to help and trust God to protect us."

Graham took a long sip of the tea. He knew he'd

just espoused a rather lengthy monologue. He glanced at Dana. She smiled in spite of herself. She still wasn't buying it. "Graham, I think maybe it's time I find another place to live. This has been a great respite for me; I needed to be on a ranch near the horses after the house I was renting went on the market. And this has been a wonderful place to heal after...the fall...and amnesia. But it's time for me to move on..."

"Temper tantrums, Dana. You and the horses have a commonality. You buck off the rider when you're upset, don't you? If you did move off the ranch, where would you go? What about your horses? You need to be near them, Dana. We both know that."

"I'll rent a place in town, near Mom. Maybe you'll let me board my horses here; if not, I guess I'll have to find somewhere else to board them." Dana felt trapped. *Me and my big mouth.* She peered over at Graham and smiled. "Can we start over? We both care about the kid; we just have different theories on how best to help him, now that he's crossed our paths. I say he should be charged for attempted theft. B & E, I think they call it. He broke into and entered the barn, rustled up the thoroughbred and was almost off and running. *I* caught him. Not *you*, Graham."

"Dana, you're clearly used to running the show. But this is *my* ranch. And I'm running the place—not you. You don't like the way I run it—maybe you *should* leave."

~

Dana was stunned. Flabbergasted. Speechless. She stood up and just glared at him. Who did this guy think he was? Okay he was a gorgeous hunk I'll give him that. ya, okay. He's also a believer and rich to boot...and a widow. Who was she kidding? The pickings didn't get any better than him. She adored his sons. Still, he was getting on her nerves. The constant harping about how much he loved Myrna and how he was never going to remarry...blah, blah, blah. It was too much, really. She had to get away from him.

Yes, leaving was definitely the best thing to do. After all, he wasn't the only man in town. She would move on to greener pastures. Okay; so maybe the next guy wouldn't be as rich, or as educated and smart and sexy and...oh what was the use... she was absolutely crazy about the man, even if his lame idea of helping the poor didn't match her theories.

A scripture popped into her mind. *It was about helping the poor and finding treasure in heaven. Maybe Graham was right. She better patch things up with him. So they didn't agree on everything. So what?*

She didn't know she was going to do it. Graham had remained standing by the door after their altercation. She threw her arms around his neck, losing herself in his cobalt blue eyes. "Graham...I'm crazy about you. I..."

He stilled her. Stopped her from continuing her speech. He kissed her...long and hard. Her knees felt like they were buckling. Her heart spun out of control. The kiss went on interminably. The sound of Will's voice broke into their passionate embrace.

Will was knocking on the door...talking through it. "Dad..." Will opened the door and stood a few feet away from them. An odd expression clouded his features. He seemed to be trying to compute the scene. "Dad...um...well...does this mean Dana is going to be our new Mom?"

~

"Son," Graham chuckled, nervously, moving toward Will and putting his hand on his shoulders. He took a deep breath. "This means that...I like Dana...a lot. But remember what I told you? We run everything by God. Why do we do that, son?"

"Because...because God knows everything. And...God knows what's best for us." Will smiled, confident he'd given the right answer.

Graham put his hands on his son's shoulders. "You're a good student, WIll. These summer Bible classes are giving you some real knowledge of the Word."

Will sulked. "I wanna know if we're going to have a new Mommy...or, like, maybe just a live-in cook... I didn't like the one you...interviewed the other day. She was snotty and I could tell she didn't like Jay and me."

"Well, I'll keep that in mind. I certainly won't he hiring anyone you boys don't like. I will probably hire a housekeeper/cook. It's a large house to take care of. The cleaning service Dana organized is great, but it would be better to have a live-in; Lord knows we have the room."

"Before you...hire any of them, Dad...like...do Jay and I get to meet them?"

Graham leaned toward Jay and spontaneously hugged. "Son, you and your brother mean everything to me. I want you and Jay to be real happy with whomever I hire."

"You do great barbecuing Dad...but your housekeeping leaves a lot to be desired." Jay smirked.

"Glad you agree we need help. Barbecuing is great for summer—winter months you might starve."

"Dad!"
"Just kidding."

Chapter Thirteen

Kileta was a half hour early. She had mountains of auburn hair. Her dark eyes sparkled with intelligence. She gave her age as thirty-eight.

"Why do you want to be a live-in cook and housekeeper? Frankly, you look too young and glamorous for the job..."

Kileta crossed her long, tanned legs beneath the short, floral dress she wore. "It's all I know. All I'm trained to do. All I want to do. I love children, cooking and all things domestic."

"So you're from Mexico City, right?"

"Originally. We moved to Kentucky when I was a child, because Mom has a sister here..."

"And you're available to live in and do housekeeping, cooking and keeping an eye on the boys...they're young teenagers... if I have business to take care of."

"Yes. I would love it." She flashed a big smile.

"And when school starts in the fall, I may need you

to pick the boys up or drive them occasionally. I'll need to find out if a school bus comes near here and I'm not saying that would be a daily chore; I just want to be sure you have a driver's license and all that."

"Since I was sixteen, Sir. Never had a ticket...or an accident. I drove myself here."

She seems too good to be true. Maybe I should look a little closer. "I'll see you to the door, Kileta. I have another woman I need to interview, also." Graham stood to indicate the meeting was over.

Kileta smiled, shook Graham's hand and left. Soon, she drove off in an older blue Nissan.

Graham did check closer and discovered she was newly released from prison. She'd been in prison for attempted murder of her former husband. *The last thing he needed was a woman who had been involved in domestic abuse. He'd rather go it alone...or lean on Dana and his sister to pinch hit when he couldn't look after the boys. He would need to be much more cautious in hiring a live-in housekeeper/cook.*

Graham gave the agency a piece of his mind. "Do not send any more candidates. I will be working through another agency," he told the owner. "Further, to protect your other clients, I suggest you check into Kileta's criminal record. You apparently failed to do that."

Graham hired Violet Hoffman. A woman in her early seventies, she was imbued with great energy. She had been a competing runner in her youth, and still moved remarkably fast. There some things he didn't like about her, but no one was perfect and she seemed to fit the bill. Her references were excellent. That spoke volumes. And his sons liked her. She captivated their hearts in minutes. Violet was a wizened old gal with a razor sharp wit.

"Take a couple of days to get settled in and oriented. Get used to the house. Find out where everything is." He'd toured her through the house and was surprised that she seemed unimpressed with the magnificence of it. *I guess she's always worked and lived in lavish estates, just like she said.*

"Why that's right gentlemanly of you, Mr. Van Rensellier. Ah sure do appreciate it." She peered over at him. The piercing eyes that inhabited the old girl's weathered face searched Graham's eyes. *She* was deciding whether she liked *him* or not.

"Get settled in for a couple of days. Buy whatever you need at the supermarket in the way of food and household supplies. Just give me the bills." He thought better of that plan. Instead, he handed her some large bills. "Take this cash and go shopping when you can. Just give me the receipts for the goods. If this works out, you will have a home for many years to come." Graham grinned and shook her hand. "Welcome to Sugarbush."

Violet's eyes sparkled with delight and humor. "If it don't work out, it ain't gonna be my fault. You'll never find anyone more hard-workin' or a better cook than me." Her eyes twinkled with merriment.

Graham loved her spunk. In fact, actually, he loved pretty much everything about her. She would be a grand addition to the family. "Tonight, Violet, I want you to be my dinner guest. I'm doing barbecued chicken. You'll meet my friend, Dana...she'll probably join us for dinner. I can likely talk her into making a salad. Oh...and...my sons approve...so you can't be all bad."

He smirked and raised his eyebrows.

"Why...you're a regular... good ole Southern gentleman, I do declare. That's mighty generous and gracious of you to...have a sort of...orientation meeting." As she smiled, the creases around her eyes seemed to deepen as they danced with merriment.

"Now, let me help you with your luggage and get you settled in. I'll get your suitcases from your car. You just relax."

"Door's open, Graham. You'll see my suitcase and an overnight case in the trunk. That's it."

Graham got Violet settled into her room. He wondered why her skin was so leathery. She looked more like an outdoors woman. "Make some tea, have a rest...do what you want...this is your home now. Dinner will be served at 6:00 on the back veranda." Graham headed down the stairs to fetch her luggage. "One problem solved...many more to go." Graham spoke aloud as he retrieved the luggage from Violet's car.

~

"More salad, Violet?" Dana glanced over at the older woman. She was a treasure. No doubt about it.

"Don't mind if I do." Violet nodded and smiled, lighting up her face.

"I picked up some Key Lime Pie after I stopped into the office this afternoon. Does anyone *not* want a piece of it?" Dana waited a few beats for the response.

"That's what I thought. I shall indulge also." Dana disappeared into the kitchen, returning with the pie. She served it to Violet, the boys, Graham and finally herself.

Jay brought out the tea.

Violet dug into the pie. "Used to enjoy a lot of Key

Lime Pie in the Bahamas. Worked for a couple there for over twenty years. Well... it's on my resume..."

"I'm so glad you showed up here, Violet. Welcome to Sugarbush." Dana smiled. Strangely, *she* was beginning to feel like "The Lady of the manor." It seemed perfectly natural to play the gracious hostess.

Violet insisted on cleaning up after dinner and serving herb tea, despite the protests. "Guess I'll watch TV and have an early night. Tomorrow, I've got a lot of shopping and housework to do. I'll be turnin' in real early." She smiled warmly at the group and headed in the direction of the staircase leading to her upstairs room.

Chapter Fourteen

Dana had fallen hard and she knew it. Whatever would she do? Moving out didn't really solve anything. He's waved the rent in exchange for her teaching his sons to ride. Recently, Graham insisted she pay no boarding fees for the thoroughbreds in partial exchange for her expertise in selecting the "perfect" racehorse...hopefully, a colt that would win the Kentucky Derby. "Once you begin the training process, we'll hash out a deal we're both comfortable with. I'll be counting on you to give it your best shot with the Derby in mind." She loved that Graham deferred to her in all matters pertaining to the equines. It kept her on her toes.

Dana called Danielle. "Well, I did it, Mom. I hung my license and gave notice to the Landlord that I won't be renewing the lease at the Real Estate office. I am going to commit to training a colt for the Kentucky Derby. Graham and I are believing God together for finding and training the Kentucky Derby Winner. I know it's a daunting goal, Mom. But have you ever known me to settle for less than the moon?"

Danielle laughed heartily. "No, honey... I have not."

Mom...I just know we can do it. It's where my heart is...maybe why I was born...I walked away after Stefan's accident...but I believe God is calling me back to the horses...it's my destiny."

"I hope you know what you're doing, honey. Real estate is a lucrative career...especially for women." Danielle always tried to be good to her only daughter, but she couldn't help feeling a bit envious. Dana always seems to get whatever she wanted in the end. It had never been that way for her, though. She was a businesswoman and she'd worked hard for everything she'd achieved.

"Mom, I need to put my whole heart and soul into the horses. Training is a full-time job. I've had a break from it. I saved some money. Now, it's time to get back to my...calling. You know, Mom... someone once said 'If you can, you should.' That says it all. "I *can* train a winner. I just *know* I can. Somewhere...deep inside I know I was born for this...gifted for it." Dana was reflective. She shared everything with her mom. "Firstly, we need to buy a special colt with impeccable bloodlines. I've been praying every morning that God would lead, guide and direct me to purchase the right colt."

"Well, I need to caution you, Dana. Don't overpay. The price these owners are asking is usually outrageous...you need to be very, very cautious and careful before...Graham plunks down his hard cash." A flash of envy rippled through her. *I shouldn't be envious of my daughter. I shouldn't be competitive with her. I need to love her. Just because I've been a widow for ten, lonely years, it doesn't mean I should resent Dana finding someone. Forgive me, Lord.*

"Thanks for your input, Mom. We will be seeking God on this. It's a challenging undertaking; but I'm up to the task...and so is Graham."

"I hope so, Dana. I...hope you're not biting off more than you can chew." Danielle couldn't help throwing a little damper on her plans. She was still waiting for someone or something exciting to sweep into her life. Dana had already found her Prince Charming. And only one year after her last romance ended.

"I've challenged Jay to a game of chess," Will's eyes twinkled.

Dana knew Jay usually won, but Will was to be commended for his persistence.

"May we be excused, please Dad?" Will glanced over at Graham. Then he turned toward Dana and shot her a shy grin.

"Of course. Enjoy the chess game." Graham grinned. A gentle breeze ruffled his naturally wavy hair as he reached over to the coffee container, pouring Dana another mug of coffee and topping up his own mug.

Sitting out here on the back veranda, the sun warming her melting heart, Dana had never been happier. *I'm sure he doesn't feel the same way. He's still grieving Myrna. I can feel it; sense it sometimes. It must be such a deep valley to walk through. Lord, please let me comfort him, let me be his friend..."* Oh, what was the use? She sighed. *She didn't just want his friendship, she wanted everything with this man—absolutely everything.*

"There's a horse auction tomorrow afternoon, Dana. I think we should go. It starts at 2:00. The auction is held adjacent to Keeneland." Graham glanced over at Dana.

She snapped back to reality. "Absolutely. But I need you to spell out your goals so that I can help you achieve them. You want to upgrade your existing horses, correct? Or are you serious about buying the best colt with the best bloodlines and the goal of competing for the Kentucky Derby? I need to be clear on your goals. You tell me exactly what your plans are. I know the equines... I'll help you get there." Dana peered into his eyes, her heart lurching. *Darn, that man is good lookin'."* She smiled at him, unable to resist flirting with him.

He grinned back. "I want a winner, Dana. I want to buy a racehorse that will win the Kentucky Derby. We lost some time with you having amnesia. Let's get back on track. Meanwhile, if we see a really great thoroughbred that we like, we can start to build a stable of really fine horses and sell off the inferior stock, like we talked about. We can enjoy riding them and if they prove to be superior...maybe enter them in contests. I need all the help you can give me...I respect the fact that you're the pro."

"Hey, thanks, Graham...for that acknowledgement. I'll be happy to teach you everything I know." Dana peered into his eyes. Her stomach lurched. *What a gorgeous hunk. Will he ever be mine, Lord?*

"I thrive on challenges. Right now my biggest one is figuring out how to run a ranch and turn a profit."

Graham peered at her.

"Sorry to give you a cold shower, Graham...but the first tip I'll give you is not to expect to make any money horse farming; though you could do well if you want to offer a boarding facility, obviously. Horse farming is a rich man's hobby. I think you fit that part of the equation. If your objective is truly to locate and purchase a racehorse that will take first place in the Derby... I'll help you achieve that goal. I know you've been following the Derby for a long time; so I hardly have to warn you of the pitfalls and daunting challenges. Still, it is a truly admirable, exciting goal. I'm with you all the way, Graham."

"You're the expert, Dana. You're the insider. I'll rely on you to bring me up to speed." He hesitated a bit before continuing. "If you commit to this project; you may want to consider taking a hiatus from selling real estate. You will need to focus your time and expertise on helping me find and train a winner...and since that's a full-time job, I'll give you suitable remuneration, in addition to your housing and boarding your horses."

"Okay, you *are* serious. It's a business proposition." She took a long sip of the coffee. There really wasn't any need to mention that she was a couple moves ahead of him and had already taken steps to end her brief real estate career.

"I had a hunch you'd say that. I'm very serious about this project, Dana."

"How does God fit into this equation? You've indicated that it's...a mission of sorts..."

"Thought you'd never ask, Dana." He grinned at her.

Her heart lurched "Well?" *Those piercing, cobalt*

blue eyes and broad shoulders made it hard for her to concentrate on the subject at hand.

"If we win the purse, I want to donate it to Israel. There are still aged, poor Jews that escaped the Holocaust that aren't being properly looked after...it's just something God has laid on my heart."

"I know the Almighty promises to bless those persons that help His beloved Israel. Thus, I believe he will lead and guide us every step of the way in this pursuit."

He warmed her heart and did a whole lot more than that. *Oh Lord, I want to spend my life with him. He...he's stolen my heart...help me.* "I...I'm a bit surprised that you wouldn't want to contribute to cancer research..." *Lord, I hope I'm not becoming too pushy.*

"I have already given extensively to cancer research...and so has my family."

"Good for you. I...I didn't realize how philanthropic you were." Dana was becoming increasingly enthralled with every aspect of this wonderful man.

"Come on...I'll walk you home. Maybe we can talk more there. The boys will head outside soon to play Fetch with the dogs...and we need to flesh out the plan." He leaned into her and hugged her.

She melted into his massive chest and whiffed the masculine scent of his cologne. The power of his broad shoulders and massive chest excited her more than she cared to admit.

They pulled apart after a short time. Graham's mood morphed into a serious tone. "There is work to be done—lots of it. If we are going to enter a colt to compete in the Derby next season, a lot of planning and training needs to take place. But first, of course, we need to locate and buy *the* finest colt available..."

"True. Timing is of the utmost importance. I need to train the colt on a rigorous schedule. He must not go past his peak. Over-training is as bad as under-training. As a licensed trainer, there are a lot of little things I gleaned that trainers and assistant trainers don't know unless they have earned a license. It's actually a gruelling course." Dana peered over at him to gauge his reaction.

Graham was an ace listener. "We'll do this. I really believe that." He grinned at her.

Chapter Fifteen

The feisty, powerfully muscled colt captured Dana the moment she laid eyes on him. The dark bay thoroughbred racehorse reared up, his nostrils flaring as the trainer sought to calm him down for the visit with Graham and Dana.

"Tell me about this racehorse." Dana peered into cold, calculating, grey eyes. The older trainer was reluctant to disclose any information. Instead, he ignored her question, leading the horse into his stall.

Dana and Graham followed him into the barn. Dana whispered to Graham. "He doesn't want his owner to sell. Maybe the owner *has* to sell. He might be in trouble financially. I bet the trainer wants to buy him and is trying to raise the money to do it."

"We're meeting the owner here, Sir. Dana Lockhart and Graham VanResellier." Graham reached out his hand to greet the odd man. Flat, grey eyes peered at them, contemptuously. He didn't give his name. "Wait outside." His voice was gravel.

Graham glanced over at Dana and then back to the trainer. "We'll be happy to do that." Graham remained gracious. He turned to Dana. "Let's go."

Dana reluctantly trailed Graham out of the barn. "I don't know what he's up to, but he's...way off base, that's for sure." They stood outside the barn, the hot sun beating down upon them.

Dana consulted her watch. "Ten minutes. Still, no owner has shown. Now what?" Suddenly, Dana twigged. "I have a hunch that trainer took the racehorse out the back of the barn to squelch the meeting we have with the owner. Chances are he's trying to buy it...probably working on raising the money...maybe getting a consortium together."

"You might be right, Dana. You know more about this business than I do." They walked around the barn and practically bumped into a tall, lean, older gentleman. Graham and Dana exchanged glances and spoke in unison. "The owner, I bet."

I know him from somewhere. Dana suddenly remembered his name. "Tanner Wessner, right?" Dana turned on the charm.

"Hey, Dana! Nice to see you again. I thought you'd left the industry."

Dana grinned. She enjoyed the recognition of folks. She'd been a star jumper, and folks knew who she was. "Only Show Jumping, Tanner. I'm back to training. Hey...any truth to the rumor you're thinking of selling *Flaming Bullet?*"

"I'm...thinkin' of selling... that's right." He assessed Graham, skeptically.

"Any chance we can take a closer look at the colt? The trainer was a little less than welcoming." Dana raised her eyebrows.

Tanner chuckled. "Uh... don't worry about him. He's a sour puss at times. Known him a long time. He's an okay guy. I'll tell him to go get a cup of coffee." He waved them back into the barn. "Come on in, Dana...and..."

"Graham. Graham Van Rensellier." Graham grinned and shook Tanner's hand as the trio strode into the barn together.

Tanner glanced over at Sour Puss. "Get yourself a cup of coffee. Come back in an hour if you want."

Sour Puss fastened his grey eyes on them. He was motionless for a few beats and then turned, lifted his head high, striding out of the barn.

Tanner led the Thoroughbred outside into daylight. The dark Bay was a beauty and contained a great deal of powerful energy. It seems to spark from him. He was sleek and muscular. Almost perfect.

Dana peered at the Dark Bay, appraising him with trained, expert eyes.

Graham looked him over with approval.

"Have you had lunch yet?" Tanner glanced from Dana to Graham.

"No." Graham couldn't decide if he liked or trusted the man. Something about Tanner bothered him. He just couldn't put his finger on it.

Dana was skeptical, too. She knew a few things about Tanner that Graham probably didn't. Still, she had a sense about the Dark Bay and she felt in her spirit that the colt was a great horse—a winner.

Over lunch, Tanner showed them a file of the history of the racehorse.

Dana was skeptical, but it seemed the colt had

done extra-ordinarily well and was headed for more wins. *So why does Tanner want to sell him?* The question niggled at her.

Graham finally cut to the bottom line. "What are you asking for the colt?"

At the price he mentioned, Graham almost choked on his chicken burger. When he recovered from the initial shock, he peered into Tanner's pale green-grey eyes. "Why so much? Is he really worth that?"

Tanner relished displaying his vast knowledge and the stellar history of the racehorse, along with his impeccable bloodlines. He talked endlessly about the colt, citing details, dates and winnings.

Dana's head was spinning. She glanced over at Graham. He seemed to be taking it all in stride.

"Why are you selling? He sounds like a perfect candidate to win the Kentucky Derby and Preakness Stakes race." Graham studied the owner's face, skeptical.

"Mah wife is ill. She doesn't have long. I need to give her all mah time and attention...I don't know how long I have her for." His countenance changed along with his voice, which became softer.

"I understand." Graham's voice was gentle, compassionate. Waves of sadness washed over him.

"Ah figure he's ripe to win the Kentucky Derby. He's got a real good shot at it. But mah wife...is more important to me...I want to spend every spare minute with her...I can't focus on prepping *Flaming Bullet* for the Kentucky Derby at this time. I believe God wants me to give someone else a crack at him."

"Have you entered him in a lot of races? Do you have a list of those and how he fared?" Graham spoke with authority. He felt nervous dealing with the man, though he wasn't sure why.

Graham has done his homework. That much is obvious. Dana was impressed by how astute and knowledgeable Graham was becoming.

"Yes, to your first question; and yes, to your second." The owner was smug.

The package is too neat; too perfect. What is the owner not saying? Graham was an astute businessman. Something didn't add up here. But what? *Maybe he was too much of a skeptic.* Graham peered at Dana. Was it a match made in heaven? Or was he missing something?

Dana was skeptical, also. "We'll need to check out everything you've told us, of course. Could we have a copy of that report?" She took another sip of coffee.

"I figured you'd want that. Here you go." He pulled out a file from a folder he'd laid on the table. He handed the report to Dana. "That's your copy."

Graham hid a grin. He loved bright, shrewd women. Myrna had been that and more. Dana was sharp and clearly a seasoned equestrian...and businesswoman. He liked and admired so many things about her.

"We're on our way to an auction. If we don't buy a horse today, we may come back for a second look at your colt...if he's still available." Dana watched the owner's reaction carefully. If there was a downside or any missing information, she wanted to know about it.

"With all due respect, Dana...and Graham, It could be gone by then. I have another buyer viewing him...in..." He glanced at his watch. "A half hour."

Graham and Dana exchanged glances. "We'll take

our chances." The words were spoken in unison. They peered at each other, unable to believe what had just transpired. They both burst out laughing and it broke the tension.

They had one more private racehorse to view before attending the 3:00 auction. The racehorse was a fine thoroughbred with impeccable bloodlines. That much was obvious. He'd won many Stakes races. Still, Dana always relied heavily on her gut feeling when it came to picking horses. She didn't have it about this one. It was just as well— she wanted to see what horses were up for auction.

Graham drove Dana and himself to the auction. A true gentleman, he opened her door. Their eyes met and Dana's heart lurched. *What is it about this man that sets my heart to racing?* She smiled, peering into blue eyes that seemed to change in color from day to day, like the ocean. She could lose herself in those eyes. She loved everything about him.

He grinned at her. Neither spoke for several minutes. As they strode toward the area in which the auction was being held, Graham finally cracked the silence. "We're going to buy a racehorse today, Dana. I feel it in my gut. And it will be the right one. I just know it." He spoke with conviction and resolve.

"Strange. I feel the same way, Graham. But we had better pray. I don't have to tell you what an enormous investment this is." Dana's voice took on a somber tone as they walked together toward the auction. Dana prayed. "*Lord, you are in control. You know our lives from beginning to end. You know the love we have for horses. Would you give us the wisdom to choose the right horse at the auction, or the direction to find the best colt? Lord, you know our goal is to win The Kentucky Derby for Your honor and glory."* Dana's eyes were closed as she meditated.

When she opened her eyes, Graham was standing very, very close to her. He peered deeply into her eyes. Then he leaned down and took her in his arms. His lips came down on hers. Gently at first, then more fiercely as their kiss escalated into great, burning passion, causing them to be locked together in a kind of timeless eternity.

Her world spun into a frenzy of wild emotion.

"Whatever am I going to do with you, Dana?' Graham's tone was sombre, thoughtful. He struggled to calm himself, cool his ardour. When his breathing finally returned to normal, he peered over at her. "Come on, Dana, let's go find a winner."

"Let's do it!" She laughed, gaily. The Derby was supposed to be fun. Joyful. Exhilerating. She wanted that. She wanted to tap back into the excitement and challenges she'd known as a jumper and trainer. She longed to part of that world again.

They were surrounded by dozens of prospective horse buyers. Dana greeted some familiar folks. Kentucky horse auctions were a social event as well as being a serious auction.

A rider paraded the thoroughbreds for the onlookers to enjoy and assess. The registration papers for the racehorses were displayed publicly, allowing the potential buyers to study them before the auction began. A pedigree specialist stood by, available for questions. This one was an old-timer. Dana knew him from somewhere. She smiled and nodded her recognition. He returned the smile.

They read the registrations papers on a few select thoroughbreds that tweaked one or the other's interest. Still, neither of them felt moved to make a bid when the auction finally began. Still, they stayed through to the end, not wanting to offend anyone. For Dana's part, she waited to see if God would suddenly nudge her to get Graham to make a bid. She kept glancing at Graham to see if he was inclined to offer on any of them.

Graham finally glanced over at Dana. He spoke in a hushed tone. "I must tell you, Dana...I do not feel led to bid on any of these fine thoroughbreds...do you?"

"No, I don't. Many of the thoroughbred racehorses have impressive accolades. But I don't feel led to discuss a bid or make one. Is that your take, too?" Dana peered over at Graham, waiting for his reaction.

"You took the words out of my mouth." Graham nodded.

They drove toward Sugarbush in silence, after the auction. Dana's cell chirped. "Any luck?" Tanner's distinctive voice was on the line.

"Could we take a closer look at your racehorse?" The words sprang unbidden from Dana's lips.

Graham turned the car around and headed back to the farm where they'd viewed the racehorse guarded fiercely by the sour trainer. "We may wind up bidding against the trainer, Graham. I have a gut feeling that he's trying to buy that colt." Dana glanced over at Graham to gauge his reaction.

"You're probably right, Dana. But if he had the money or had managed to raise it, I assume he would already have bought it." Graham shrugged.

"True." Dana agreed.

"I know you get that buying the right pedigreed

racehorse is merely the beginning. Expenses to keep him, and continue working with him will be astronomical." Dana warned.

"And based on past events, we may need to hire 24/7 security. There will be a lot of money tied up in him."

"You're absolutely right, Graham. In fact, I was going to suggest you hire some security."

"Aw, come on, Dana...you're just sayin' that." Graham grinned over at her.

"No, I'm not." She chuckled. "As it happens, I need my beauty sleep, you know." Dana smiled over at him.

"I have deep pockets, praise the Lord." Graham shot her a saucy grin.

It must be nice. Dana glanced over at him and couldn't resist flashing him a big smile. *Probably too big.*

They met the owner at the barn at Horseshoe Stables. The trainer was not present. It wasn't long before the registration papers were transferred and the seller had a certified check in his possession.

As Dana and Graham stepped out of his jeep, Will and Jay rushed up to Graham, ignoring Dana. "Hey, Dad...like...you were gone pretty much all day..." Will sulked.

Jay was silent for a few beats but then spoke up. "You bought a racehorse, didn't you Dad?" Jay spoke excitedly. He was grinning. He followed Dana and Graham up the front staircase to the house. Rover and Roamer barked their greeting as they bounded up the staircase close on their heels. Graham leaned down and tousled his son's hair, playfully. "You don't miss much do you, Jay?"

"Try not to. Learned it all from you, Dad." He smirked.

~

A couple of hours later, a handler driving a horse trailer showed up. Sitting next to him was Tanner Wessner, the former owner of *Flaming Bullet*. The handler, a lean, tanned cowboy jumped out of the cab of his horse trailer as soon as he stopped. A few strides took the lanky cowboy to the back of his trailer. He unlatched the door, let the ramp down and let the colt out.

Dana and Graham watched the handler assist the finicky colt down the ramp. "Frank's the name. That's a mighty fine lookin' thoroughbred you got here...don't come no finer than this..."

"That's what we thought." Graham grinned, feeling steadily more confident about the expensive purchase. "I'll show you the way to the barn." Graham grinned and strode toward it. Soon, they reached the large, red barn. Graham let them it and pointed to a stall. "Hey, the colt gets the very best stall in the barn." Excitement welled up inside him. *This is a long held dream. I sure hope it turns out well.*

Dana excitedly began watering him and giving him treats, being fanatically diligent about what she fed him and measuring the exact amount and types of feed to keep the champion and keep him in optimum shape.

Graham got his nose out of joint. Fast. "So, what's the deal, Dana? You don't think I know *anything* about racehorses? As it happens, I've read practically every book written on the subject."

"So...reading and studying books on racehorses

and attending the Kentucky Derby annually makes you an expert," Dana snapped.

"Knowledge is always power. God grants the favor and the wisdom. There are rich folks that have chased that golden dream all their lives...and never win...I know...I've met them." Graham observed Dana closely.

Dana finished feeding the colt. She peered over at Graham. "And yet you believe that you can win the Triple Crown. In fact, you've already decided what to do with the winnings. More power to you, Graham." Dana had kicked into her professional mode. "Knowledge is only a part of it; Graham. It's personal experience—hands on... years of training...and working with the thoroughbreds...and then...somehow, you develop that gut feeling that a particular colt with a winning pedigree is *the* one."

"I get that you have more actual experience than I do, Dana. That's why I hired you. But I don't expect you to talk down to me when I get involved in the care of my own racehorse!"

"Oh lighten up, Graham! You take yourself so seriously. You're rich. Super rich. I get that. And it's gone to your head! I get that, too." *Woops, maybe I got a little carried away.*

"Gone to my head? Whatever do you mean, Dana?" Graham stood glaring at her. Fuming. Hurt. Shocked.

"He who has the money, makes the rules and weilds the power. You forget one thing, Graham; you're *paying* me to advise you. We agreed on which racehorse you should buy. Now we have to come to terms with how we're going to proceed from here..." Dana despised feeling powerless; particularly when it came to the equines. She had developed a sixth sense about them. Her instinct about the animals had proven uncannily accurate time and time again. Almost infallible. Graham was a newbie in the business. Though she had to admit, the man was one fast learner.

Chapter Sixteen

Graham arose early, taking his mug of coffee onto the front porch. He picked up the Bible he kept in a wicker basket next to the rattan sofa. Studying Ephesians six, he claimed it over his life, his sons' life and Dana's life. Every day, he put on the whole armor of God. He claimed success for his God-given dreams. Satan and his minions doubtless would scheme up a strategy to derail his goal of winning the Triple Crown Stakes race. As a believer, he knew he had to fight a daily battle of spiritual warfare.

Graham was always mindful of the spiritual battle that raged over him and every believer. With his goal of contributing the winnings to Israel, he knew God was on his side, but he still needed to be alert and prayed up. He had been given much, and God would require much from him.

He was always mindful of the fact that he'd been born with a silver spoon in his mouth and a thirst for knowledge. Horses had been in his blood for as long as he could remember. He'd even toyed with the idea of becoming a polo player when he was younger, though he'd never pursued it. Still, owning a polo field and opening a polo club would be a great way to be involved in the sport. Plus it would be a legacy for his sons.

It would be easy to kick back and enjoy the good life on the ranch; but God had placed this burden on his heart and he knew that when the Holy Spirit led him, he had to follow. He'd missed the leading of the Holy Spirit only once in his life, and as the Good Book warned, *"Woe, to that one who ignores the leading of the Holy Spirit." He'd paid a bitter price for that misstep.* How much better it is to walk in the spirit, following the leading of God.

He would love to go riding, hang out with Dana and the boys and not have the pressure of prepping a colt for the Kentucky Derby. Still, he was up to the challenge, in fact he thrived on challenges. He had disappointed people along the way...he was only human...but he wasn't going to disappoint God. In fact, with all that he'd been given, he felt a burden to be a magnanimous giver.

Recently, during intensive prayer, he had sensed God nudging him to proceed with his plans to buy a colt and train it for the Kentucky Derby.

He believed with all his heart that his colt would win The Triple Crown. He and Dana would enjoy the celebration and victory. Then he would publicly announce that the winning purse would be a gift to Israel. Oh, he knew the rules; don't let your right hand know what your left hand is doing; but sometimes God led individuals to do things in unique ways. This was one of those times.

Jay ambled over to Graham who was in the Tack Room. *He seems restless.* Not like him. He was a solid, grounded kid. "Morning, Dad." Jay shuffled his feet and peered down at them.

"What's goin' on?" Graham was routinely checking the saddles. You couldn't be too careful. He tried to read his son.

"Well, like...Dad...Will and me had a fight. A real bad one. He said he's never gonna forgive me..." Tears sprouted from Jay's eyes.

Graham had rarely seen tears in Jay's eyes. He reached over and hugged his son. "I love you, son. What's goin' on?...we'll pray...nothing is too big or too hard for God, right?"

"R...right, Dad. That's right." Tears trickled down Jay's cheeks and he sniffled.

Jay rarely cried; rarely got really upset. "What did you fight about, son?" He grinned, trying to lighten the mood.

"I don't know if I should tell you, Dad. Like...you might be...irked with me."

Graham grinned. "So what? Whatever it is, we'll deal with it. So spit it out."

"Well...like...it's about Dana, Dad."

Graham took a deep breath. He hadn't expected that. "Let's have it."

"Will and me got into a fight. He said you would probably end up marrying Dana. And I said it would never happen..."

He had Graham's attention. Big time. He stifled a smirk. "Where is Will?" Graham peered at Jay.

He...he's sulking in his room, I think." Jay sniffled.

"We need to talk." Graham's tone was serious.

"I'm listening." Tears trickled down Jay's cheeks.

"Do you mind rounding Will up for me? I'll meet you both in the family room in about ten minutes." Graham lovingly raked a hand through Jay's hair, tousling it.

"Sure, Dad." Jay was gone in a flash.

In the family room, Jay and Will settled onto the Wing Back chairs, Graham sunk into the candy-striped, canvas sofa.

"You need to understand something, guys. Dana and I are friends. Period. She's a trainer, as you both know...she's going to work with the colt and prep him for the Kentucky Derby. We're going to win. That means that Dana and I will be working closely together on a daily basis. I'm... fond of her. But marriage is not in the cards if that's what you're thinking. I've told you boys that before. Why do you think that's changed?"

"Because...because..." Jay squirmed around in his seat, uncomfortable. "I just have a hunch...because I think...Dana...is in love with you, Dad." He blurted the words out.

Graham was stunned. Silent. Finally, he spoke. "What makes you say that, son?"

"Well...like...Dad...you'd have to be blind not to notice that she looks at you...with love-struck eyes...and hangs on your every word..." Jay glanced down at his feet, shuffling them.

Will became very serious. "Ya, Dad. I see a lot of movies. I've watched how she looks at you. She's got designs on you, Dad. You better watch out..."

Graham chuckled. "She's a trainer—and a good friend. She's going to help us win the Kentucky Derby, as I said. God sent her to us for that...and...yes... maybe some companionship, as well." Graham's voice took on a serious tone.

"You're kidding yourself, Dad." Jay peered closely at his dad. "I think..." He blurted the words out. "I think you love her, too. You just don't want to admit it." He smirked, chuckling.

Graham was stunned. His sons had grown up overnight. He gaped from Jay to Will for a couple minutes before speaking. "I think this conversation has run itself out. I'll rustle up some breakfast for us. I'll be meeting Dana later this morning to go over the training schedule, etc... I'll ask her—flat out—if she has designs on me. Then I'll just let her talk. We should learn quite a bit from a confrontational line like that, don't you think?"

"Unless...unless she conceals the truth, Dad." Jay looked real serious.

"You read too much Shakespeare, son. Not everyone is complicated...nor do they have evil...or ulterior motives. I read Dana as a straight shooter. "

"What do you know, Dad? Don't you get that women can be devious?" Jay smirked.

"I suppose...can I rely on *you* to teach me the ropes?" Graham grinned at Jay, a twinkle in his eye.

"You got it, Dad. Glad to be of service." Jay saluted with all the pomp and regality of nobility.

Chapter Seventeen

Dana took the colt through his paces. Graham rode along *with* them, observing her methods. After a gruelling morning of training, Dana was exhausted. "I'm going to take a break, guys. If you need me, you know where to find me." She smiled at Graham and his sons and strode back to her house. *Flaming Bullet* had been up to the task of being trained. In fact, he seemed to revel in it. Dana felt good about the progress they'd made on their first day of training.

Will and Jay watched Graham feed the ravenous racehorse.

Lord, I sure hope this is not a waste of time and money. Quickly, Graham repented of his unbelief. *Hadn't God led him to the colt that he and Dana had chosen? "Oh ye of little faith..."* spun through his mind and pounded at his heart.

It *was* going to work out. Graham had to admit that every day he spent with Dana, his admiration for her grew. He had a sneaking hunch that she was the best trainer in Kentucky. Sure, okay, he'd come to that decision based primarily on gut instinct; which, of course was backed by her stellar record. Then there was that mysterious hunch he'd grown to trust in himself and Dana. *Yes, Flaming Bullet would win the Kentucky Derby. He had to win it and by the grace of God, he would.*

Graham had always thrived on challenges. His current one was without precedent—and because of it, he'd thrown his heart and soul into it. The endeavor *had* to be successful. He found himself praying more often and more diligently than ever before. *They had* to win. And they absolutely would win.

Dana pounded on the back door at the top of the back steps of the old mansion.

Graham heard the knocking now. He didn't hear it before. He hurried to the back door which was locked and opened it. He took one look at her face and knew that something was terribly wrong. Whatever it was, it had to be serious. "Come on in, Dana. What's goin' on?" He studied her harried face."Why didn't you come to the front door?"

Dana ignored the question and started bawling. "The...colt. He's..he's... gone. Stolen. He's not in his stall...and he's not in the field. Let's go, Graham... we better ride out and see if he's somewhere on the farm..." Dana fought to keep a handle on her emotions. She straightened up. "If someone stole him, he won't get away with this." She speed dialed the sheriff.

"Sheriff Donaldson here." His voice sounded strained. Tired.

"Dana Lockhart. I'm at Sugarbush Farm...Graham Van Rensellier's place. I've been training a racehorse for the Kentucky Derby. I live on the property. Suddenly, the colt has gone. Vanished. I...I don't know how they managed it. I didn't hear a sound last night...and my house is close to the barn..."

"I'm sorry, Dana, there's been a spate of these horse thefts lately. We don't know if we're lookin' for a lone wolf or more than one thief. I'm on my way. I need a description of the colt and any other information that may help us..."

Graham had to be strong for her. Dana was verging on hysteria. "My times are in His hands. *The Lord giveth and the Lord taketh away. Praise be the name of the Lord."* God was in control and he refused to allow fear to overtake him. "We'll get him back, Dana. Jesus is Lord. The enemy doesn't want us to win, because the purse will bless Israel." He turned to the invisible but real enemy. "Take your hands off my mission and purpose. Greater is He that is in you, than he that is in the world." Graham spouted Eph. 6:10 to 17. He bound the enemy and prayed the prayer of protection over Dana, himself, his sons and the horse farm.

"I have a hunch who might have stolen her, Graham." Dana peered into Graham's eyes. They were pools of wisdom...depths she could lose herself in. She melted. *What was it about this man that sent her emotions whirling and twirling...not to mention her heart soaring into orbit? "I could have danced all night,"* played in her mind.

"Well, don't keep it a secret." Graham grinned.

"I think it might have been that weird trainer. He seemed fixated on the colt."

"I don't."

"Why not?"

"Maybe because it's too easy...too obvious...I'm betting something else is goin' on..."

"Okay. Like what?" Dana peered into Graham's eyes. They were soft and tender. She could easily lose herself in them. Peepers unlike any she'd ever known before. She'd long been a believer of the old adage stating that the eyes were the windows of the soul. She had glimpsed his and she liked what she saw.

"So what's your take, Graham? Let's have it."

"Your buddy. The one who sold it to us. The one with the sob story, that's who..."

"What! You've *got* to be kidding?"

"I'm afraid not."

"So you think he sold it to us and then stole it back?" Dana was incredulous.

"Yes. It makes perfect sense. Who else would *Flaming Bullet* go with? His former owner...that's who..." Graham spoke with conviction.

"So you're saying he's a con artist and horse thief?" Dana frowned, trying to assimilate the new information.

"I'm afraid so, Dana. I wish I would have figured it out sooner. I didn't have a good feeling about him. But that was overshadowed by the fact that I had a great hunch about the colt." He shook his head in disbelief. "Is the sheriff on his way?"

"He is."

Graham and Dana answered the questions the sheriff fired at them. Twenty minutes later, he roared off in his sheriff's vehicle.

Jay lounged on the sofa in the living room, buried in thought. "Dad, I've been reading *Ephesians, chapter six.* I'm learning how to put on the armor for spiritual warfare. Like...I guess it's spiritual warfare when you consider that you want to contribute financially to Israel. But Satan wants to keep that small country in war...and like—poverty... and turmoil."

Hey, I'm proud of you, son. That's true. "Satan's insidious, sinister plans are in opposition to what we're trying to do. But never forget that we have greater power than the opposition. Remember: *"Greater is he that is in you, than he that is in the world."*

Chapter Eighteen

Tanner was nowhere to be found. He'd left town, maybe the country...maybe even with *Flaming Bullet*; who no doubt would be renamed. Dana sat outside on her patio seeking God, the Almighty, maker of heaven and earth. *"Lord, how could we have been so deceived?"* She turned again to the book of Ephesians. Paul had warned his followers repeatedly to put on the full armor of God daily. But she hadn't done that. She'd been too busy training *Flaming Bullet* and caring for him to do spiritual warfare. And...too busy making eyes at Graham and appeasing his precious sons...to spot the enemy throwing flaming arrows at her.

What had Paul said? The enemy has strategies against your passion, against God's dream for your future. Against your mission and purpose. She had not been rising early and seeking Him with her whole heart, the way she had intended to...and because of it, she was unarmed, allowing an opening for the enemy to strike her through her weakness and unpreparedness.

Dana likened it to an alarm clock. If she *had* built herself up through prayer and saturating herself in the word of God, if she *had* put on the whole armor of God, would she have seen the horse thief coming? Would the power of prayer have thwarted the theft? *Lord, open my spiritual eyes that I might see.*

Graham sat down next to her. Wordlessly, he handed Dana a mug of coffee and one for himself. They sipped the coffee in silence.

Dana sensed a renewed strength in Graham. *Had he been praying with all his heart and mind and soul that Flaming Bullet would be found?* There seemed to be a peace about him. She took a sip of the fine brew. "You sure know how to make great coffee, Graham. Do you grind your own beans? It tastes amazing."

"I do. And I'm glad you like it, Dana. Now... about the horse thief. He won't get away with this. Maybe he's a serial...chronic horse thief. Maybe he changes his name...his identity...his story...his country. We may be dealing with a master of fakery...and the only way we can catch him is by looking to God for wisdom. After praying about this for some time, I received an image...it was like... a mask, a bizarre mask... we could be dealing with someone who has multiple personalities or at least a dual personality."

"Interesting take, Graham. So where do we look? Where do we go from here?" Dana's face suddenly lit up. "A thought just crossed my mind, Graham." Her face shone brighter. "I bet he's in show business. I bet he's an actor. He dons a personality, studies the characteristics of the persona he intends to depict and then parades around in-character." Dana peered at Graham's face, waiting for his response.

He nodded. "You know—I have a hunch you're right. Let's go to the theatre tonight. Let's drive into town and see a play. Maybe systematically attend all the theatrical events in town, and let's see if we can hook up with some actors that know our boy as an actor...not a horse enthusiast."

Dana arched her brow. "I have a hunch we're on to something. Maybe we should play amateur sleuths and see what we come up with."

Graham grinned at her, nodding. "Let's do it."

He managed to snap up a pair of tickets to *Raz Mah Taz,* a new musical. "We lucked out, Dana. We've got tickets to opening night. There's a gala after the show. It should be entertaining."

It was. After the show, Dana and Graham mingled with the opening night crowd at the champagne reception, held at a nearby restaurant. Dana traded business cards with a horsey couple she'd met previously and had lost touch with. She recognized other horsey folks and acknowledged them. More than one woman eyed Graham, and spotting her, shot her a look of envy. I wish he *was* mine. So far we're just very good friends.

They got lucky. A black actor, young and dynamic, chatted gaily with an older male character actor she recognized from the show. According to the program, the young actor's name was Bobby Starr. Catchy name. Dana smiled at him. Young men always seemed to like her and vice versa. And they all, somehow, reminded her of her late, younger brother, Stefan. "Great performance!" Dana smiled at Bobby. "You must be Bobby Starr."

"That's me. And hey, thanks. I sure appreciate the

compliment. And you are?" He'd turned from a couple he'd been chatting with, focusing his attention on Dana.

"Dana Lockhart. Horse trailer." She easily engaged Bobby in conversation as they sipped champagne.

A young, female server sashayed by them, pushing more goblets of champagne. Dana encouraged Bobby to chat about himself and his career, soon sneaking in her hidden agenda. "Do you know many character actors? Older dudes?"

"Of course. Why do you ask?"

"Any of them have horses for a hobby?"

"Are you kidding? In this town? Absolutely."

"Any older dudes that are horse enthusiasts spring to mind?"

"A couple. Hey...seems like you've got somethin' on your mind..." The actor studied her face with curiosity, grinning.

"Yeah...just wanting to hook up with an old friend." Dana tried to sound casual. She took a sip of champagne from the elegant flute.

"Do I get a name?" The actor peered over at her, curious.

"Well, you know actors...they change names... appearances... cities...." Dana took a sip of champagne and waited for his reaction.

"Throw me a few. I know a lot of actors."

"Tanner Wessner."

He thought for a minute. "He's just been cast in a show in L.A... read about it in the trades."

"Really? Well...good for him." *So he is an actor.* "So, what show? What theatre?" Dana tried to sound casual.

"Oh no, Ma'am, it's...a film role. He...uh...he plays

a Mafia type." The actor took a sip of champagne from his crystal flute. "It's called *The Light.*"

Chills tingled up and down her spine. *Only God could have led them to their target this quickly.*

"The trades said he starts shooting next month. I tried to get on the picture...no luck. It's the story of a hit man who becomes a Christian after a supernatural encounter with God... and a near-death experience."

Dana took a deep breath. She could hardly believe her luck. "Sounds fascinating."

"If you ever need to know anything about horses, I'm your gal. Been at it a long time." Dana slipped her business card into the actor's hand. Something about the intelligent, sensitive actor resonated with her. She slipped two crisp hundred dollar bills into his hand, along with her card. "There's lots more where that comes from." She whispered. *Where did that corny dialogue come from?* She gauged his reaction: It was positive. She smiled. Good actors were highly sensitive, and the smart ones saved their money when they worked, since they never knew when their next job would be.

"Hey thanks." He flashed a smile revealing a full set of sparkling, white teeth. "I need new pictures so this comes in real handy. Thanks. Oh, and...I think your guy likes shooting pool. There's a pool hall not too far from here. Over on Robertson Way."

Graham and Dana exchanged glances.

"Hey, when I get to be a star, I'll remember you." A grin lit the actor's face. His eyes sparkled. "Thanks, I really appreciate it. My new photos are lookin' better all the time."

At the pool hall, Dana and Graham immersed

themselves in the game. Graham knew how to play. Dana didn't. He showed her a few basic things like chalking the cues and the proper way to hold it. Next, he cracked the balls in the triangle and they started the game. He was a show-off and in no time ran the table.

Dana was really impressed. They played for a couple of hours, because aside from looking for their man, she actually enjoyed the game. So did Graham. They were just about to leave when Tanner walked in.

Dana locked eyes with him. She saw that stunned moment of something close to horror, sweep over him. It was followed by an attempt at composure, as he strode nervously across the room toward Graham and her. "Dana, what are you doing here?" Shock registered in his voice. There was a nervous twitch in his left eye. She hadn't noticed that before.

"I could ask you the same question. We went to the theatre and Graham suddenly decided it was time I learned pool. It's one of his favorite games. So here we are." Dana smiled, shrugging. "Do you play?" She tried to sound nonchalant, as though she hadn't been given a heads-up by the actor.

The stunned expression on Tanner's face gave him away. He turned his back to her and moved to the wall, picking up a cue and then chalking it.

Dana noticed his right arm and hand shaking slightly as he finished chalking the cue. Somber-faced, he turned toward the pool table.

Dana caught twitches flickering in his eyes. The man was nervous...real nervous.

Another man, big and burly, somewhere in his sixties, joined Tanner. The husky guy broke the balls in the triangle and they started a game.

It soon became obvious that they were both Pool Sharks and doubtless playing for big bucks, given their intensity. Graham and Dana continued their game. Graham won, naturally. "Come on, Dana. Let's go." He leaned into her, whispering. "We need a game plan." They waved goodbye to Tanner and his buddy, exiting the pool hall.

Reaching his Jeep in the parking lot, Graham turned to her. "He knows we're on to him. We need to let the sheriff know where he is and let him handle this." He started the Jeep and drove directly to the nearest sheriff's station.

~

Graham told the sheriff he suspected Tanner had stolen back the racehorse he'd bought from him. The sheriff frowned. "Have a seat. Let me do some research. See if he has any previous horse theft charges or whatever else might show up on the radar. Unfortunately, there *have* been a few cases like this. "

Twenty minutes or so later, the sheriff strode out of his office and over to where Dana and Graham were seated in the reception area. "The man is a suspect in several horse thefts but he's never been caught and charged. We'll put a tail on him and see what we come up with. We've been trying to nail this guy for some time. There have been several other complaints about him, and there have been some formal charges."

Dana and Graham, having been dismissed, drove back to the ranch. Dana had a nice warm feeling somewhere deep in her gut. She was falling hard for Graham and if the truth be known, she was not only crazy about *him*, but his sons, as well; despite knowing she and Graham clearly had no future.

"An evening out requires a gentleman to treat the lady properly. Hold on, while I get the door." Graham came around to her door and offered his hand for her to take.

Dana stepped out of Graham's Jeep and directly into his warm embrace. Strong arms encircled her, holding her close. His lips came down on hers. He pulled her closer and closer to him. His passion matched hers. They ignited like a fiery rocket. Unstoppable. Defying nature and time and everything earthy. *This* was heaven...what heaven existed on earth, she was tasting it, testing it, savoring it. The love she felt for him was way beyond anything she had ever know. *This* was what the songs were about, and the lyrics, and life. *This* was love. She could never go back to pretending they were just friends. And if he tried to do that, she would know that he was not being honest with himself.

Finally, it was Dana who wrenched herself from him.

Graham was in orbit, or he seemed that way to her. He appeared dazed and greatly unsettled. She watched him come back from the euphoric state they'd been enveloped in. Somehow, she'd snapped back faster than he did. Maybe it was the power of the shock she'd felt learning how much he actually cared for her.

Graham pulled himself from Dana and walked her to her house from the parking roundabout in front of the mansion.

Dana wanted him like she'd never wanted another man. Forever. She was somewhere close to heaven when his arms encircled her. *"Oh Lord, I want this man...I need this man...I can't live without him. He's like no other man I've ever known. Everyone I've ever met pales in comparison to him. Please, Lord, cause a miracle to happen...a miracle that entails the two of us becoming one in holy matrimony.* There. She'd prayed the desire of her heart that had been etched on her heart and mind for months. She couldn't fight this attraction forever. She had to either move from Sugarbush Farm and never see him again...or...please, God...marry the man!

He pulled her close to him on her doorstep. She knew he wanted to kiss her again, and felt him restraining himself. Somehow she summoned up the strength to pull apart from him. They stood on her doorstep gazing, love struck, into each other's eyes. *He feels the same way I do. I can tell.*

"I'd better go home, Angel."

"Angel?" *He called me Angel.* "A... nick name?"

Graham turned the key in the lock of her door and then turned back to her. "Maybe it is." He smirked. "Good-night, Angel. See you tomorrow." He turned and left.

Dana basked in the warmth and glow of Graham's attention and the new endearment. Stepping into the house, she knew instantly that someone had been here. Something was askew but she couldn't put her finger on it. But she would. She moved into the bedroom. The drawers in the dresser were open, the clothing inside, askew. Hardly the way she'd left it. She was a neat freak. *Someone has been in the house in my absence.* They'd been looking for something...but what? Rattled, she turned on her heel, calling Graham. He'd just left, he wouldn't have gone far. "Graham...someone has been in my house! Someone has rifled through the drawers...of my dresser..." She started shaking.

Graham hurried back to her. Soon, he reached her, wrapping strong, comforting arms around her.

"Honey...I...okay...let's get over to my house and then I'll call the sheriff."

Dana revelled in the warmth and comfort of his strong arms. *Thank you, Lord, for sending this wonderful man into my life.*

They climbed the steps of the old mansion together. "We need to report this to the sheriff right away. Whoever it is, they're going to be stopped. Fast. Nobody messes with my girl." Graham led her inside to the warmth and safety of his house.

Dana was tired. But not so tired that she didn't appreciate yet another endearing term he'd just used to describe their relationship

It hit her then. "The insurance papers. He must be after the insurance papers, Graham. He rifled the drawers. Maybe he planned to sell the colt and forge his name on the insurance papers...I don't know what his hair-brained scheme is...or what he was actually looking for. I suppose it could have been the kid...maybe he broke into the house searching for cash or valuables..."

~

The boys were still up, lounging on the sofas in the family room, engrossed in a late movie on TV. Dana and Graham poked their heads inside the door to let them know they were back.

"Hey, Dad. Don't keep us in suspense." Will peered over at his dad. Like...we watched over the place while you played detective. So...what did you find out?"

"We'll talk about it tomorrow. Dana and I will be in the kitchen. Finish your movie."

Graham put on a pot of herb tea and set out cheese and crackers on the table. "I'm not going to rattle the boys about this tonight. But you're staying here until we can get a handle on this. I'll tell the boys in the morning."

"I thought you said you knew Tanner from horsey circles, Dana? Strange that you didn't have even an inkling of his checkered past...how does that work? It hardly computes..." Graham was uncharacteristically rude.

Dana's blood rose. "Are you accusing me of...not doing my homework? The colt we bought from him, if properly trained, could and should win the Kentucky Derby! I had no idea he had skeletons in his closet. I couldn't have imagined...in my wildest dreams, that he would steal it back! If it *was* him, that is."

"Ya, Dad. Like... how do you know for sure it was him? It could have been someone else." Jay and Will had followed them into the kitchen and were snacking on the cheese and crackers. A serous expression clouded Jay's features. "I've been on the computer the whole time you two were gone...and I've learned a few things..." His tone was serious.

"Like what, son." Graham was dismissive.

"Like the fact that he has a twin who is an actor and has done time." Jay smirked.

"No kidding! The sheriff didn't say anything about that. Or maybe he didn't know. Crooks change their names all the time..." Graham peered at Dana.

"So...are you saying that Tanner is who he says is and sold us the colt...and maybe the twin brother stole it back?"

"I don't know...I just don't know. All I know is that we've got to get him back. Fast. Before he gets too far off our radar...of course the sheriff would know this...they keep their cards close to their chest."

"Would Tanner have enough nerve to try to sell him at a horse auction? Isn't there one more coming up...soon?" Will was thoughtful.

"There is...there's a small thoroughbred auction...early next week, I believe..." Dana's mind was racing.

"Tuesday." Jay announced. "It's at Horseshoe Farm in the valley. Not far from here according to Map Quest online..."

"You've been busy. Fine piece of detective work, Jay." Dana was impressed. "Except for one thing..."

"Yes?" Jay's curiosity was peaked. He grinned at her, an unspoken challenge dancing in his eyes.

"Tanner and his twin brother Troy wouldn't be that stupid. They could be caught red-handed..." Dana sipped the herb tea and nibbled on the cheese and crackers. "I think...personally...I think they've stashed him somewhere or transported him to another city." Dana glanced from Graham to Jay.

"Oh great, Dana. Thanks for that good news. So...what do you suggest?" Graham was crestfallen and stared numbly at her.

"Pray. We need to pray. That's all we can do. The enemy does not want us to have a winning horse. He doesn't want us to help Israel or anyone for that matter. We need to pray against the onslaught of the evil one." Dana peered over at Jay.

Jay wordlessly scurried out of the room. Minutes

later, he was back, clutching a black leather Bible. "Do you really think this will work? Prayer?"

"No, I don't *think* it will work, I *know* it will." Dana's tone was serious, intense.

"An unseen spiritual battle is raging over the noble quest of this potential winner. There is wickedness in heavenly places wanting to stop our progress. If we had wanted to win to stroke our own egos and pat ourselves on the back with our fine judgement...and then just squander the winnings frivolously...the colt would probably not have been stolen; but because of our noble cause...the enemy wants to bring us down. We need to be alert and prayed up...in fact, Paul says we should pray unceasingly...that's a remarkable statement, actually." Dana glanced over at Graham.

"Well said, Dana. That's an impressive discourse on spiritual truth. In retrospect, I think we made our mistake by not laying hands on the colt and committing him and the gruelling training schedule...the entire process...to the Lord. Our hearts were in the right place, but I guess we need to remember the ominous words. *"My people perish for lack of knowledge."* That is a sombre warning to all of us that we need to be in the scriptures and meditating on them continually. We live in perilous times." Graham glanced over at Dana.

Dana rose. "Well, I guess I better take courage in hand and head back to my house."

"No." Graham's countenance was stern. He was adamant. "I don't want you going there alone. I don't want you staying there tonight...in fact, I don't want you staying there at all until this case is solved...you might not be safe."

"Are you serious?"

"Dead serious. There's big money at stake and a potential Kentucky Derby winner has mysteriously disappeared...your house has been rifled...you're not going anywhere near the place right now." Graham's tone was grave.

Dana rose from her chair. "Don't be silly, Graham. God will protect me. What's he gonna do...break in and kidnap me?" She raised her eyebrows, smiling cheekily.

"Maybe. Maybe that's exactly what he'll do. If you're out of commission; and the colt is gone, that's one less very determined competitor. I don't have to tell you how lethal this horse racing game is...and I think we need to wise up. You'll sleep in one of the guest rooms here...Lord knows we have plenty of room." Graham gazed into her eyes.

Her eyes met his gaze. She was transfixed to him. Her heart raced frantically. *Stay overnight under the same roof as Graham? This must be somewhere close to heaven.* Still, Dana hated wimps. She wouldn't give in to fear. The Bible says *Fear hath torment.* She would march bravely home, take a relaxing bath and sleep like a baby. No two-bit horse thief was going to cause *her* to run in fear.

She stood then. Defiant. She had a mind of her own, after all. She had no future with Graham, so he kept telling her; but she was supposed to obey all his instructions? *I don't think so.* "Good-night, Graham, I appreciate your concern, but I'll be just fine. If anyone tries to break in, I'll...call you and the sheriff. I'll scream bloody murder..." She stood, smiled and headed for the front door.

Graham stood also, his features sombre. "You're not staying in your house, Dana. I meant what I said.

You're staying here tonight. I'll show you to a guest room." He towered over her. His powerful presence had an intimidating effect on her.

Dana stared at him. "Do you really think I scare that easy? We may have ruffled some feathers by showing up at the pool hall...but Tanner and his twin brother will need some time to figure out what they're going to do..."

"You're not getting this, Dana. I...*forbid* you to stay in the guest house. You're on *my* property, and I don't want anything to happen to you on my watch. You got that? You're staying *here.* And I don't want to hear another word about it." His voice was cold steel.

"Guess you don't have a choice, Dana." Jay smirked at her from the club chair he occupied in the family room.

"Anyway, it's fun having you here." Will enjoyed teasing her, as he kicked back on the long, L-shaped tan sofa that dominated the family room.

Dana stared at Graham. His face looked as though it were etched in concrete. She burst out laughing and it broke the tension. "I guess I'd better stay. You're bigger than me—if we got in a fight, I would lose."

Graham lightened up, "Hey, Dana. I'm not trying to be difficult, I just know that if foul play has occurred; and I think it's pretty obvious that it has—we need to hunker down and figure out what's goin' on here. I...I just don't want you to be vulnerable."

Chapter Nineteen

The next morning Graham served coffee in the rambling country kitchen, surprising everyone by whipping up Belgian waffles. He served them with maple syrup, topped with blackberries.

"Who knew you had this kind of talent?" Dana smirked, as she dug in to the waffles. *The man is a keeper for some lucky gal.*

"I know how to do breakfast...it's lunch and dinner I find challenging." Graham grinned from his place at the head of the circular kitchen table.

"I can help you out there. I'm actually a pretty decent cook, but I need some coaxing to get back to it." Dana dug into the waffles." Mom probably wouldn't agree with me, but she sets the bar very high. She's a serious gourmet cook."

"You've been keeping your culinary skills a secret. Why is that?" Graham peered into her eyes and held them captive.

Her heart lurched. "I...I didn't want to

infringe...you've hired Violet...and she's an amazing cook."

"Yes, she is. You just missed her. She got up early and went to the supermarket. Speaking of staff, I should maybe hire a ranch hand, also. The boys are going to be busy with school in the fall. Right now, obviously, our focus is on getting *Flaming Bullet* back. I want to go visit the sheriff this morning, Dana. I'd like you to go with me because you know Tanner and the thoroughbred. He's bound to ask questions that only *you* can answer...I just hope and pray that we get our colt back."

Jay peered at Graham. "I've been prayin' half the night, Dad...and I feel that the Lord is showing me that you're going to get him back. Tanner is a game player. If we can figure out what game he's playin' the colt will magically appear back on the property."

Graham spun around and stared at his oldest son. "Are you serious, son? You've...been praying half the night...and you got that... word of knowledge."

"Ya Dad. Like...you're the one who taught us the power of prayer. So...like... why should you be surprised I'm using it?"

"You're... absolutely right, son." Graham was stunned. "Absolutely right." He stared at his son with a mixture of pride and awe. "There's a scripture that says God will pour out his spirit in the last days. *Games, eh?* Tanner just met his match. I'm a master chess player and you're pretty much as good as I am...Jay...I think between the two of us, we should be able to figure out his silly games." Graham grinned at his eldest son, bursting with pride. "I have an idea, Jay. And anyone else that wants to join me...may do so...we need to do a prayer huddle. There's a spiritual battle raging over this enterprise. The adversary does not want us to have a winning racehorse, because the purse will be used to help impoverished people in Israel..." Graham stood. His sons did the same.

Dana rose, also. "I'm going home to see if I can come up with a brainchild...figure out what game he's playing. I have a hunch...we'll see if I'm right."

"I'll go with you. I know it's daylight — but I still don't like the idea of you being alone in your house...at least until we get a handle on this mystery. There's big money involved and unscrupulous characters at bay. We should proceed with caution." Graham moved to the door, opening it for Dana. They walked the short distance together to her house.

Graham glanced through each room , scouting around for anything suspicious. He also checked for bugs and scrutinized the door locks. "We need to change the locks for starters. Get a power lock and a security system with video cameras. I don't know if they're ever comin' back here...but if they do, we'll nail them...so Dana... we need to crank up the security here...or you'll have to become a semi-permanent house guest at my place..."

Dana was speechless. She wasn't sure if she imagined a sly grin crossing his features or not. "Right...I...don't know what to say. I...guess... I'm in shock."

"Sure. Meanwhile, you don't go into your house alone. That's the way it has to be for now..."

"I have a book I keep hidden in the house. Don't ask me why I hide it...because I can't give you a straight answer...but...let me show you my secret hiding place..." She picked up the lightweight cushion on the lime green and white wicker sofa and gasped. And then froze. "The book...it's gone. It's...it's been stolen. Graham. It can't be. The book isn't here. It's gone! That book has over twenty years of my personal observations...and information I've gleaned about horses. It.contains copious amounts of notes and... details about thoroughbreds, blood lines, etc. It was filled with notes, bits of wisdom gleaned over decades of working with horses! And now it's gone!" Tears welled up in her eyes. She fought the urge to bawl. "Recently, I'd been thinking about bringing it over to your house and storing it there, but then I thought that was rather silly; because I refer to it quite often." She turned to Graham. "Whoever broke in, wanted that book." She shook her head in dismay. "Maybe Tanner's game is that he takes the colt out late at night, rides it under cover of darkness and then brings it back before morning."

"Why would he go to all that trouble? Particularly if he intended to return it." Graham glanced over at Dana, a look of puzzlement clouding his features.

"Because he wants us to lose valuable training time, that's why. He likely has another colt he's grooming to compete for the Triple Crown. Maybe his game is to get us off track and cause us to lose time and get off course." Dana was excited. She stood. "That's it. I bet that's it! Maybe we should saddle up and ride out a fair distance on the farm. You never know what we might discover."

Someone was pounding on the door. She glanced through the peep hole. It was Jay. She opened the door. Jay stood there, his young, husky voice laced with an exciting edge. "I think I know what the game is!" Excitement mingled with a serious under current seemed to soar through him.

"Well?" Dana posed at the door, waiting to hear what Jay had to say. "Come in." She gestured for him to enter the house and take a seat on one of the matching pair of yellow wicker sofas.

Jay plopped down on one of them, his long legs sprawled out in front of him. "I think he's planning to sell *Flaming Bullet* at auction. Just that simple. We go there and we can prove that we own him, we have the registration; no one will be able to buy him. I think he knows there's something special about that colt, the "x" factor that could make him a big winner."

"It's worth a shot. The auction is today. It's...Dana glanced at her watch. "Starting in under an hour. But any serious buyer will want to see a prospective horse's papers...Tanner doesn't have them." Dana shrugged.

"True. But we can't under estimate the man. He would doubtless have some logical reason why he doesn't have them in his possession today, and he'll promise the buyer he'll have them tomorrow...or whenever." Jay grinned. "One of the zillion things I love about God...he often waits until the last minute to show up and cause a miracle to happen. He just whispered this possibility into my spirit...maybe a half hour ago. He *does* move in mysterious ways." Jay turned to leave.

"What is your take, Graham?" Dana deferred to him. She was doing that more and more frequently of late.

"Let's head out to the auction. Pronto." Graham stood, ready to roll.

Dana grabbed her purse from the glass-and-wicker side table by the door. "Let's go. I'll tell you my take on the way there. It's a bit bizarre, really." She chuckled.

The three of them strode to the Jeep. Jay sent a text to Will. He showed up in a flash, jumping into the back of the Jeep with Jay.

Graham started the engine, cruising down the long road to the gate. Once on the main road, he turned to Dana. "So, what's your best guess about Tanner's next move?"

"You're going to think I'm nuts...but here goes..." Dana expounded her theory to Graham.

He was silent for a few long beats before he spoke. "Is Tanner off his rocker? I mean, none of this behaviour is in any way normal."

"He could very well be. I took him at face value, but not anymore. Looks like we're dealing with a devious, unconventional...bizarre horse thief. We need to catch him before he creates any more havoc."

At the horse auction, there was no sign of the colt and no sign of Tanner. Finally, disappointed, they all climbed back into the Jeep. Dana turned to Graham. "There must be a way we can catch him..."

"Wait! There is. It just came to me." Graham smirked. He hadn't started the engine yet. He grinned over at Dana.

"Well, don't keep it a secret." Dana raised her eyebrows, her face a question mark.

"Maybe he has a second, secret ranch where he stashes the stolen horses. The ranch we know about... The Z Thoroughbred Farm is his cover. We need to find the *secret* ranch." Graham was smug. "And...and that fits in with his games. He fools everybody. He likes disguises. He's an actor."

"So...how did you come up with that?" Dana peered at him, skeptical.

"I don't know. It...just makes sense that he might think to do that." Graham glanced her way. Their eyes locked for a beat.

Her heart raced. *He is so incredibly gorgeous.* "Okay, let's say it's true. How do we find this secret ranch?" Dana peered over at him.

Graham started the engine. "Simple. We hire a tail. The detective can pick him up at one of the pool halls. It's a cinch." Graham shrugged. He looked in the rearview mirror, backed up and started driving off the property.

"I don't think that will work. If he thinks we're onto him, he may have left town already." Dana played Devil's advocate.

"We're going to find out. We're going to get this guy. Arrogant guys like him are fairly easy to trip up. They suffer from over confidence...and that will be what trips him up." Graham's eyes remained on the road ahead as he spoke.

"Well, I think it's a fool's errand. He probably knows we're onto him and he's a couple steps ahead of us." Dana sighed.

"Maybe not. If he's addicted to gambling at the pool halls, he might make poor choices." Graham kept his eyes on the road ahead as he drove.

"I think we should pray that God will protect *Flaming Bullet...*find a new colt, hire 24/7 security and move forward. We've filed the theft report with the Insurance company...they'll be doing a lot of close

checking...they might come up with something. If we
don't get him back, you can use the insurance money to
buy another colt. Do you believe in women's
intuition?" Dana peered over at him.

"Very much so." Graham nodded.

"Well, I have a hunch that if we keep frequenting
the pool halls, we're going to get to the bottom of
this..." Dana glanced out the window.

"Let's give it a shot...as many shots as it takes...as
it happens, I put a lot of stock into women's intuition.
Myrna had it in spades; and you know what? She was
always right."

Dana rolled her eyes. *Mryna.* "In checking the
internet yesterday, I printed out five pool halls in the
outlying areas. I have that sheet right here in my purse.
The closest one is Lily Play Pool Hall on Johnston
Road. It's maybe seven or eight miles from where we
are now..."

"Let's go." Graham programmed the location into
his GPS and soon they were headed there. Forty
minutes later, he drove into the parking lot of Lily Play
Pool Hall. It was jammed with cars. "Must be a popular
spot...judging by the number of vehicles on the lot."
Graham finally found a spot and parked. "Let's go,
gang." He glanced at his sons in the back seat and then
at Dana."

Inside the pool hall, the foursome played snooker.
There was no sign of Tanner. Finally, they grabbed
sandwiches at the bar and hopped back into the car to
continue their mission.

"Our game is noticeably improving." Graham
grinned as he wheeled out of the fifth parking lot at the
pool halls. "Willow Tree Pool Hall out on Willow Road

is next," Dana announced, checking her list.

Dana glanced over at Graham. *He is incredibly handsome...remarkably charming. If I want to be honest with myself, I am absolutely crazy about him.*

Graham glanced her way, grinning, as though reading her mind.

Her heart lurched. *I want to reach over and tousle your hair and pull you into my arms and hold you close...so very, very close.* Of course, she didn't. Instead, she smiled demurely at him.

"Music?" He grinned, flickering his eyes her way.

She shot him a big, warm smile. *Get a grip, girl.* "Yes, music. Definitely."

Graham flicked a switch ushering in classical music. He sped down the freeway. Using his GPS navigator, he took the South exit and drove several miles to their destination.

Dana and Graham played at one table; the boys at the other.

Dana became enthralled with the game and found herself revelling in it and challenged by it. Graham's sons were already pool sharks and he wasn't far behind. She was catching up. Fast. This little adventure was turning out to be a whole lot of fun.

Dana glanced toward the entrance as the door opened. Two older men, identical twins, clad in fine sports clothing headed directly to the wall to get cues. *BINGO! Tanner and Troy.* She could hardly believe their luck. A quick flicker of her eyes toward Graham, and then Will and Jay, and she knew they'd spotted the pair as well. They all immersed themselves in their pool game, ignoring the twins, an unspoken understanding between them.

"Dana and Graham! What a surprise!" Tanner's expression reflected as much. "Say hello to... my twin brother, Troy. Troy, this is Dana Lockhart and Graham Van Rensellier... "He glanced at the young boys, unsure if they belonged to Graham.

"My sons, Jay and Will." Graham gestured toward them.

Troy nodded his acknowledgement before settling into his game with Tanner. The table adjacent to the one Dana and Graham occupied was the only one available. They stepped over to it. Troy broke the balls in the triangle, starting the game.

Graham and his entourage continued playing, stealing occasional glances over at Tanner and Troy.

~

It was well after midnight by the time Graham wheeled his Jeep out of the parking lot and headed down the freeway to drive everyone back to Sugarbush Farm.

"Well, now we know for sure that Tanner knows we're on to him. So, what happens next?" Dana glanced sleepily over at Graham.

"I have a hunch we'll hear from him." Graham parked his Jeep in front of the old mansion and everyone jumped out. Rover and Roamer barked frantically in greeting. They raced around in circles going nuts.

They'd begun walking toward the front steps when Dana stopped suddenly. The outline of a tall figure was illuminated slightly by the dim lights at the side door. *No wonder the dogs are going nuts.*

Graham had spotted it, also. Simultaneously. Wordlessly, he hit emergency on his cell and motioned for Dana and the boys to stay put while he headed for the side door. Whomever it was had run off into the night or was hiding somewhere in the house. He lurked in the shadows hoping to nail the intruder. No one emerged from the house. He finally strode back to the others, turning toward Dana. "He's hiding somewhere in the house... or maybe snuck out through another exit. I won't play his game. The sheriff should be here soon. We're going to stay outside until he gets here." Graham shivered. "Cool out here...exhilarating though." He glanced over at Dana. "Take my jacket." He took his jacket off and put it on top of the one she wore.

"That's better. Thanks, Graham. But what about you?"

"Don't worry about me. I'll be just fine."

Dana began to wonder if they had inadvertently stumbled upon a sizeable underground operation in the horse industry. This was hardly the time to discuss that possibility.

A sheriff's vehicle drove up near the house, kicking up dust. The Sheriff and Deputy Sheriff jumped out. The Sheriff hurried to the rear door, while the Deputy Sheriff covered the front door. "Stay in the front...all of you...for now." The Deputy Sheriff barked the orders.

Graham, Dana and his two sons stood outside shivering in the cool night air. They watched as all the lights in the house blazed suddenly. The Sheriff and Deputy Sheriff were inside the house doing a sweep. Graham turned to Dana. "It's an easy house to hide in...and there are four exits on the main level, as you know. I'm guessing Tanner has some boys working for him...I don't think he would dare break in himself...but

I have to wonder what they're looking for..." Graham was weary. He struggled to stay awake and alert.

"You're kidding, right?" Dana peered at him but it was dark and she couldn't make out his expression.

"No..." Graham glanced at her.

"The papers, of course. The ownership and insurance papers for Flaming Bullet."

"Oh...right, of course. They're in my safe at the bank. Did he really think I would just leave them somewhere in the house where anyone could take them? He sure underestimated me." Graham shook his head in disbelief.

~

Dana breathed a sigh of relief. For one fleeting moment, *she* had underestimated him—foolish girl that she was. He was a very clever man and she'd discovered no loopholes in his way of living. Well, except for the annoying fact that he didn't seem to get just how right she was for him.

About forty minutes later, as the old edifice morphed to life with a myriad of blazing lights. The sheriff strode down the front stairs, waving everyone inside. "Not a trace of anyone. You sure you didn't...just imagine you saw someone moving? You left a couple lights on, right? Maybe...it was just some shadows...from the furniture or whatever..." The sheriff peered over at Graham, skeptically.

Graham shot the sheriff a look of disdain. He was miffed at the insult, but he didn't respond. Instead, he glanced at his sons. "Jay... Will... did you see someone move in the house?"

"Well, ya Dad. Like... for sure...a dark figure hurried toward the side door. Like...we all saw it..." Jay glanced from Will to Dana and then to the Sheriff and Deputy Sheriff.

"Sheriff... I saw it, too." Dana knew the sheriff and was surprised at the insult. *It's late. He's tired and probably on overload.* We should all just let it go.

"Good-nights' overlapped, while Graham and his troupe scampered inside. The boys shot up to their rooms like bullets.

Dana smirked as she cast a glance toward Graham. "I'm in the same guest room tonight, right?" She knew there was no point in arguing with him. He had made up his mind that she would be safe only with him in his house. As long as she was a tenant on *his* property, she had little choice but to follow his instructions. A part of her enjoyed that immensely. And that was a surprise. She usually insisted on total independence.

Graham broke into a wide grin as he studied Dana with male appreciation. They stood in the regal living room, its' ancient, massively high ceilings towering above them. It was her favorite room and she suspected it was his, also. He couldn't stop his impulse to thrust his arms around Dana, nor did he want to. He pulled her close to him, nibbling at her ear. "Whatever am I going to do with you, Dana?"

Even in the dim light, she could see his eyes dancing with admiration. The sly smile he flashed at her caused her heart to soar like giant wings on a massive bald eagle. *Lord, I want this man. With everything that I am, I want him. Is there any chance for us? Any chance at all?*

As though in answer to her silent prayer, Graham spoke. "Myrna would have wanted it this way. She would have insisted you be our house guest...forever if need be."

House guest? That's the extent of my attraction to you? Dana lost it then. Okay, she was frazzled and overtired, but this last, lame line pushed her over the edge. "Will you give it a rest, Graham! Myrna is gone. She's in glory. We're here...on earth. You and me... and your sons. Stop holding onto the past! Haven't you ever read the scripture *"I will do a new thing?"* God is constantly bringing new things and new people into our lives...opening new doors. We are admonished not to look back. We are not to relive our tragedies or our past. He wants us to live full, rich lives in the here and now...only then can we be a powerful witness to those who do not know the Lord...to those who need...salvation and a new life..." Dana fairly spat the words out. "If we don't lead blessed and full lives, why would anyone want to follow Jesus, anyway? We need to be an example of what a blessed and prospered Christian looks like." Jesus said, *"I will give you life and give it to you more abundantly."* "That's His promise, Graham." She'd had had enough of him living in the past. Surely, he could see how futile and dishonoring to God that was. Not to mention herself.

Graham was speechless...immobile. He seemed to drink in every word she uttered. Finally, he spoke. "I...I guess maybe you're right, Dana. I *do* need to move on."

Dana took a deep breath. *There is hope.* Suddenly the lights blazed and something akin to a grand symphony swept over her. Imaginary, of course. Still, it was as real as the vast, blue sky above. *Lord, you are faithful...so very faithful. I've cried out to you, sometimes silently...not even knowing what to say...but you've heard my plea...you've heard my cry...and now...yes...I'm in love with Graham, Lord. I wish I weren't in a way...but it's too late for that now...*

Dana suddenly felt bone weary as she glanced around the charming, ancient bedroom. Pale yellow wallpaper was peeling slightly in some areas and discolored in other sections. Still, there was something magnificent about the Turn-of-the-Century edifice and it's quaint, high-ceilinged, ancient rooms. She glanced at the ornate chandelier hanging from the high ceiling. *This must be the premiere guest room.* There was a private bathroom which had mottled grey marble floors adjacent to her room. A grey marble fireplace flanked the wall across from her four poster bed. Grand, old prints graced the walls, one of which was a Parisian scene; adorned with a light above it. *Graham was so blessed to have purchased the house turn-key. He'd paid dearly for that privilege but he'd wanted to enjoy the house and its' furnishings the way it was meant to be.* Suddenly, she felt bone weary. Too exhausted to soak in the tub. She might fall asleep there. She crashed.

Dana awakened as daylight filtered into her room. It was early. A quick glance at the bedside clock told her it was 6:00 a.m. She stretched, strolling to the French windows which opened onto a private deck. She glanced outside. It was still. Quiet. Peaceful. *Lord, thank-you for the privilege and joy of being here. Thank-you for bringing Graham into my life.* No matter where it went, God was in control. And Graham had become a wonderful blessing in her life. In fact, she couldn't imagine life without him.

The mini bar in her room was stocked with bottled water, coffee and a coffee pot. She wondered when

Graham had had time to restock the supplies in her room. A sprinkle of joy soared through her being. *He's quite a man.*

She brewed a pot of coffee, poured herself a mug of it and ambled outside onto the deck, mug in hand. Soon, morning sun began gradually filtering in. God had given her a new day. She basked in the privilege of worshiping and seeking Him and sharing the Good News with others. "Thank you, Lord, for this day. And thank-you for keeping me safe and protecting me from harm and evil." *"This is the day that the Lord has made. I will rejoice and be glad in it!"* Her heart sang for joy. And then she knew. Knew, absolutely, without a shadow of doubt. She was deeply, passionately, irrevocably in love with Graham. Whatever would she do?

Returning to her room from the deck after sipping coffee, she pulled the drawer open in the night stand. Graham had told her that he'd placed Bibles in the night stands of all the guest rooms. She picked up the well-worn King James Bible from the drawer, carrying it out onto the deck. Settling onto a chair in front of the small wrought iron table, she immersed herself in the scriptures. Slowly, strength seeped through every part of her, refueling her and recharging her. She drew all her strength from the Bible. She pitied those folks who claimed they didn't have time to seek God. She knew that someday soon, that small window of opportunity to draw near to Him would be shut. It would cease to exist. Today—Carp Diem—seize the moment; and she would. Oh yes, she would.

Dana's cell chirped. The sound of Graham's rich, husky voice was like a symphony to her ears. "You comin' down for breakfast, Dana? I made French toast and squeezed some fresh orange juice..."

"Hey, thanks, Graham. I've just been...revelling in some solitude and enjoying the view up...checking out the Hanging Moss tree. I'll be down in a few minutes." Somehow, she found it exciting to sleep in the premier guest room of his house. She'd slept soundly. *That mattress must have been made in heaven. Very luxurious. If she had to hang out here for a while, it wouldn't be painful.* She dressed hastily. After hearing his voice, excitement soared through her. She smeared on a quick coat of pink lipstick and flicked on some mascara before descending the long, winding staircase.

Graham was waiting for her at the landing, grinning and watching her descend the staircase.

She hit the last step. "Well?" Her eyes twinkled in amusement. *Lord, if he was even a sliver more handsome...she would surely faint.*

Graham was clad in a turquoise T-shirt of the finest quality, along with his jeans. *Every inch the gentleman farmer.*

"Well, I think having those insurance papers in my safety deposit box saved the day. Wait until you see today's news! You're not going to believe it." Graham shook his head and strode with her the short walk to the massive country kitchen. Today's newspaper lay in the center of the kitchen table.

Graham held out the chair for Dana like a true Southern gentleman—an aristocratic one at that. "Check out the front page news, Dana. You're not going to believe this article." He poured Dana a mug of aromatic, rich, dark coffee and then set down French toast at her place setting.

He served himself and took a seat at the table, opposite her.

Dana glanced at the newspaper glaring up from the center of table. She picked it up. Quickly, her eyes moved to the scathing article. She scanned it as she sipped the coffee. Riveted.

She finished reading the article and set the paper down. "Well, isn't that something? He's been charged with the theft of a Thoroughbred colt he sold to someone...he's been released on bail set at three million...pretty hefty figure." Dana poured maple syrup on her French toast and dug into them. "I hope he's convicted. I'm betting he's guilty."

Graham took a long sip of coffee from his mug. "Okay. So we know he's a horse thief, but we still have to prove that he stole back the racehorse he sold *us*—though it should be significantly easier to do now that he's been charged with horse thievery."

"I think we need to move fast. Hire a detective. Have him tailed. See if he comes up with anything. If we don't nail him on this right away, we may never do it." Dana savored the French toast, adding more maple syrup.

~

"I'll phone the sheriff right after breakfast." Graham studied Dana. *She looks gorgeous without make-up. It was exciting having breakfast with her.* He needed to stay focused on the challenge at hand. "Maybe he'll be able to recommend a good detective."

"Yes, I bet he will." She finished her second mug of the aromatic brew. "Thanks for a terrific breakfast, Graham. Where are the boys?"

"I don't know. I guess they're somewhere around.

When Jay read that report earlier this morning, he practically freaked out...called Tanner a scoundrel." Graham chuckled.

"He's that and a whole lot more. I feel so foolish." Dana peered over at Graham. "I trusted him. I thought the man was a straight shooter." She shook her head in disbelief. "And after all my years in the business..."

"He's an ace con man, Dana. You couldn't have known how deceptive he was." Graham shook his head.

Graham signaled for Dana to follow him to his office where he placed a call to the detective the sheriff had recommended. "Pick up the extension, Dana. We'll have a conference call."

Dana knew that she was responsible for Graham's decision to buy the colt from Tanner. She needed to do everything in her power to get him back and assist in every way possible to get Tanner out of the horse industry and back to prison where he belonged.

Chapter Twenty

Luke Pato was Italian. Stocky, and sullen, he suited his mop of ebony hair. Piercing, dark eyes assessed the information Dana and Graham gave him. Dana noticed he seemed to assimilate it rapidly and was clearly eager to begin the assignment.

Nick's Pizza wasn't Dana's favorite spot. But what did it matter? Nailing Tanner and what appeared to be an underground operation was what *did* matter. "We've filed the insurance report. I don't know if or how fast they will actually pay out on it." Dana shared this information with the P.I. as she sipped her iced tea.

"Okay. I think I have everything I need to get started. Thanks for the cash advance. Time for me to get to work."

Hand shakes concluded the brief meeting.

Two Weeks Later

It was early Saturday morning. Graham and Dana

were feeding and watering the horses in the barn. Will and Jay assisted. Graham's cell chirped. "Hey...Good morning, George. Do you have anything?"

Dana couldn't hear what was being said. She was a couple of stalls over from Graham, but she saw the disappointment flash over Graham's features. Soon, he ended the call.

"Well? Any news?" Dana arched her brows, moving toward him.

"Not good news, I'm afraid. He's already found the secret ranch. We were right about that. From what he could see using a powerful telescope, there are dozens of magnificent horses roaming around the property. He wants to meet us for breakfast and show us some photos. He'll drive us out there. You might be able to assess the horses...see if maybe he's attempted to get rid of some of the competition so he would have a clear path to victory at the Derby."

"This is incredible, Graham. I've always had an over-active imagination...and I just thought maybe he had a second ranch somewhere...I had no idea he had a thriving operation..." Dana was flabbergasted.

"The place is tucked away...it's in a remote area. This Nick character really knows his stuff and moves fast. God only knows how he found it this quick. It also proves he's honest. He could have taken at least a couple of weeks to find it/and or share the information with us." Graham was incredulous.

"Wow! So it's a huge, thriving operation. I wonder if the authorities know anything about this. I'm guessing they don't." Dana shook her head in sheer amazement.

~

After the chores, Graham and Dana drove to the breakfast house. Nick was sitting in a booth near the front door. They joined him. Over scrambled eggs and hash browns, he brought them up to speed. "How would you like to proceed?" He glanced from one to the other as he waited for their reaction.

Graham and Dana exchanged glances. "Does the sheriff know about the ranch?" Graham studied Nick. The man was razor sharp. He definitely possessed the fine-tuned instincts of a seasoned investigator.

"Don't think he does." Nick ate hungrily. "The food is real good here. I'm starved. Bin up since 5:30."

"We'd better inform the sheriff first. Get him involved and derive a master plan to storm the place." Graham peered at the detective. This was all new to him. He was winging it and he knew Dana was, too.

The Sheriff, Deputy Sheriff and a group of local ranchers including Graham assembled at Sugarbush. It was time to mastermind the covert operation. The Sheriff went over the game plan.

Soon, the makeshift posse was ready and poised to storm the secret ranch. The designated time was set for 8:00 a.m. Dana calculated that the thoroughbreds would be grazing in the corrals around that time. She would quickly figure out which horses were the three-year-old colts that might be in training for the Derby. Maybe a trainer would show up, scheduled to work with one of the colts. Maybe even *Flaming Bullet.*

The posse of men assembled on horseback near the entrance of the covert operation. They milled around until the designated time. At exactly 8:00 a.m. moving full speed ahead, ten armed men charged forward onto the farm like an Indian Band in attack mode.

A corral which housed several fine Thoroughbreds loomed into view. Two horses reared up as Dana and her men galloped toward them. Dana spotted the missing colt right away

Flaming Bullet grazed in the pasture, magnificent in his beauty and grace. He recognized Dana and Graham immediately, moving friskily toward them.

Dana called out to him. In minutes, she led him out of the corral. They were being guarded by the Sheriff and his men. So far, they hadn't encountered the ranch hands. Woops...she spoke too soon.

Three strapping young dudes ambled outside a small building near the main house, which wasn't much larger. "Hey, what's goin' on? Whatta ya doin?" The taller man spoke in a gravely, shaky voice. He appeared to be trying to sound in control.

The Sheriff flashed his badge. "We're here to crack an illegal horse operation. You wouldn't know anything about it, I guess." He smirked.

"No, of course not." The biggest and burliest of the three seemed to be the designated spokesman. "We work for Tanner. He owns this ranch. He pays us. We do what we're told."

"Even if it's illegal? The Sheriff looked him over.

"What do you mean; illegal?" The large, rugged cowboy seemed genuine.

"Some of these Thoroughbreds are stolen. Did you know that?" The Sheriff studied the ranch hand.

"Stolen? No kidding. I thought Tanner was...a big player...a rich dude...and a straight shooter."

A medium-sized older guy clad in jeans that were too tight and a cowboy hat that had seen better days, spoke up. "I knew there was somethin' off base goin' on... but I jest couldn't put mah finger on it."

"We have a warrant to confiscate all the horses on the property. We'll be doing a detailed search on each one, in order to determine the rightful owner. We have horse trailers due any minute and we'll be loading them on. Where is Tanner? He was released on bail pending his trial." The Sheriff glanced over at the older guy.

"Beats me. I do know he has a girlfriend...lives in a trailer on a couple acres near here...and he's got a twin brother..."

The Deputy Sheriff peered at him, computing the new information. "How do we know which one is Tanner? I guess we need to check the driver's license..."

"Maybe one of the ranch hands will give us the information we need. We could try pumping them." The sheriff glanced over at his partner, speaking softly.

The Deputy Sheriff spoke in hushed tones as he moved toward two lanky cowboy types chatting, their elbows resting on the fenced corral. "Where is Tanner?" The Deputy Sheriff glanced at the ranch hands.

Both men shrugged, disinterested. They remained at the fenced corral gazing at the sky.

The Deputy Sheriff dug into his pocket and handed a large bill to each cowboy.

"Maybe he's not too far from here—you never know." The tallest and lankiest of the two flashed a sly grin and shuffled his feet nervously.

The deputy sheriff dug into his pocket and placed another large bill into the man's hand.

"Drive straight down the main road leading here

from the highway—Langham Road—watch for a road that looks more like a trail....Holt road it's called...drive a few miles...the road turns and then you'll see the Trailer park. Don't know why it ain't marked from the main road. There's jest a few trailers there...I bin there once. I think most of 'em are abandoned...maybe all of 'em...rumor has it that Tanner bought 'em all and owns the Trailer park. Now, I'm not sayin' he's there or anything, and he does drop by here from time-to-time..."

"Very interesting." The Sheriff glanced at the Deputy Sheriff. The ranch hands might be trying to divert them; or maybe it was a genuine lead. He pressed some more bills into the informant's hand, grinned triumphantly and peered at his partner. "We'll check it out after we keep a close eye on the horses and determine what's here."

Graham and the P.I. stood next to the Sheriff. The P.I. glanced at his cell phone. "If the ranch hand is tellin' the truth and it's only a few miles from here, maybe Graham and I should swing by and see what's goin' on. We'll be back before the Possee shows up."

"Sure. Go Ahead." The Sheriff nodded.

Graham jumped into his Jeep. Minutes later, they pulled up at Red Creek. Graham zapped the window down and heard trickling water from the creek. A pair of black crows circled overhead. Their drive into the area apparently startled a few other birds, as well. They chirped and flitted among the tree branches. Masses of blackberry bushes obscured the entrance somewhat. The road was little more than a cow path, but he managed to drive his Jeep onto it. "I don't think there's anything here. Maybe it's a wild goose chase and they wanted us gone for some reason. I think it's just...maybe an old cow trail." Graham glanced around at the overgrown bushes.

"I have a hunch the ranch hand was telling the truth. Maybe it's an abandoned trailer park...unused for some time. Let's check it out. We're here now." Nick egged him on.

"Sure. Why not?" Graham plowed through, bumping over potholes with his Jeep, Nick guiding him. They came to a clearing after a short drive on the makeshift road. "Look at that...a few, obviously abandoned, run-down trailers and one that looks significantly better than the others." Graham drove slowly over the rugged terrain and multitude of pot holes. He parked in front of the nicest trailer. "Definitely abandoned. Must have been used at one time, I guess." Graham shook his head. "Let's get out of here."

"Not so fast. There might be more than meets the eye here." Nick jumped out of the Jeep and peered in the windows of the nicest trailer. He rapped on the door a couple times. Nothing. "Let's go around the back."

Graham followed Nick as they peered through the curtained windows. "The place is abandoned. That ranch hand sent us on a wild goose chase. Let's get out of here." Graham started walking toward the Jeep.

"Maybe not." Nick scanned the area carefully and thoroughly. "Maybe the sheriff will get a search warrant. Something valuable could be stashed here. Something he didn't want to keep on the ranch. Maybe...drugs he administers on thoroughbred racehorses...to hinder their performance in stakes races. It *looks* abandoned. That may be deliberate. It wouldn't surprise me if it's real nice inside. Yup. I think it's a stash house and a hideout. Incredible that the ranch hand dared to tell us..." He peered over at Graham. "Unless he's in over his head...and is rooting for us to nail Tanner."

The P.I. glanced at Graham. "I bet it's a hideout...maybe used occasionally. If he does have a girlfriend, he probably has her stashed in a penthouse somewhere. This place is just some kind of...maybe an occasional hideout. It makes you wonder what else is goin' on. Let's get back to the ranch. Those horse trailers should be showin' up real soon. Maybe the sheriff can get a search warrant and see what's hidden inside here."

In minutes, Graham and Nick drove onto the ranch just in time to spot the first horse trailer driving up. Glancing at the driveway, Graham spotted several more horse trailers following.

"Mornin', Sheriff." The young, beefy man at the wheel grinned. "Let's load 'em up. Which ones do we take?"

The sheriff studied the list he'd brought with him. It contained a description of the thoroughbred, his name, the owner's name and contact information, along with the insurance papers. "There are eight horses in question. They will all be confiscated until the authorities can determine legal ownership and whether or not they've been stolen back after they were sold. Quite a scam he's got goin' on. I wonder how long he's been doin' this?" The sheriff shook his head and directed the handler to load the horses onto the horse trailer.

After four thoroughbreds had been loaded onto the

large trailer, the handler nodded to the sheriff and deputy sheriff. "I'm on my way." He climbed into the cab of the horse trailer and drove out in a cloud of dust.

Another handler drove up with his horse trailer. Soon, he was loaded and drove off. The men waited until the last four thoroughbreds were loaded onto a trailer. "Mighty fine lookin' horses." The sheriff was filled with admiration for the majestic animals.

"Real fine. Among the very finest in Kentucky." The deputy sheriff nodded.

Graham spoke up. "What happens now?" He'd been watching the process, still in shock. "Do you think it's possible that he skipped town despite the hefty bail?" Graham peered at the sheriff.

"Seems like this Tanner character is slippery. He might have flown to the Bahamas or somewhere else exotic. Maybe he has a house there."

"Why would you say that?" Dana peered at the sheriff, surprises.

The sheriff grinned again. "Just...takin' a wild guess. Well...truthfully, I just have a hunch that's where he is. I've heard some rumblings about him flying there now and then. He likes to stay a couple steps ahead of everyone. Might be a possibility. It's near Palm Beach and the Polo matches. And some world-class race tracks. It's incredibly beautiful there. That's where I spent my honeymoon."

"A lot of luxury yachts cruise those waters. If Tanner moves in the Jet Setter circles, he's bound to show up there sooner or later. We're just getting into fall weather. Maybe he decided to enjoy some balmy weather with a hot babe."

"The Bahamas isn't very large. And once there you

can probably find out anything with a little ready cash. Why don't we take a little trip?" Dana glanced over at Graham. He seemed to be computing the idea. She thrived on challenges. No way was she going to let Tanner slip out of their hands. He needed to be strung up. She was up to the task. She was betting Graham would agree. *Yes! She loved the idea. The more she thought about it, the more she warmed to the idea of hunting him down.*

Graham peered at her. He was very quiet. "I... think the idea might have some merit. Obviously, that's up to the Sheriff...if he has the manpower to dispatch a pair of undercover cops. If you really want to go...maybe Nick will accompany you. I can't leave the boys, of course. And I sure don't want to take them on this expedition."

"Of course not, Graham."

~

Graham barbecued steaks. Dana made a salad. They dined outside on the veranda. August was coming to a close. Soon the boys would be in school. Over coffee, Dana glanced at Graham. "It's settled. Nick. has agreed to accompany me, and the sheriff has conceded to send a pair of undercover cops with us. We'll see what we can dig up." Dana was pleased that she'd orchestrated all this.

"We don't even know that he's there. He could be anywhere. But knowing the sheriff, he must believe Tanner is there...or he certainly wouldn't be sending his men there." Graham peered at Dana.

"Oh, sorry. I forgot to tell you. The sheriff called and told me that one of the hired hands on the ranch had tipped him off. I don't think it's a wild goose chase, but it will be challenging to find out where he's holed up and figure out what he's up to."

"No kidding." Graham nodded. "You shouldn't be going on this mission, Dana. You're way out of your league. Since when did you become the equivalent of an undercover cop?" Graham raised his eyebrows accenting the question.

"Graham...it's just a real strong gut feeling I have. I told the sheriff...there's that women's intuition thing again...I told him I had a hunch Tanner was going to skip the country despite his hefty bail...maybe he has a house in the Bahamas and he has some last-minute business to take care of before he skips the country. Wouldn't it be fun to catch him in the act?" Dana peered over at Graham.

"So...the sheriff figures that despite the three million bail, he's going to flee the country...well, how would he be able to?" Graham peered at Dana.

"I don't know. I'm guessing the scam involves his twin brother. And maybe the horse theft operation is just the tip of the iceberg. There might be a much bigger scam here...and...possibly the judge got wind of it and made the bail real high to discourage him trying to leave the country." Dana shrugged.

Chapter Twenty-One

Dana and the P.I. flew into Freeport, Bahamas, arriving just before 7:00 p.m. No one had ever mucked her around as much as Tanner had. She didn't like being deceived. She would find him and string him up. Further, she was embarrassed and angry that she'd assured Graham that Tanner was a reputable horse guy. *Reputable! What a joke that was.*

They checked into the Bahamas Hilton under assumed names. They would meet with the undercover cops at their suite the next morning. Nick Pato bid Dana good-night at her room on the fourth floor; but not before insisting he enter the room and do a sweep first. "Stay in the room until morning and don't order room service. We don't know how far reaching Tanner and his boys are. My room is adjacent. And there's access from both sides." He chuckled. "Good thing you trust me."

Dana arose early the next morning, keen to take a swim in the Olympic-sized pool before their 9:00 a.m.

meeting. It was already warm and balmy, the temperature soaring into the late seventies. Idyllic weather. She towelled off after an invigorating swim and kicked back on the luxurious chaise lounge, basking in the welcoming warmth of the sunshine. Someone was calling her name.

"Dana?" A brawny guy, somewhere in his forties, grinned at her, striding toward her. Large sunglasses and a baseball cap masked his identity. Dana sat up and stared at him, suddenly recognizing him. "Graham! What are you doing here? I thought you weren't coming." She glanced around. There were a few folks swimming and a smattering of people lounging on the chaises in the early morning sunshine.

Graham kept his voice mellow as he moved onto the chaise next to hers. "Did you really think I was going to throw this problem onto your lap and then just vanish? Okay... so you've got the P.I. with you and a pair of undercover cops, as well. I think you could use a friend. You've taken it upon yourself to look after this issue...I know, I know...you feel responsible for me buying the colt. And you thought you knew Tanner and could trust him." He peered at her, taking both her hands in one of his. "We're in this together, Dana. Sis has agreed to move into the house until we get a handle on this." Graham's eyes swept over her. He had to admit she was getting under his skin. In fact, if he wanted to be brutally honest with himself... he was falling hard for her. Still, he would never commit to marriage again. Once was enough. Besides, Sis kept reminding him how much women changed once they tied the knot. She'd seen it with her best friend, Eloise. She didn't want her only brother to be trapped in a bad marriage. She loved him way too much for that.

"I couldn't resist. It's a whole lot better than reading a mystery novel or watching a suspense movie on TV." Graham chuckled, plopping down on the chaise next to hers. The balmy breeze picked up speed. "Maybe a wind storm kickin' up...I love this tropical climate."

His musky after-shave wafted her way. She found herself strangely more relaxed now that Graham was here. *Maybe he's right. This is not a good place for a woman alone.*

Graham glanced at a long row of large terra-cotta pots sprouting vivid coral, flowered plants. Masses of the exotic plants lined the edge of the gated poolside. The wind carried the fragrance of the exotic, reddish plants wafting toward him.

"I don't think it's a good idea...you being here." Dana's tone was sombre. She wasn't going to let her attraction to Graham deter her from her mission. She was working with a team. Why had he shown up here?

Regardless, Graham continued peering at her and grinning. He ignored her message, settling onto the chaise.

Dana was suddenly cognizant of the skimpy leopard bathing suit clinging to her curves, still wet from the swim. Reaching for the matching cover up, she shrugged into it. Being around Graham was hugely distracting to say the least. And there was no time for diversions. She was on a serious mission.

"Why don't you think I should be here?" Graham peered at her. Stunned.

"Because...I *do* know something about Tanner. And if we're lucky enough, I may be able to get him alone...he's been known to have a few drinks...and when he does, he gets chatty. If I'm alone... and I'll be wearing a wire... he might give me all the information we need without even pumping him for it." She spoke in hushed tones.

Graham saw red. "So...I guess you want me to turn around and just head back to Kentucky. Well, guess what? I'm not going to do that. I'm going to stay here and protect you as much as I can. Don't worry— I won't get in the way. I'll just be nearby, in case everything goes haywire." As exasperating as the woman was, she needed protection whether she realized it or not.

"Right. So you're going to assume the role of cop and sweep in and save my life. A pair of cops are assigned to this case, plus the PI we hired. Don't you think you would just be interfering?" Dana sat up on the chaise, defiant. *Didn't he get that she wanted to handle this with the pros?*

Graham lost it then. "It was *my* colt that was stolen...on *my* ranch. Yet, you're saying *you* get to make all the decisions about this! I don't think so."

"Well...I...I'm the one that talked you into buying the colt from Tanner. And as I said before...I have some insight into the man..." She leaned toward him, whispering. "I have a wire on...I think I can crack this case myself...and I'd like to..."

"Oh, so your dream is to be an amateur sleuth, is that it?" Graham was livid, but he forced himself to speak in a whisper.

Dana stood up. She'd had enough. This argument was going nowhere. She forced herself to speak softly and lean close to him. "Oh come on, Graham. You know that's not it. As I said, I created this problem when I recommended you buy the colt from Tanner. And I intend to get to the bottom of it." Dana fought the desire to yell at him. *What part of this doesn't he understand?*

"If Tanner is as lethal as you say, Dana, it could cost you your life...I know, I know...you're wearing a wire and you have lots of backup. Don't underestimate that you're dealing with a very sophisticated crook...you don't know who he's connected with or what he might do...especially if things don't go his way..." Graham leaned in toward her, placing large, strong hands on her shoulders. He hadn't intended to, but he drew her close to him and kissed her. He couldn't seem to stop the impulse. He pulled apart quickly, whispering to her. "Dana, I'm...sorry to be so tough on you...but I just want to protect you. I have a hunch that things may not go according to plan. Is God warning me about that? Maybe. I felt led to come here...to protect you. I'm in room 321 if you need me." He turned to go, then turned back to her, peering into her eyes. He held them captive.

Neither of them moved. Dana continued gazing into his vivid blue eyes as excitement coursed through her entire body. *Why couldn't he have stayed home?* Her knees felt weak as mush. *Suddenly, nothing seemed to matter. Nothing but Graham and her. Here. Together. In this tropical paradise.* All her resolve vanished. She wanted this man like she'd never wanted another. She'd never known excitement like this. Being in his presence was heaven on earth. She wanted to dance on the ceiling, shout to the rooftops. A classic, old show tune sprang to mind. *"I'm in love, I'm in love with a wonderful guy!"* She was emotionally entwined and enthralled and dizzily captivated by everything the man was. Everything he stood for. His Christian principles...his dreams...his desires...the stuff that made him tick. And like it or not, his sons had forever stolen her heart, too. They were tender and trusting. Vulnerable. Precious.

There was no turning back. She could not return to her former life. He *was* her life. Graham and his sons meant everything to her. Even the horses didn't matter as much as they once did. At one time, *they* were her whole life. *What was she saying? What had she been thinking? Temporary insanity? Yes, that must be it.*

Graham gazed into her eyes and held them captive. He reached for her hand and gently clasped it, helping her up from the chaise. His arms encircled her in a tender embrace. He was gentle at first, soon pulling her much closer as he wrapped powerful arms around her and held her close.

She melted, and was transported to another world...a world that only true lovers inhabited. A world where there was only deep, abiding love, joy, passion...a place where lovers could forever embrace each other and know incredible, heavenly joy. Yes, God had allowed her to feel love deeply, passionately, to experience a level of euphoric joy that would always be unexplainable, except to those lucky lovers that shared similar experiences.

Time stood still. They were locked in an embrace as though frozen together permanently. Dana could neither think nor move. *Graham...darling...only, ever, always... Graham. Oh, my darling, if you knew how much I love you, need you, want you...if you knew that without you I would curl up and die. If you knew that you are my whole life. If you knew that I live for the moment I glimpse you, for the great joy of basking in your presence...to look at you, beloved. And to hope and pray...that somehow God has ordained that we should be together forever...*

She had never truly known what it was to love. Not until now. Not before Graham. Dana remained in this euphoric state suspended somewhere between the galaxies of the heavens and the earthly, physical presence of the Adonis-like male so near to her she could feel his breath on her lips, sense he was about to kiss her eyes, maybe caress her fingertips. *So this is what Song of Solomon understood and embraced...love that captivated his heart and mind and soul...love that would be etched for all eternity in the Good Book for everyone to read and enjoy...this euphoric experience that only lovers are allowed to glimpse...*

After some time, Graham eased out of the embrace. It took a great deal of effort. He wanted to hold her forever. Never let her go. But they were here on a mission and he felt God had nudged him to come here to protect her. He gazed at her. His heart brimmed with love and concern for her. "Dana. Let me walk you to your room." He was still riding high on the heady cloud of love, but he had to be her protector. God had sent him here, of that he was certain.

Her heart lurched. *Oh Graham. Don't you know how wild I am about you? I came here because I love you. I botched things up by recommending you buy the colt from Tanner. I assured you he was honorable. I caused this problem. That's why I need to fix it. Don't you get it?* She had already told him that countless time. No point in flogging a dead horse.

The tropical breeze was gaining in strength, becoming a forceful gale. Dana and Graham strolled toward the entrance of the swanky hotel. Dana's long, blond tresses danced in the breeze. They moved wordlessly through the swanky lobby. It was sparsely furnished with grand, white sofas interspersed with tall, potted Palm tree varieties, and a white Baby Grand. An older gentleman plunked out classic music on it.

Wordlessly, they stepped into the elevator from the lobby. Dana pressed number four on the panel. Soon, they alighted. At room 421, they stopped. Dana handed Graham her plastic entrance card. He slipped it into the door's slot. When the door opened, he strode into the room ahead of her, motioning for her to remain at the door.

She had to admit that she breathed a whole lot easier knowing that Graham had entered the suite before her to check it out. She hadn't asked him to accompany her. He'd shown up anyway. Quickly, she realized that he had done the right thing...even the wise thing. *Lord, where is this going? I want this man. I was just settling in to going it alone here in the Bahamas, but now that he's shown up, I realize how much I need him... and want him. Oh Lord, whatever am I going to do?*

"Dana, I don't trust anyone or anything in this town. I want to make sure no one is in your room...and that everything is secured. I told the P.I. to take the adjacent room. It's extra security for you." Graham moved in front of her and did a sweep of the room, checking the bathroom, under the bed, the closet and finally the balcony. Theoretically, the room could be bugged. If Tanner was working with other crooks—

who knew what they might do, given that their operation was in jeopardy? "Okay, I did a sweep. It's clean. But...that doesn't mean anything... the room could be bugged. Tanner could be on the inside. If he is working with other crooks—who knows what they are capable of doing, given that their operation is in jeopardy." Graham impulsively pulled her close. "You're vulnerable, Dana. I...I don't like leaving you here alone." His eyes met hers and held them captive. He fought the urge to embrace her. "Good-night, gorgeous. Sleep well." He grinned, turning to go. "I'll...I'll be praying for your safety..." A serious look stole over his features. "I don't like leaving you here alone...as I said...we should make other arrangements. Fast. Maybe right now."

"I think you're over-reacting, Graham. Security is reputed to be excellent in this hotel. I'll be just fine."

Graham peered over at her. He was uncharacteristically silent. "You just never know. I don't like leaving you alone...maybe...well, why don't I rent a two-bedroom suite and we'll share it? I'll pick up the tab, of course. I just think...it would be a good idea. We don't really know what we might find ourselves involved in...

Dana yawned. "I've got jet lag...I've got to get some sleep...we'll talk about it in the morning, okay?"

"I think we should act fast. We may not have the luxury of time." Graham's tone was stern.

"Graham, I'll be fine." She smiled at him. "I'm going to say good-night." She yawned.

He stared at her. Silent. *Myrna always obeyed me She said I had uncannily perceptive and accurate insights into most situations. What is it with Dana and her independent streak? Sometimes I think I could get serious about her. But I don't think she's wife material, actually.*

~

In her room alone, a strange kind of loneliness spread through her like wildfire. *He really cares about me. I think...I actually think the man is in love with me! Is that possible, Lord?* He was gorgeous, tender-hearted, caring...oh what was the use...he'd told her repeatedly that he had no intentions of getting serious with anyone. Still, the man possessed the broadest shoulders she'd ever seen. She could admire his build. No harm in that. And his eyes...well if the eyes are the windows of the soul, his reflected a deep tenderness...and compassion, great intelligence...and, well... she wasn't sure there were words descriptive enough in her vocabulary to describe how...incredible and wonderful he was. And sexy. Very, very sexy. She could lose herself in his arms...get drunk gazing into his eyes...which were like fathomless pools of love...wisdom, compassion, tenderness, caring. She gave her head a shake. She needed to forget about him...at least for now. She was on a mission and not even Graham could deter her from it.

Dana arose early as usual. It was just past 6:00. She had slept remarkably well. The room phone rang. She picked it up.

"Graham here. Something weird happened last night. Someone tried to break into my room. I heard some noise on my deck...in the wee hours of the morning. I resisted the temptation to see who it was. Instead, I grabbed a robe and my wallet and cell phone...called security and hurried to the elevator. By the time I reached the front desk, I was told that security was on it and they would report back to me. They moved me to a different room on a higher floor. So far, I don't have an update."

"Fast thinking, Graham. You could have stepped right into a trap if you'd gone to investigate the noise." Dana breathed a sigh of relief. "I...I guess I'm fortunate they didn't get onto *my* balcony...I wonder why they targeted *you*?" Dana was groggy, still waking up.

"You're joking, right? My best guess is that they wanted to get rid of me first. You're much more vulnerable. I rather like the idea that they have to get past me to get to you. They figured it out pretty fast, though." He chuckled. "Buy you breakfast? Not here. Maybe we'll go for a little drive."

"Yes, please. Let's get away from the hotel for a while."

"I've heard about this quaint spot on the hillside overlooking the ocean. The food is reputed to be amazing..."

Chapter Twenty-Two

Breakfast was just that. Amazing.
Actually, more than amazing. Incredible. *Or was she so
crazy about him that she was euphoric just being in his
presence?*

The view was breathtaking. She could stay here
forever. They were just finishing breakfast when she
spotted Tanner. A quick glance toward Graham and she
knew he had, also. Or was it his twin brother? In
seconds, the man stood in front of them at their table, a
Beretta pointing at Graham's chest. He'd seen it
coming and ducked, just as the loud pop of a gunshot
reverberated throughout the cafe.

Instantly, Dana grabbed the heavy, decorative vase
standing on the floor next to their table. She rolled it,
heaving it into Tanner or his twin. It smashed into him,
disabling him. Blood spurted everywhere. Shocked and
writhing in agony, he screamed hysterically.

The shrill sound of police sirens blared, mingling
with the eerie wail of an ambulance. In minutes,

paramedics arrived, wheeling the bloodied perpetrator onto a stretcher and into the waiting ambulance. A pair of cops grilled them and everyone else in sight, scribbling down notes. Finally, satisfied that Graham and Dana had been the intended victims and were clean, they departed.

"Let's get out of here. Do you still think you're not vulnerable, Dana?" Graham's voice shook as he spoke.

Her heart was brimming with tenderness and relief. She had to admit, it *was* a blessing to have him here. "Thank-you, for coming Graham...thank God you came..."

"I hope I'm wrong, Dana...but I think this is just the beginning...Tanner may be part of a larger organization...I don't know...but what I *do* know is that you shouldn't be alone...not even for a second.

The meeting was scheduled for 2:00. They met in the suite shared by the P.I. and the two undercover cops. Everyone sat at the conference table in the modest-sized room. Dana and Graham sat next to each other. Ken, the older, seasoned cop presided at one end of the table. Jalen, a strapping, black cop who had just turned fifty, sat next to him.

Jalen reminded Dana of a bull. He looked to be as strong as one. *She* wouldn't want to tangle with him and neither would Tanner. *He seems sharp, too. And focused. God has sent us his best. Thank-you, Lord.*

Nick served bottled water all around. Then the P.I. made his recommendations. "Everyone wears wires at all times, except, of course, when you take a quick shower. God must be watching over us. Lady Luck just dropped a gift on us."

"Well, don't keep us in suspense. Share the hot

news." Dana peered at Nick, curious.

"Tanner is dining in the King's Dining Room tonight; which, of course, means it was his twin brother that opened fire while you were having breakfast." He glanced over at Dana and Graham. "Tanner will be dining with a stunning gal—a New York model." The P.I. grinned. "Slipped the Matre D a couple hundred and he suddenly remembered this important information." The P.I. shook his head. "One possible motive for horse thievery might be to have stacks of cash to buy beautiful broads."

"How would he have met her?" Dana peered at the P.I.

"Probably at the Polo matches in Palm Beach. Who knows? The guy gets around." Nick shrugged.

Graham's mind was racing. "So, what's the game plan?"

Nick gazed at Graham. "I'll call an escort service and get a date...slip a couple more bills to the maitre'D and get the table right next to Tanner and his arm piece. See what I can find out. I'm bound to pick up something useful."

~

The King's Table was rated five stars. It was the epitome of elegance. Nick had already checked it out. He liked this part of his job. The P.I. had told the escort agency that he wanted this evening's date to be quiet and soft-spoken. As long as she wasn't real fat, he wasn't fussy. He had no criteria for looks or body type, though he stressed the importance of a quiet woman and a good listener. He was prepared to tip them well if they did a good job.

The P.I. met his date at the bar in the hotel, as

they'd arranged. She was quiet and genteel, and very sweet. Long, honey-colored tresses and enormous green cat eyes gazed at him. She smiled, shyly.

This was much better than he could have hoped for. He liked her instantly. Her sweet smile warmed his heart. It had been years since anyone had sparked any real interest in him. In fact, he'd given up on women after the last one cheated on him.

Miranda wore a lime green dress with matching pumps and several gold bracelets on her left wrist. He wondered if the large diamond ring she wore was real. If it was, it was worth a pretty penny. He resisted the urge to tell his dinner companion about the spy mission he was on. It would be more natural if she didn't know. And, of course, he didn't know her—he couldn't trust her. As long as she didn't talk much and kept her voice soft when she spoke, he would be able to eavesdrop effectively. They would be close enough that his wire would work beautifully.

God had blessed him with more than his fair share of good looks. The mirror told him the grey flecks in his dark hair gave him an air of handsome elegance. Ladies often gave him a second look. He knew that Tanner's reservation was for 7:00. He made his booking for 6:30. He wanted to be relaxed with his date and ready to glean whatever he could on this prospecting mission.

Nick asked his date a number of questions trying to set her at ease. *If she's relaxed and comfortable, he'll be able to focus on his mission. Also, they will seem like a real, genuine couple.* Despite, their unlikely meeting, he found himself quite attracted to his blind date. He hoped the feeling was mutual. He grinned, chuckling at a few comments she made. The lady was witty. *Woah. That came as a big surprise.* He wanted to see her again. He couldn't get side-tracked though, he needed to stay on purpose with his mission. That had to remain at the forefront of his brain.

The P.I. glanced at his clock. It was almost 8:00 and there was no sign of Tanner and the model. He was used to being patient. Staking places out and waiting interminably were part of his job description. Patience was a prime requisite for his work.

They dined on rack of lamb with a good red wine. The soft music in the background was perfect to dine by.

He could see the front door in his peripheral vision from where he and his date were seated. Suddenly, Tanner and his date walked through the door. The stunning brunette beauty was draped on his arm. She was clad in a short, clingy dress in a tropical mango shade with matching pumps. Tanner was grinning, his eyes dancing. Clearly in high spirits despite his predicament. *Maybe he's late because he visited his twin brother in the hospital. He was probably taken in for questioning as well.*

Nick gave his date the pre-arranged signal, indicating she should be silent. He sensed his date had an inkling of his mission.

His date focused on the gourmet food on her plate, soon taking a sip of the wine. She was silent.

Tanner pulled out the chair for the beauty queen. She played the Grande Dame as she slid into her chair, flashing a big, flirtatious smile at Tanner.

Nick could hear their idle chatter. He was listening for dates, locations and details. He pretended to focus on his dinner, taking a few bites and grinning at his date occasionally. The spying mission seemed like a write off, Tanner was ordering fancy desserts for himself and his date. They would soon be leaving. Suddenly, like a gift from God, he dropped a gem. "I really wish you would reconsider and join me at the Polo matches in Palm Beach next week..."

The beauty queen cooed, leaning into him as she caressed his arm with a slender hand, enticingly. "Darling." She flashed him a sexy smile. "I wish I could... but I...I just can't turn down a lucrative modelling assignment in Milan. A girl has to eat, you know."

Nick couldn't hear the whisper. Common sense told the P.I. that Tanner had upped the anty. Money talked. It always had.

"Well, darling...it would be wonderful to spend more time with you...and not have to do the dumb modelling job..." The exotic beauty smiled, leaning sexily into him, batting long, dark eyelashes.

Nick figured the smile must have matched the lucrative bribe.

"I'll be flying to Palm Beach on Friday. Let me know when your flight gets in from New York, and I'll pick you up." He leaned closer to her, whispering "I'll make it worth your while if you come with me to B. A." He grinned.

"Yes...I'm sure you will." A flicker of nervousness played on her face as she smiled.

Tanner slapped cash onto the tray holding his bill and escorted the model out of the fine eatery.

The P.I. and his date made their exit after a few minutes, taking the elevator down to the main floor.

Nick tipped his date generously. "I'll get a taxi for you...I enjoyed your company."

The blind date slipped Nick her card. "Thank-you for a lovely dinner...and excellent company." She smiled at him.

"It was fun." A thrill of excitement rippled through him. He hadn't expected to be smitten with his blind date. Nick helped her into a taxi, noticing her long shapely legs as she settled into the back seat. She smiled, gazing into his eyes.

Nick leaned toward her. He wanted to take her in his arms and kiss her. Of course he didn't. "Good-night, lovely lady," he whispered, peering into her eyes.

Nick made a conference call to Dana and Graham, as soon as he found a private area around the side of the hotel. He got them up to speed, ending with: "Honestly guys, I think y'all should just head on home. Cracking this operation isn't going to happen overnight. God only knows what he's got goin' on in Palm Beach. He is going to try to make a run for it. That much we know. Sounds like he's headed for Argentina. Just how he intends to do it, I don't know. Maybe he is going to arrange for a falsified passport while he's in Palm Beach...and travel under an alias. Maybe the model will join him later."

~

"You're not going to dismiss us, Nick. We're paying you, remember? It's *our* chase— not *yours*. You may want to control it, but...really, that's *your* problem. Because, guess what? We're gonna nail this guy—crack this operation and see him strung up. Guys like him need to get out of the horse business and stay out." Dana was proud of herself for speaking up. She glanced over at Graham. The man had the equivalent of smoke emanating from his ears. He was seething.

"We need to talk, Dana. You shouldn't even be here. This is not territory for a young, beautiful...woman." He glanced her way and melted. *Maybe it's too late, God. I'm hooked on this woman...hooked big-time...* He circled his strong arms around her and held her close. "Honey, I know you want to nail this guy, I get that you want to be part of this operation, but...we can't function effectively as long as we're worried about *you*..." His lips came down on hers. Some force significantly stronger than his own weak will, over-powered him. His breathing got heavier as he pulled her even closer into his massive chest.

Dana had never felt this way before. The embrace was powerful; but sweet...oh so very sweet. She wanted to stay in his arms forever. He was everything she'd ever wanted or needed. The subtle, tangy male scent of his cologne wafted over her. Her knees felt weak. *"Lord, I never knew I was capable of loving this way. And now that I know, I don't ever want to stop...loving him...I don't know if I can stop, God, it's too late...I need... want this man more than I've ever wanted anyone before in my life. If I don't hook up with him, God...I...I don't know what I'm going to do. Maybe just devote myself to the horses. Be an equestrian... and live solo for the rest of my days...because, Lord...I don't want anyone but him. Now, at last, I truly understand what love is. And in a strange way...I identify with Graham...and the fact that he felt he could never love anyone like he loved his wife, Myrna. Because after my college sweetheart broke my heart, there's never really been anyone of lasting interest in my life, either. But now there is Graham. And he's everything I ever wanted or needed."*

God spoke to her then, his voice almost audible. *"My precious, precious child, don't you know how much I love you? Don't you know that I want the very best for you? Don't you know that I created you, fearfully and wonderfully? I have good things up ahead for you. I want you to enjoy prosperity, love, fulfillment...so many wonderful things. I died so that you would have life and have it more abundantly. I want you to reign as a queen in life; I want all my people to reign as kings and queens. Press into all that I have in store for you. Know that nothing shall be impossible unto you."*

Dana was jolted to her senses. *What an utter and absolute fool I've been, Lord. Please restore me, Father. Give me wisdom, show me the way...* As their embrace broke up, Dana made a snap decision. *If this mission means so much to Graham and he really doesn't want me here, maybe I'll... take the next flight home...*

She pulled herself up higher. A smile broke over her face. She glanced up at Graham and peered into his penetrating, vivid blue eyes. "I can tell when I'm not wanted, Graham. I guess...maybe I'll head back to the farm...maybe give your sister a hand with the boys and look after the horses...check on Wilbur and see if he's been caring for them properly..."

Graham's countenance changed dramatically. Tenderness was laced with the sexy timbre of his voice. She stared at him.

They locked eyes. He stared at her, barely able to believe his ears. "You...you would do that for me? You would...obey what I said...what I believe...?" *Maybe there is hope for us.*

Dana broke into a huge grin. "Yeah, I would. I'd do that and whole lot more for you."

He swung her around then and burst out laughing. "Tell you the truth, Dana. Women like you scare me...because you're so... clever, so capable, so... determined...and yet you're all female..." He shook his head and grinned.

"Shush." She placed two forefingers on his lips. Her voice was soft. Mellow. "You talk way too much."

His lips came down on hers again and she knew she was a goner. There could never be another man for her. She was absolutely, totally, crazily in love with this guy...and...truth be told...she enjoyed being feminine and letting him call the shots. *Woah. That was a new one.*

When they simultaneously moved apart from the embrace, Dana spoke from somewhere deep inside. "Graham, I'll head back on one condition...that you don't leave anything out when you tell me how you rounded Tanner up and exposed his lies and deceit and the covert operation." Dana peered at him, her eyes full of mischief.

Graham chuckled. "Yeah, I'll tell you everything. I'd be real happy to do that. Just...pray that we nail him."

Chapter Twenty-Three

Graham rode the taxi with Dana to the airport and waited with her until she boarded her flight. He hugged her. "Have a good flight, Dana."

"I'll call you as soon as I get back to the ranch." She smiled at him, turned and melded into the lineup for the flight boarding for Lexington, Kentucky.

Graham called a working lunch meeting at the suite shared by the P.I. and the two cops. Over sandwiches and coffee they brainstormed, working out a plan of operation. Now that Graham felt somewhat in charge and didn't have to worry about Dana, they would smoke out Tanner and glean as much information as they could about his operation.

After breakfast, Graham donned the wig and glasses he'd purchased earlier at the gift shop. He slipped into a yellow Alpaca sweater and crème slacks Nick had bought at the hotel boutique earlier that morning. He remained strictly in the background. He couldn't risk being spotted by Tanner. Still, he was the only one in the group that had met him and could identify him.

As Graham checked the mirror in his room, he gave his disguise a thumbs up. The blondish-brown wig he had donned, along with the sunglasses and the touristy togs made an effective disguise.

Nick also wore a disguise consisting of a black wig, glasses and checked Bermuda shorts topped with a casual sport shirt in a tangerine color. *Being a P.I has its' moments.*

Graham and Nick sat in the lobby, ostensibly reading the newspaper. If Tanner was staying in the hotel, it would be just a matter of time before they would spot him.

Friday morning. Three Days Later

Finally, Tanner surfaced with the elegant model draped on his arm. They seemed to be oblivious to everyone and everything around them.

Perfect. Graham glanced over at Nick. He had the touristy items with him: a camera, some maps, a couple of *"What's on Around Town"* magazines. They both touted shopping bags with their change of clothing hidden inside. "The girls are late as usual," Nick commented, loud enough so that Tanner and his lady friend would think the guys were waiting for their wives and had a day of tourism lined up.

Tanner and the model were fixated on each other. Graham and Nick could have been standing on their heads and he wouldn't have noticed. *Bonus.* Graham and Nick exchanged glances, a silent understanding flashing between them.

"He's hailing a taxi out front, we need to follow

him." Nick spoke softly, as he watched Tanner and his girlfriend. He texted the undercover cops. "Guys, meet me in front of the hotel. Graham, take a separate taxi, tell the driver you're going to the airport; though you may be changing routes. We'll let you know where we are."

Tanner's limo driver dropped him and the model at the airport. Graham, Nick and the two cops were close behind. Once they spotted him and his girlfriend line up for the flight to Palm Beach, Graham and Nick disappeared into the Men's room.

Nick texted Graham. "Change back into your street clothes, take off the rest of your disguise. We'll need to pass security and go through the airport check. We need to look like our passport photos." Earlier that morning, Nick bought two Tote bags at the airport. They stuffed their disguises into them, padding them with "gifty"-looking items like sporty hats and T shirts purchased from the airport kiosk. Graham found himself immensely enjoying the elaborate ruse. *Maybe he should have been an actor.*

~

Tanner's limo driver pulled up to a fancy restaurant in downtown Palm Beach. Tanner and his date entered the restaurant.

Nick and the undercover cops, Ken and Jalen, along with Graham, waited until they saw Tanner and his date were seated. Graham suddenly wished Dana was here. He missed her. It would have been fun to have lunch with her. *No, that's crazy thinking. Sending her home was a wise decision. She was safe. Thank God. He could only guess at the kind of people Tanner knew and what trouble might lie ahead.*

Nick had discreetly tipped the Matre'D upon entering the restaurant. Nick and Graham, along with the undercover cops, were seated at a good table in a booth adjacent to Tanner's. They yakked about politics which was interspersed with intense listening up for any little gems that would help them break up Tanner's operation. Their wires were intact, of course; but with the music and chattering of the guests, Graham wasn't sure how effective it would be.

When Nick spotted the waiter setting down Tanner's check, he requested his. The server promptly brought it. Nick threw down some bills on the check.

Nick and Graham, still enjoying their disguises, followed Tanner and the model as they drove a fair distance away from the core area of Palm Beach, finally stopping at a somewhat grand old building on the outskirts of town. Tanner and his date stepped out of the Jaguar and strolled, hand-in-hand into the building.

Graham turned to the P.I. "Nick... make sure your wire is secure, I have a hunch we're about to strike gold."

"Think so?"

"Didn't I just say that?"

"You did. I just hope it's that easy."

They waited a few minutes after Tanner and his date entered the back of the building. By now, they could see it was a pool hall despite a lack of signage. The place was tucked away. *Was it private? Maybe a private pool-hall club? Would they be able to get in?*

Graham opened the front door. An attractive woman well into her sixties posed at a small desk. She was dressed expensively and meshed with the elegant decor and furniture. Graham realized it was a boutique hotel with a private pool hall. *Most unusual.* "Good evening, gentleman." The hostess's eyes travelled over them, assessing them. "I don't believe I've seen either of you here before, have I? You will need to become members to play here." Her smile seemed more like a sneer to Graham, as she assessed her new guests thoroughly. "Would you like to join the club?" Her smile showcased even, white teeth. *Expensive dental work. Caps, no doubt.* Her hazel green eyes missed nothing. The light from the chandelier overhead caught the diamond's fire, causing it to sparkle brilliantly.

Graham didn't hesitate. "How much is it? Can we join for a week? A month? We're visitors to the area. A friend told us about this place."

"Ah...You're looking for a day pass. I can do that." Ms. Charm's smile didn't reach her icy cold eyes. She pulled another form out from the small, antique desk. "Two hundred, fifty dollars each. Pay before play, naturally." She gazed at them, waiting for their response.

Graham coughed and sputtered. "Naturally, Ma'am." *Maybe they would be wiser to wait this dance out.* He had a sense that the woman didn't miss anything. Further, he had a gut feeling that she was bad news. He glanced over at the P.I.

The P.I. shrugged. "It's only money." He pulled a money clip from his pocket and counted off the cash in large bills, paying for both of them. *Five hundred bucks. They'd better glean something for this investment, aside from the kick of it all.*

Miss Charm smiled big when her greedy eyes landed on the cash. She obviously took great delight in receiving the bills. She plucked the cash from Nick as though taking emeralds or diamond, quickly recounting it. She seemed to almost caress the bills. Satisfied that it was correct, she nodded to her guests. "Come with me." Her smile was professional, cold, devoid of all emotion. She showed them to an empty table, turned and left. She glanced back at them, for just a fleeting moment before disappearing out of sight.

Graham and Nick pulled cues down from the wall and chalked up. At the table, Nick broke the balls and they started their game. They were two tables over from Tanner and his buddy. They hoped their disguises were as effective as they believed them to be.

Tanner and his male companion, a middle aged, intense man, were focusing on their game. Tanner spoke in a murmur. "You sure you won't join me in Buenos Aires? I'll be staying at the Eldorado Polo club. There's some fine players there...bet you'd enjoy watching them."

"Nah. I'm not into travelling. I've got everything I need right here in Palm Beach." His buddy focused on his cue and the shot.

"Yeah. I guess you do." Tanner focused on his shot. He ran the table.

Nick didn't trust it. The information was just too readily dumped into his lap. But on the other hand, Tanner and his buddy hadn't given them a second look. Their disguises were, after all, pretty good.

The model glided past the pool tables, taking a seat which afforded her an excellent view of the table on which Tanner and his buddy were playing. Tanner broke the balls for the new game and swung into action. He glanced at his date, flashing a big, flirtatious smile.

"Hey, doll. You're lookin' good." Tanner's voice had an icy edge to it. He took a moment and gazed at the gorgeous creature he'd brought with him. Leaning toward her, he whispered. "You should reconsider and join me in Argentina, gorgeous. Maybe I'll buy you a house there..." He pursed his lips and planted a kiss on her pouty lips.

"I'm sorry, darling, I have bookings I can't get out of. I don't want a lawsuit on my hands." She smiled. "I'll miss you, darling, but it's just not a good time for me to travel. How long will you be gone?"

This time, Tanner glanced around the room quickly, almost as though it were a cautionary routine that he was accustomed to using. He leaned closer to the model, whispering.

Graham could not hear his whispers this time. He doubted Nick could either. Would the hidden wire pick it up? He'd have to wait and see. His best guess was that Tanner said something to the effect that he had no intention of ever returning to the United States.

"Maybe you'll change your mind. I hope so." The model smiled, weakly.

Graham stole a long glance at her. Beneath her weak, shaky smile, he glimpsed relief and joy. *She's scared of him. She wants the money. She's likely taken it already, but now she wants out. I have to wonder how that's going to play out.*

Tanner's face changed. His expression became grim. Hard, like concrete. "You're comin' with me, doll." His eyes were dead, his voice flat.

Fear flushed over the model's features. She trembled. "I...I have to go to the Ladies' room."

Tanner leaned into her. His voice strained. Hard.

"Make sure that's the only place you're goin'."

Graham really believed it was a miracle that he could hear the whisper. In the natural, there was no way he could have heard it. And the whisper would have been too faint for the wire to pick up the sound.

The model's countenance was grim. Sad. She stole a knowing glance at Graham and Nick as though she knew their mission and was sending a silent signal that she was in over her head. She took a deep breath and strode to the back of the pool hall, down a hallway where the restrooms were located. Once there, she planted herself in front of the door like a statue, unmoving.

Graham, sensing the model was in trouble headed toward the restrooms.

He'd sensed she'd been trying to give him a signal as she walked by his table. Nick showed up, also. He whispered to the model. "We'll try to get you out of here, if that's what you're trying to do." He flashed his ID briefly and stuck it back in his pocket. "Come on, Ma'am, we gotta move fast. Follow us." Nick moved speedily toward the back door.

The model hurried, following them, nervously. It was too late. Tanner appeared, aiming his Beretta at the P.I.'s chest. He fired. The bullet bounced off his bullet-proof vest. Tanner swore under his breath and aimed at Graham. Graham had seen it coming and ducked, narrowly missing the bullet. The P.I. aimed his Colt 42 at Tanner who was using the model as a human shield, while she struggled frantically to free herself from his deadly grasp. He twisted her arm, causing her to scream with pain.

Graham realized with a sinking feeling they'd been

had. Tanner had been two jumps ahead of them. He had set them up...manipulating them into following him. He likely owned the club. The hostess was probably in on it with him, maybe somehow part of his operation. He'd planned to murder them both. That much was obvious. Maybe the peculiar woman who had greeted them in the foyer of the club would dispose of the bodies and just keep smiling and collecting money from the new suckers who joined the club.

A chill swept over Graham. Had Tanner *really* intended to murder them both? *Dead men don't talk.* Would he actually go to that extent to avoid incarceration? *Prison is not a desirable place to spend a large part of one's life. Living the high life in Buenos Aires with a gorgeous woman would be far more pleasurable.*

Tanner fled, keeping the model in the line of fire until he reached his waiting car. He dragged the model with him into the back of the sleek, black Jaguar, despite her kicking and screaming protestations. The driver speedily wheeled the Jaguar out of the parking lot, roaring off into the pitch-black night.

Fitting, Graham thought. Tanner was like the Jaguar. Stealthy. A Pouncer. Calculating. Fast, like lightening. Tanner's buddy was nowhere around. *He must have raced out the front door and drove off.*

"We've been had. No time to waste." Nick was punching in the number of the local sheriff, quickly apprising them of the situation. After he ended the call, he turned to Graham. "You can believe it or not, but this is my first failed operation. It's not over yet. We're going to snatch victory from the jaws of defeat." Nick was seething. "I've been trained in chases and surprise attacks... all aspects of my chosen profession. He jumped into the car, Graham grabbed the passenger seat. Nick gunned, chasing the speeding Jaguar through the streets on the outskirts of Palm Beach.

Graham had been briefed on modus operandi in the unlikely event of a scenario just like the one they found themselves embroiled in. He was on his cell, talking to the sheriff.

The sheriff took control. "I've got you on a conference call so you'll know what's happening. An All Points Bulletin has been sent out. Road blocks are being assembled. We're going to nail this guy before he gets to the airport or marina. He might try leaving by boat. Tanner has a woman with him. He's taken her by force and is using her as a human shield. Looks like he's planning to jump bail and leave the country, maybe to Buenos Aires."

Chapter Twenty-Four

The road block that was set up was effective. Tanner was nailed with his driver and the model at Palm Beach Yacht club in the process of chartering a small yacht and a captain to cruise them back to Freeport. Police showed up, handcuffed Tanner and stuffed him into the back of a police car.

The model began to sob uncontrollably. "I just want to go back home to New York. I don't know how I got involved with him..."

The police weren't buying it. One of the cops glanced out over the sea of yachts and then back to the model. "How *did* you become involved with him, Ma'am? You'll be coming down to the station with us. We've got a lot of questions for you."

"B...but I have modelling assignments in New York," she sputtered, lamely.

"You should have thought of that before you became involved with this slime ball." The cop was unmoved by her tears and pleas of innocence. They pushed her into the back of a separate police car for the drive down to the station.

At the police station, Tatiana was bombarded with questions, most of which she could not answer. Finally, after a couple of hours of grilling her, she was released. "What about...the witness protection program...shouldn't I get a million dollars and a new life..." She peered over at the Deputy Sheriff.

He chuckled. "Yeah. Right, lady. You and every other gangster's girlfriend would love that freebie. It's not going to happen. You showed poor judgement of character. That's your problem. You'll have to live with the fallout. By the way... the man has a long history of dating gorgeous broads once or twice and then sending them on their way. Get back to work and forget you ever knew this creep. Consider this a warning...a lesson. The world is filled with undesirables—wolves in sheep's clothing. You need to learn how to discern the good from the bad..." The deputy sheriff saw the crestfallen look on the poor girl's face. Okay maybe he went too far. "There ain't no easy money, lady. You gotta work for your money, same as everybody else." He shook her hand. *Darn, she was one good lookin' woman. Too bad he was married.* He handed her his card. "If he contacts you, give us a call." On that parting note, he grinned. "Good luck, beautiful." Well, he just couldn't resist acknowledging her beauty. Yeah, she affected him. He just didn't want her to know it. He was a married man and he intended to stay that way. You didn't get everything you wanted in this life. His wife was a good broad. He loved that woman. Didn't mean he was blind, though.

~

Graham flew home ahead of Nick and the undercover cops. They assured him that they would look after the details. After all, he had a horse farm and two sons to get back to.

As soon as Graham cruised through the main gate at Sugarbush Farm and drove down the long driveway toward his house, a peace and joy swept over him. He took a deep breath. *Lord, thank-you. It's like...the caress of a tropical breeze. I'm in love with Dana.* The reality of that hit him like a ton of bricks smashing onto his head. *Lord, whatever am I going to do?* He could hardly wait to see her.

Dana greeted Graham at the front door of the mansion with a hug. Soon, his sons were jumping up and down gleefully, mussing up his hair and cracking jokes.

Graham's sister, Sybil, cast her brother a knowing smile. She moved in close to him, whispering. "It's too late, Graham. You *do* know that, don't you?" She grinned at him, her eyes twinkling as she waited for his response.

Sybil had prepared lamb with roasted potatoes and veggies. She'd found the wine cellar and set a good bottle of red on the table. There was plenty of reason to celebrate.

"I stayed in the house like you told me to, Graham. Sybil and I went to my house during the day just to check on things. Everything looks good. The sheriff took a closer look at the secret ranch...said he just had a hunch there was something they'd missed. He's been working covertly on the case and just discovered a separate, secret, small barn hidden behind a cluster of trees a fair distance out on the acreage and away from the main barn and coral. He discovered two other stolen colts that had been missing for over a year." Dana took a sip of her iced tea. "Isn't that incredible?"

"Nothing would surprise me where Tanner is concerned." Graham shook his head. Over dinner, he brought everyone up to speed regarding Tanner. Soon, he moved onto to their common goal of training *Flaming Bullet* for the Derby. "We've lost over three weeks of training; we'll need to make that up as fast as we can. But now that we've got him back, we need to set up a rigorous training schedule...and pray that we can make up for lost time." Graham peered over at Dana.

Dana slowly nodded. "It's going to be challenging to make up the lost time."

Graham knew he'd gotten it right. This whole Kentucky Derby fever was now in *his* blood just like it was in Dana's. They *had* to win.

~

Sybil drove out from Sugarbush Farm early the next morning after a bombardment of hugs and kisses by her nephews and a hug from Dana and finally a long embrace from Graham. "Hey, Sis. I owe you for this. You really were an enormous help. Thanks for everything." Graham hugged his sister again and waved as she climbed into her white Jeep and drove off.

~

Dana cracked the whip. "We can do this, guys. We can train *Flaming Bullet* to win The Kentucky Derby. The only good thing about all this is that Tanner's intense interest in the colt is verification that he's a hot property favored to win the Derby. Don't ask me how I knew that particular colt was the one—I just did. Of course he has impeccable bloodlines—but so do other colt. I really think it's a God thing. And, yes, you develop a kind of...sixth sense about these thoroughbreds when you work with them as long as I have."

During the next weeks and months, Dana not only devised a brutal, taxing training schedule for *Flaming Bullet,* but she adhered to it rigorously, using steely determination and discipline—the brand of discipline that took her decades to develop and was now a deep part of her psyche. Decades of equine knowledge, plus focused daily training would pay off. She knew exactly how hard she could push him. *Flaming Bullet* would take home the roses! It was his destiny. She was sure of it. And God had set her in the colt's path to help him claim the victory. *Glory to God in the highest!*

Chapter Twenty-Five

Tanner had been plucked from the Palm
Beach Yacht club by authorities and driven to the
county jail and booked for attempting to jump bail. He
was held in the local jail and later transported back to
Lexington, Kentucky and his farm. He was scheduled to
reappear in court for attempting to jump bail and skip
the country. Doubtless, significant additional time
would be added onto his sentence. The law didn't take
skipping out on bail and attempted murder lightly.

~

Sybil had always been a social butterfly. She
opened a good bottle of red from the wine cellar. She
pulled a pot roast from the oven and surveyed her
masterpiece. The medley of roasted carrots, onions,
potatoes and other yellow veggies made the roast look
picture perfect. She took a whiff of the aroma wafting
from the dish. She glanced over at Sybil. "We have
good reason to celebrate. We thought we would be
celebrating victory...winning the Kentucky Derby.

Instead, we're celebrating Tanner's return to incarceration. He'll be in a place where he can't hurt any more horses. This is a worthwhile reason to celebrate."

~

Dana took a peak at the formal dining table. Sybil had set it beautifully. Tanner would be headed back to prison. Many years would be added onto his sentence, no doubt.

Graham presided over the head of the long, highly polished, Chippendale table. Sybil had set the table beautifully. She occupied the place of honor to his right. Dana sat on his left, with one of his sons next to each woman. Sybil proposed a toast. "To the end of Tanner's web of deceit." She shook her head. "All these years...all the missing colts...who would ever have imagined we would stumble onto a major underground operation like the one he's been running...".

Graham and Dana joined in the toast. "To bringing integrity and joy back to Kentucky Derby. May God grant protection on the colts, their riders and their owners...and preserve this magnificent sport." Will and Jay lifted their glasses, which contained red grape juice, joining in the toast.

"I wouldn't normally celebrate someone's downfall, but this celebration is unique. We stumbled onto a covert operation and broke the cycle of abuse and deceit with the thoroughbreds. He should get a stiff sentence...particularly since he tried to skip the country." Graham shook his head.

~

Dana rose early as usual. She glanced at her bedside clock. It read 5:00 a.m. Half-asleep, she spooned coffee into the filters, added water and turned on the machine. She would be awake after a couple of cups of rich roast. A couple of scrambled eggs and a piece of rye toast and she was ready to start her day.

Moving into her bedroom, she slipped into a pair of jeans and a fresh, white linen shirt before plunking down at the kitchen table to enjoy more coffee and read her Bible. Over a couple more mugs of coffee, she meditated on the scriptures. She was reading the Bible in a year and used an online Bible plan to keep her on track. God had richly blessed her since she had committed to seeking Him with a whole heart. As long as He was leading her day and guiding her life, good things would come her way. *I need to trust in Him and lean not on my own understanding...in all your ways acknowledge him and he will direct your paths.* Over time, she was brimming over with scriptures, the words burned into her mind and heart.

It was easy to get side-tracked, easy to tell herself she would skip reading the Bible just today, but she was determined to press in to all that God had for her. He said she should meditate on his word day and night. Well, that's what she would do. Dana put a tick mark on her wall calendar, indicating that she had read the portions of scriptures designated for the day. Regardless of what else *didn't* get done, she would read the entire Bible in a year. She had accomplished that task for the last four years. She would do it again this year. God had shown up and favored and blessed her more than ever since she'd committed to meditating on his word day and night. *God was honorable, right? He said what he meant and meant what he said.*

At the barn, she fed Flaming Bullet the special

food set aside for him. Somehow, he has to catch up. Somehow she had to make up the lost time when she should have been training him. It hit her, then. Tanner must have hired a trainer to come to the ranch daily to work with the colt. He knew the horse business, despite the fact that he was sleazy. Flaming Bullet probably continued intensive training after Tanner stole him back from her. Naturally, Tanner had hoped to steal the insurance papers and enter the colt into the Kentucky Derby and Preakness Stakes race. She would know soon. Today. An hour or two with Flaming Bullet and a short gallop and she would just know if he'd been in rigorous training or if Tanner had neglected it.

Bonus. After working with the colt for a couple of hours, she knew absolutely that Tanner had kept the colt in training—which just proved his intent to enter *Flaming Bullet* in the Derby. She wasn't surprised.

~

Billy, a ranch hand at the secret ranch, leaned into the corral. He hated being two-faced, it went against his grain. But he was in much too deep to bail out now. Plus, he'd gotten used to the dirty money. He'd finally been able to get his ex off his back. Margie and the kids had finally stopped whining about his support payments being late or non-existent. With her off his back, he could finally move on with his life.

Billy hated to double-cross his boss. But what the heck? He deserved it. Tanner was not a nice guy. Everybody knew you could not screw people over and expect God to bless and prosper you. So he wasn't perfect. Maybe the Big Guy upstairs would give him a nod for squealing on his boss. Tanner didn't need more money. He needed more integrity. He was helping the guy progress spiritually, actually.

He'd handed *Flaming Bullet* to Dana. She was a great broad. Maybe she'd get tired of the would-be cowboy Graham and look his way. He knew women liked him. He wasn't really good-looking but he had a certain, rugged charm women seemed to gravitate to. He could figure out an excuse for driving out to Sugarbush, maybe he'd remember some important information about *Flaming Bullet. Maybe* before you know it, they might bond and then who knew what could happen.

Billy didn't waste any time. He would cook up the story as he drove to Sugarbush. He was a master at winging it. After hanging out with Tanner for almost a decade, he'd picked up more than one trick. He slicked his hair back and slapped on his favorite cologne, shrugged into a fresh, blue Western-styled shirt and the jeans he saved for special occasions such as this one. Polishing his well-worn cowboy boots, he whistled in anticipation of his foray.

Billy phoned Dana when he reached the gates at Sugarbush Stables. The large, black vehicle he drove had been his buddy for more than fifteen years. He'd named the vehicle *Rugged Roger* because of everything they had been through together. His call to Dana went directly to voice mail. He phoned again. "Hey, Dana. It's Billy from the ranch...Tanner's ranch. Got some information for ya. Any chance I could...ah... talk to you in person for a few minutes? I'm at the gate."

What information could he possibly have that she and Graham did not already know? I'd better check with Graham before I let him in. "Gee, Billy. It's not my ranch. I need to check with Graham. I wish you would have called first, before you made the drive..."

"Hey, I won't take much of your time, Dana. If I didn't think this information was important, I wouldn't have driven out here. I'm...a busy man." *He figured it always looked good to act like you had more goin' on than you did.* Billy prided himself on being clever. He always did his homework. He'd staked out the place earlier that morning. When he spotted Graham's Jeep with him at the wheel and his two sons in the back of it, he knew he was kissed by the stars. Dana was likely alone on the farm. It was time to make his move.

~

Dana waffled on calling Graham. He probably wouldn't trust anyone who worked for Tanner. And maybe he'd be right. She remembered Graham was heading out early. She didn't want to bother him while he was driving. She was a big girl. She could make her own decisions. *Maybe I'll make points with Graham if I glean some important information about Tanner. What harm could it do to let Billy visit her? She thought better of it. Why couldn't he tell her whatever it was over the phone?*

She knew Graham was driving the boys over to the school to register for the fall term. He had told her that he had some business in the city after that. He would be back at the ranch in the afternoon. What harm could it do to see Billy?

~

Billy wasn't born yesterday. He knew every trick in the book. He'd anticipated her next question. He'd always prided himself on how smart he was. Tanner had even acknowledged how clever he was on occasion. "My phone might be tapped. I don't trust it. Not to mention I'm on limited minutes on my cell phone..." Billy rattled on.

Dana was busy. She had a tight training schedule to adhere to. She would get this guy and his information out of the way and get on with her day. She buzzed him in.

Billy grinned. He slapped his fist on the steering wheel in excitement and spoke aloud. "It's my charm. Hot dang! That woman likes me. I knew it. I just knew it. I gotta chance with her." He was still grinning as he drove his rickety, old truck down the long road leading to the farm.

A pair of barking Shepherd dogs yelped, racing straight toward his vehicle. He leaned out the window. "Hey guys, relax. I'm a friend..." He was usually good with animals, but these hefty, healthy looking dogs weren't dissuaded. They barked frantically. He stayed in his vehicle, having little choice.

He tried tapping in Dana's cell number again. It went straight to voice mail. He hadn't realized there were vicious dogs on the property. He chided himself for not anticipating that. He stayed in the truck, biding his time. Dana would come out to the truck. By now, she was probably eager to glean the new information he told her he had. He rehearsed his story as he waited for her. That good lookin' woman would show up here sometime soon. He glanced over at her white Mercedes SUV parked in front of her small, white house. Graham drove a jeep so this had to be her vehicle. He rehearsed his story as he bided his time, waiting for Dana to show up. He needed to have a darn good reason why he'd shown up here.

He checked the time on his cell phone. 8:01 a.m. Dana would soon be out at the racetrack training Flaming Bullet; putting him through his paces. He could help her. He had some information she needed. Some inside stuff he'd gleaned from Tanner. His cell chirped. He glanced at the call display and saw Dana's number flash on the screen. *"Yes."*

~

"Why don't go ahead and tell me the information. I'm busy." Dana got right to the point. The faster she could find out what he wanted, the sooner she could get him off Graham's property. *Was it just coincidence that she was alone on the farm?* She didn't like hanging out alone on the farm. It made her nervous. More so now that the oddball ranch hand had unexpectedly shown up here. *I shouldn't have let him onto the property. What was I thinking? I better make another pot of coffee. Well, it's too late now. I'll just get rid of him as soon as I can.*

He grinned from his perch inside the cab of his truck. "How about calling off the dogs. You won't be able to hear a word I say, if you don't." He yelled to be heard over the barking sound.

"Sure. Okay." *I'm going to hear what he has to say and get him out of here.*

He jumped out of the cab when she called off the dogs. "Hey, good-lookin'... got some insider tips I gleaned from Tanner. Figured you could use 'em. I'm not here to waste your time—lovely lady—I jest want to help...I ain't proud of being associated with that...sleeze ball...but...well, you know how it is...family obligations, and all that stuff..."

Dana cut him off. "Get to the point, please." She

226

stood a safe distance away from him, becoming more uneasy by the minute. *Why didn't I at least alert the sheriff? Mind you he's so busy, who knows when he would be able to get over here.*

He smirked.

For one, brief minute she realized the man had a certain earthy, raw, sex appeal...a kind of cunning savvy some woman really liked. Bu what was he doing here? How fast could she get rid of him? "Would you cut to the bottom line, please?"

Billy turned on the charm. He enjoyed towering over her. She looked so feminine and small. He knew he had raw sex appeal. *Dana was the perfect woman for him, and he was perfect for her. She just didn't know it yet.* "Sure, of course. Aren't you going to invite me in for coffee? I've got quite a bit to share with you."

It took her a nanosecond to come to a decision. Something about him was making her nervous. "No. Definitely not. I want you off the property right now. Graham will call you and if he decides we should meet, then the two of you can set up a meeting. So...you either drive off the ranch or I'll call the sheriff..."

"Hey, hey, hey...no reason to get snitty. Ah'm tryin' to help you. Like I said, I got some inside information I'm sure you'll be interested in knowin..."

Dana was actually tempted for a brief, fleeting moment. Then she snapped back to her senses. What had she been thinking? The man was a scoundrel. He worked for Tanner. Maybe he'll wind up in jail, too. He might be considered an accomplice. Still, she couldn't help being curious. Maybe she should talk to him. Time was of the essence, after all. Maybe he DID know something important. It was daylight. She had her pepper spray, a shotgun she knew how to use and of course, her cell. He wouldn't dare try anything stupid. Still, she'd play it safe and remain standing outside near his truck, protected by her yelping dogs, which were temporarily silenced. She was safe. And she was curious about the information he claimed to have. She was glad she'd left a voicemail for the sheriff to drop by, not that he would have time. But she could ask anyway.

The cowboy tipped his hat and grinned. "Sure could use a cup of coffee. I wanna make sure I remember all this important information." He turned on the charm. Women liked him. They always had. She was no exception. Maybe prettier and smarter than most of the women he'd known, but she was still female. And he was all male. *Don't opposites attract?* He smirked.

She noticed for the first time how good-looking and sexy the man was as he tipped his battered cowboy hat and grinned.

She was being overly cautious. Silly, actually. The sheriff was routinely monitoring a few large farms in the area, given the recent spate of thefts. Sugarbush was on his list. He would probably show up here today. She waved him inside. "Come on. I'll make some fresh coffee." She'd grown up learning good Southern manners, it wouldn't hurt to be neighborly. She shrugged off her feeling of apprehension.

"Thank-you, Ma'am. Sure do appreciate it."

Dana put on a fresh pot of coffee and set out homemade peanut butter cookies on the table with two mugs. In minutes, she poured the coffee.

The lanky cowboy had plunked down at the

kitchen table on a chair opposite her. He grinned and bit into the cookies. Nodded. "Mighty fine, Little Lady. Seems like you got way more than your share of talent. I'd..." He stood then. "I'd like to share that..." He suddenly grabbed her and held her close, kissing her passionately.

The man is a chameleon. He ripped her shirt and bra like it was a piece of paper, picked her up while she screamed and yelled and pushed her down onto the sofa.

Oh God, help me. The man is about to rape me. She fought like a wildcat, digging her long nails into his skin, trying to get to his eyes.

The cowboy just laughed. Loudly. His lips came down on hers, his kiss fierce, demanding.

She lost it then. Furious and terrified, she managed to get her foot free, despite being encased with a cowboy boot. She kicked him in the groin.

He flew from his position of attempted rape, off of her, in a flash. He yelped and went crazy, writhing in pain. He managed to push her to the floor and pin her there, despite his apparent, excruciating pain.

"No!" She yelled.

Just then the door burst open. The sheriff stood there, taking a picture with his cell phone. "What have we got here?" He handcuffed the yelping cowboy while the deputy sheriff herded him outside. The man was yelling and writhing in agony. The sheriff and deputy sheriff showed no sympathy.

Dana had never felt so embarrassed in her entire life. She straightened herself up and hurried into the bedroom, emerging shortly in a fresh outfit; jeans with a fresh, pale pink linen shirt and a lightweight jacket.

No two bit horse thief was going to get the best of her. He may have won the first round but she would win the second and third and fourth round...

~

Graham's voice was stern. "What were you thinking...inviting the man into your house? What do you use for brains?" He was livid. He hadn't meant to spit out such harsh words, but it was too late. The damage was done.

Graham had burst through the door in the nick of time, his presence unexpected. "How had he known she was in trouble?" God must have prompted him to check on her. She'd been merely curious about what the ranch hand claimed to know. She could handle herself—she'd thought so. Now, she'd embarrassed herself, shocked the sheriff and deputy sheriff — and worse, alienated Graham...just when things were starting to look promising for them. She felt like banging her head against the wall. What had she been thinking?

Chapter Twenty-Six

Dana awakened after a fitful, restless sleep. She had a splitting headache. She didn't get headaches. *Good Lord, did the cowboy slip something in her coffee without her knowledge?* She phoned Danielle. "Mom. I'm in big trouble. I hope I haven't blown it forever with Graham..." She told her Mom about the nasty incident.

"It's not worthy of you, Dana. You stepped out of character, somehow. You and Graham have been under a lot of pressure. First, the amnesia, then your colt goes missing and the whole Tanner fiasco... You need to cut yourself some slack. Just get focused on your mission and purpose....and keep praying that Graham will see you as his future wife...don't give up on that idea, no matter what. Can you do that, Dana? Can you get yourself focused on your mission and goal? A scripture springs to mind. *"For I know the plans I have for you, saith the Lord, plans to prosper you and not to harm you. Plans to give you hope and a future..."*

"Oh, Mother...you always know what to say. You always have the right words..."

"You will too, honey. I really believe you have a future with Graham and his sons." Danielle infused her with positive, faith-filled words. Still, a part of her was competitive with Dana. Maybe it was because she was adopted. She'd given up so much to nurture Dana. She'd met a special man after her hubby died. But Dana had needed her and she'd been there for her. But she hadn't been available for the new man, between running a business and caring for a teenage daughter. She'd lost him. There hadn't been another man since him. Part of her wanted happiness for her daughter—the other part was bitterly resentful that Dana always seemed to just walk into favor, blessing and God's richest rewards. Oh, she knew she had to work on her attitude. She'd talked to God about it. Still, she was a relatively young woman herself. Wasn't *she* entitled to meet a wonderful man, too?

Dana laughed bitterly. *Was she her own worst enemy?* "I might have had a chance...but after this ugly incident...all because I was merely curious to find out what the ranch hand had to say..."

"You made an error in judgement, honey. We all do that. Even Graham. I believe God put Graham and his sons into your life for a purpose. But never forget that the adversary, Satan, lurks around like a roaring lion seeking whom he may devour. Have you been doing spiritual warfare every day? Have you been putting on the full armor of God? You can't let up...not even for a second, honey." Danielle spoke with seriousness. It was a battle she herself had not always won. But she wanted Dana to win it.

"How can I make amends with him, Mom?" Dana sobbed.

"The way to a man's heart is through his stomach. I know it's a cliché. And that's because it's true. You need to make some effort. Cook up something amazing tomorrow morning. Then call him and tell him you would like to bring it over for him and his sons. He'll ask you to join him...he's a gentleman from the old school. Wear something *other* than jeans...like maybe a dress and pumps. Tell him how much you appreciate him and his sons..." Danielle rattled on and on, giving her daughter tips she'd gleaned over the years.

"You're joking, right? He would throw me out for sure!" Dana laughed.

"I am absolutely serious, Dana. Graham wants a feminine woman. All men do. You've been so busy running the show and proving how clever you are, and what a great trainer you are...blah blah blah..." She paused for a couple of beats. "If you want him to see you as a woman he could get serious about, you need to act like one..." Danielle was on a roll. She was about to continue when Dana cut in. "Mother...I'm hanging up if you don't change the subject!"

"No, you're not. You're going to hear me out. I'm...just getting started, actually."

Dana sighed. *She had never known her mother to be like this. What was going on?* When Dana could get a word in edgewise, she spoke up. "Mother! What has gotten into you?"

"Simple, darling. I don't want my daughter to end up an old maid!" Danielle blurted out the words, describing her thoughts about Dana of late. Not to mention herself.

Dana was stunned into silence. It was the cold shower she needed. She realized with sudden clarity that she'd focused all her time and energy on getting *Flaming Bullet* ready for the races. But she hadn't nurtured her relationship with Graham. In fact, she rather took him for granted. And *she* called the shots. After all, *she* was the expert, not Graham. So, actually...where did that leave *him*? Straggling behind her? What man wanted that? No wonder he had started going out at night. Maybe there was already another woman. Maybe it was too late. Please, God. Don't let it be too late. I'm crazy about that man. And Mom is right. I've been taking him and his sons for granted. I better sharpen up before I lose him. "Mom. You're right. You're absolutely right. I just hope I'm not too late. I want to be feminine for him... I want to look amazing for him... I *do* want to cook for him." Tears flickered in her eyes as deep emotion surfaced.

That night, as Dana fell asleep, she knew that tomorrow she would turn a new leaf. Tomorrow, she would swing into action and make a plan to be feminine for Graham. But tomorrow was a training day. The countdown was on. The Kentucky Derby would take place in three short months. She didn't have a minute to lose. She tossed and turned all night. She had a dual mission. Both were equal tasks. Both were of primary, pressing importance. Could she do both of them justice? Or would she have to give up one or the other? She fell asleep and slept soundly until the next morning.

Chapter Twenty-Seven

Graham wasn't in the barn; neither were his sons. She suddenly remembered that he was registering the boys for school this morning. Why hadn't she remembered sooner? "Wilbur, I'm trusting you to do the chores. You know the drill. You have the special diet for Flaming Bullet. You're an ace groom, and I shall see to it that you get a raise, provided you take special, extra good care of Flaming Bullet. He is going to win the Kentucky Derby and the Preakness Stakes race. According to Mark 11:23 & 24, I am calling things that are not as though they are."

Wilbur stared at her, dumbfounded. He quickly recovered, grinned and retorted with: "Yes, Ma'am, Flaming Bullet is a winning horse. I knew it the moment I laid eyes on hm. There is something extra-special about that thoroughbred. I'll watch over him and take good care of him until you return." He grinned and moved toward the precious colt.

Dana stood in front of his stall. She leaned over

and stroked *Flaming Bullet,* murmuring secrets to him. She was programming him to win. She prayed over him and called things that are not as though they are. "You will win every race you enter. You are a winner. You are special. Jesus loves you. Graham and his sons love you. I love you. I am proud of you. You are going to move ahead of all the competition. I can just see it. Heaps of roses will be thrust upon you and your jockey as you win the Derby."

She kept stroking him. "It's no accident that your jockey is named Jacob. Names from the Bible have special significance..." She nuzzled against his long neck and sensed his warmth and appreciation toward her. She *loved* him. She wasn't sure when it began, but lately... ever since Flaming Bullet had come back to Sugarbush, they had powerfully bonded. She sensed the colt was more relaxed. He knew he was home.

Dana sensed that the colt wanted to be with her and Graham and wanted to hang out with the other thoroughbreds at Sugarbush. He wanted to roam the gorgeous, hilly greens of Bluegrass country. He had come home. She knew it. And the colt knew it. She also sensed that the colt shared her passion for winning. It was in his blood. In his genes.

She whispered to him again. "I'm praying for your protection, handsome. I plead the 91st Psalm over your life. That supernatural Psalm of protection is my best insurance that no evil or harm will come to you. I pray that you will enjoy the training process. Though it is gruelling for both of us; I know you get it, you have a winning pedigree and you are a born winner. I can just see the heaps and heaps of roses being thrust upon you and Jacob when you win!" She leaned into his long neck and caressed him. Then she kissed him and flashed him a big smile and turned to go. She glanced back at him. "I won't be long, handsome. Take it easy until I get back. We still have a lot of work up ahead."

Dana flashed Flaming Bullet a big smile, nuzzled against his neck and hurried to her car. She'd better move along if she intended to get involved with Will and Jay getting registered and organized for school. They needed her whether they realized it or not. And if that meant being a little pushy or aggressive...well, maybe that's what God wanted her to do. He moves in mysterious ways and she felt led by the spirit to leave the beloved colt and join her favorite guys.

Jacob, the jockey for Flaming Bullet had just entered the barn. He looked like he was raring to go. "Good morning, Jacob. Ready for training? You're here early. Good for you."

"Raring to go, Dana. Raring to go. "The small man with the slight build had a huge spirit. He was enthusiastic and a natural sportsman. The jockey was as hard working and dedicated as Dana had ever seen. It didn't get any better than this. Everything was moving in a positive flow.

Dana flashed Jacob a smile using the "thumbs up" gesture to show her positive feelings about him. "He's all yours, buddy. Take good care of him." She smiled, turned and hurried toward her SUV parked near her cottage. No time like the present to show her interest in Graham and his sons. God had given her a nudge and she needed to act on it.

Graham registered surprise and delight when Dana showed up at school. So did his sons. *Thank-you, Lord.* He seemed to have fully recovered from the ugly incident. His sons meant everything to him, and with her showing interest in them, she sensed she was gaining points. And the Good Lord knew she needed lots of points to win Graham's favor once again.

Back at the ranch, Graham seemed to be wary of Dana. As though he didn't know what to make of her...or maybe could not trust her. Still, somehow, she had his attention *as a woman,* not just as a trainer. It wasn't solely about business and the goal of winning. There was a romance here whether he wanted to acknowledge it or not.

If Dana wanted to be totally honest with herself, having the winning colt was a secondary goal for her. Her primary goal was winning Graham's love as well as his sons' love. But could she do it? Did she really have the mettle required to pull it off? *Lord, maybe it's just too much for me. Too much to handle. Maybe I've bitten off more than I can chew. Do you really expect me to train Flaming Bullet while simultaneously cooking for Graham and his sons? I thought that's why he hired Violet. She needed to focus all her time, thought and energy toward training the colt.*

"*I gave you a wonderful man, my precious daughter. And I expect you to nurture him, look after him and be good to him and his sons. If you can do that, I will cause the two of you to become one. Walk in my ways and do not look either to the right or the left...but straight ahead. I want you to nurture him, look after him and be good to him and his sons. If you can do that, I will cause the two of you to become one. Walk in my ways and do not look either to the right or to the left...but straight ahead. I have so much blessing in store for you if you follow my ways. You do not even begin to know the treasures I have for you. But you need to walk into the blessing and walk into your purpose. Stay close to Me. Abide in Me.*" Dana could hear the still, small voice of the Holy Spirit. God was leading, guiding and directing her. She gazed heavenward in utter amazement.

It hit her then. Violet needed some time off. She had a lot of work keeping the house clean and organized. Maybe *she* needs some home-cooked meals and some time off. That thought had never occurred to her until now.

Chapter Twenty-Eight

Dana swung her SUV into the school parking lot. She didn't see Graham's Jeep anywhere. *It must be parked somewhere around here.* She parked, shot up a quick, fervent prayer and marched into the school. A couple of times she stopped, half way there. *"Lord, what I am doing? I'm interfering...aren't I?"* But in her spirit, she just knew she was where she was supposed to be.

Inside a large room, she blended in with dozens of moms and their kids. A few Dad's as well. She still hadn't spotted Will, Jay or Graham. She began to feel quite foolish. *Lord, you sent me here...at least, I think you did. What's next?*

Will called her name. "Dana! Hey, cool! You showed up, too!" He grinned and hurried over to her. Soon, she spotted Jay who reacted the same way. She found herself spontaneously hugging both boys. *Lord, what is going on? Graham will not be amused. But, on the other hand, God led me here and I'm going to be brave and go with the flow.*

Graham looked bewildered. She finally spotted him at the Admissions desk filling out forms. He glanced her way a couple times and managed a sort of half-grin.

It's a start, Lord. It really is.

He finished the paperwork and then gave her his full attention. He seemed to be fighting an urge to grin at her. "What are you doing here, Dana? Why aren't you...at the track training..."

She cut him off. Then, it had to be the Holy Spirit speaking through her, because she neither had the presence of mind nor the inclination to come up with something wonderful to say. She blurted out words she hadn't thought. "You and your sons are more important..." She couldn't believe she'd spit those words out. What had come over her? Was the Holy Spirit prompting her? Had to be. The Good Lord knew she wouldn't have had the nerve to be so aggressive.

He grinned. Big. Then, right there in front of everyone, he hugged her, ever so briefly...but there it was. A real big, genuine hug. The embrace broke the ice and they both chuckled.

At that moment, Dana knew she had turned the corner with him. They could move forward in this burgeoning relationship...romance, really...and maybe, just maybe things would work out between them.

Back at Sugarbush, Dana drove the horse trailer to the track and worked diligently putting Flaming Bullet and the jockey through their paces. Working the colt up to the one and a quarter mile race was a challenging task and one she thrived on. As a seasoned equestrian and an insider, she was privy to pretty much every trick in the book.

Earlier that morning, she'd contacted another horse farm knowing the owner was training a three-year-old to run in the Derby. She brought Flaming Bullet and the groom to the farm, as she had arranged. She knew it was good training to let the colts compete against each other. They needed to get used to letting the dirt fly in their face and other colts racing in close proximity.

Dana pushed herself to continue adhering to a gruelling schedule with her colt. He *had* to win. And he would. She refused to entertain any thought but that. Winning. Win. Win. Win. That's what it was all about. Still, she realized today that her colt needed a lot more time competing against other colts. He was nowhere near used to it. He had a long way to go. And he had to get there fast. And he would.

The jockey was optimistic. "The longest journey starts with the first mile. We've got our work cut out for us, that's for sure. But we're up to the task. We are definitely up to the task." Jacob spouted this knowledge from the cab of the horse trailer, while Dana drove them back to the ranch.

Was he trying to convince himself? Something about the colt bothered her. She just couldn't put her finger on it. Had Tanner done something to her, unbeknownst to her...maybe when he thought they were on to him? She sent up a silent prayer. A shiver raced through here. *Lord, this win is for you. For your honor and glory. If I'm missing something, please help me to figure out what it is.*

Chapter Twenty-Nine

It was the moment of reckoning. It was time. Ready or not, the three-year-old colts were about to race in the Derby. Dana was breathless.

Graham and the boys seemed unsettled to her. It was as though everyone held their breath. *Flaming Bullet had* to win. He just *had* to. There had never been another colt like him. He was prepped, ready and chomping at the bit to get into the race. She sensed he was ready to compete for the roses and win.

All eyes were on the colts. *Flaming Bullet* was sleek, shining, in glorious, magnificent form. He was rested and prepped. She'd done everything she knew to do. Dana held her breath. *Lord, I pray that the gruelling schedule and careful diet have paid off. Flaming Bullet has to win the Kentucky Derby.* It had to happen. It absolutely would happen.

The Jockeys paraded their colts around in a circle as was customary. Jacob sat proudly on *Flaming Bullet.* Soon the Starter would call them into a line and the world-famous Kentucky Derby race would begin.

The Starter's loud, energized voice barked the exciting announcement. It blared over the loudspeaker as he called out the jockeys and the colts by name. Zero hour. And...they are at the starting gate. And they're off!" Flaming Bullet is in the lead...."

Something was wrong. Terribly wrong. *Flaming Bullet* leaned and waved as though drunk. He seemed to sway... he stumbled and fell as Jacob toppled off of him.

"Ladies and gentleman, there's a problem with *Flaming Bullet.* He was slightly ahead of the competition but he's...the horse is...downed...." The announcer's voice droned in Dana's ears. Waves of shock and horror rippled through her. *Lord, no... what is going on?*

She heard the announcer's voice. It sounded surreal. Her colt was downed but the race continued.

Dana and Graham ran from the Owner's box into the holding area near the starting gate. Jacob was shaken but he was okay. He led Flaming Bullet into a paddock. The jockey was stunned. Dazed.

The veterinarian on hand hurried to the colt's side and began examining him.

Dana and Graham, horrified, hovered over them. Neither spoke. The announcer's voice was a blur, droning overhead. An annoying distraction. Their colt was downed, out of the race. She was horrified. Dimly, she heard the cheers as the race ended.

"Dana, Graham..." The vet glanced at them, his face a mask of concern. "The colt... has been poisoned, that much is obvious. What kind of poison... and how and when it was administered...well, that is tricky to determine. I'm calling in an expert to run some tests so that we can try to figure out exactly what happened..." The vet shook his head in disgust.

The sheriff and deputy sheriff showed up, bombarding the vet with questions. They looked over *Flaming Bullet* themselves and snapped some photos of him. The men turned their attention to Dana and Graham. "Do either of you have any idea what might have happened? He was the odds on favorite to win first place...somehow he became weak and stumbled..."

Dana peered into the sheriff's eyes. She lowered her voice to a whisper. "Do you think Tanner is behind tampering with Flaming Bullet?"

"That would seem too obvious, since he knows we're onto him and he's been charged with horse theft and attempted murder...and he's off the circuit. Unless he orchestrated the dirty deed through accomplices, we might be looking at someone else. I don't actually think he is behind this. No, my hunch is that while we were focused on tracking Tanner down, someone...maybe someone who wanted to buy Flaming Bullet—maybe his previous groom orchestrated this. You told me about his reluctance to let you anywhere near the colt. I don't have any answers...just a lot of questions."

Dana shook and began sobbing. She'd never broken down emotionally before with a horse she'd trained. Somehow, this colt was different—and Graham's involvement made it special..." She turned to Graham. "I...I'm never this emotional with the horses...but this...this...is horrendous...this is foul play if I've ever seen it. I just hope the Vet can figure out what might have happened..." Dana caressed Flaming Bullet's long neck as she wept bitterly.

While the Vet put him through a series of tests, Dana whispered to the colt, encouraging him. "You're going to be fine. We're going to get you into the Preakness Stakes Race. We're going to figure out what happened...we're going to get to the bottom of this. How dare someone muck around with you...and you're going to get better...you're going to be fine...whoever has messed with you is going to pay dearly..." Dana went from weeping to cold resolve. She would find out what went down. She would get to the bottom of it. And by the grace of God, if foul play was involved....and it was hard to believe it wasn't...the scoundrel involved was going to pay. Oh yes, he was going to pay big time. *Lord, you see this injustice. You are a great and mighty God. Nothing is too hard for you. Please God, let Flaming Bullet be miraculously healed...and let him go on to victory in other races. Lord...you gave him to me...*She sobbed and her voice broke. She wiped her tears and spoke aloud. *"*Lord, you are a God of miracles. I call out a miracle..." Dana wiped her tears from her face and peered at Graham.

Graham stood by stoically. He fought tears of his own as his mind raced a mile a minute.

"Heady High-Minded won by a half a length." She'd heard the announcer call it out over the loudspeaker, but it was as if his voice was coming down a long tunnel. Like this wasn't really happening. It was just a bad dream. But it was all too real. She began sobbing, at first just a bit and then uncontrollably.

Graham wrapped her in his strong arms and she settled down somewhat. His sons remained at his side. Stoic. Silent.

She vaguely heard the thousands of excited fans leaping to their feet. Yelling and cheering sounds resounded throughout the horse racing facility. The winning colt and his jockey paraded proudly for the cameras and crowd while heaps of gorgeous red roses were thrown upon him. Cameras moved in close, filming the winner. It was all shown on giant screens interspersed throughout the facility. The million-dollar purse went to Heady High-Minded and Windy, his jockey. Dana fainted in Graham's arms.

Graham carried Dana into his Jeep. When the boys got settled into it, he drove them home. He didn't ask Dana if she wanted to stay at the mansion. He took her there, carrying her up the steps. She was still out like a light turned off. He set her onto the bed in the guest room upstairs she usually occupied. He covered her with a down-filled comforter and turned off the light. She would sleep until daylight. Still, he would check on her throughout the night. She had been verging on hysteria. He'd never known her to react like this. Maybe someone had slipped something into her coffee or food. Or maybe his mind was racing and he had an over-active imagination. They'd both been shocked and disappointed and needed to recover.

Dana slept soundly through the night as far as Graham could tell. He was up much of the night. He wanted to be there in case she needed him. He knew then that he could never live without this woman. He loved her. He really loved her. And he wanted her so much he ached. Ached, somewhere deep inside. He wanted to protect her from the wicked, harsh world. He wanted to love her and take care of her...he wanted...absolutely everything with that woman.

Dana finally came downstairs at around ten the next morning. She was silent. No words would come.

Graham had sent his sons outside. He wanted this time alone with her. He didn't speak, he just gazed at her, waiting for her to say something.

After considerable silence, she spoke through her tears. She was sobbing, softly, silently. She glanced up at him with a half-smile. "It...it just wasn't meant to be...all that work...all that focus and dedication...all for naught..." She looked to him for answers. "Why, Graham? Why?"

He fought overwhelming emotion. "I don't know, Dana. I just don't know. I don't have any answers. But we still have each other, don't we, Dana?" He looked at her intensely. It was the moment of truth and they both knew it.

She reached for him, then. She thrust her arms around his neck. "Hold me, Graham. Just hold me and never let me go. I love you. Don't you know that? I've always loved you. You took my heart the moment I laid eyes on you. You are all that matters to me. You. God... and your sons. It's not about the horses, it was never about the horses. It was always about you."

He held her so close she could barely breathe. "Will you marry me, darling? I want to love you like you've never been loved before. I want to teach you about love."

She was in a daze. A heady, billowy, heavenly kind of daze. There would never be another man for her. She'd known it the moment she'd laid eyes on him. She'd tried to convince herself that it all about the horses, all about winning the purse...but it wasn't. It was all about him. All about the deep love she'd fought, a love so strong, it just kept rising higher and bolder like the morning sun, a love so powerful that it could last throughout all eternity. A love that only God could have orchestrated.

Graham was on his knees. He was from the old school. Had been brought up that way. He pulled the ring from his pocket. An enormous, pear-shaped diamond solitaire. He'd bought it just a couple days ago. The day she had surprised him by showing up at school. He'd known then that he had to marry her, couldn't live without her...as long as she would have him.

Gentle tears spilled down her cheeks. She reached up and held him. "Oh Graham, I love you so much. I've wanted you from the first moment I laid eyes on you. I want to be your wife. Yes. I want that with all my heart. I've fought the attraction, but to no avail. I tried to tell myself it was all about the horses. All about winning...but it wasn't. Deep in my heart I knew it was all about you. I didn't know if you felt the same way. At times, I thought you were very attracted to me. At other times I wasn't so sure. I knew you fought the attraction. And so did I. Maybe God had to give us both a wake-up call by moving the colt out of the equation. Maybe he wanted us to just focus on each other for a while."

Chapter Thirty

Dana was on cloud nine. She called Danielle and shared the good news. Danielle was ecstatic.

Back at her house, Dana relaxed. Finally. She actually watched some TV and read a novel she'd bought some time ago and had not had the time to even begin it. She mulled around in her head as to whether or not Tanner was involved with the foul play. The tests hadn't come back from the lab yet. She didn't yet know what the colt had ingested. Tanner may have been involved, or one of his buddies; but without hard evidence, it was pointless to speculate. He would be in prison for a long time anyway, between attempted murder, and an aborted plan to skip the country and forfeit bail.

Sybil looked after the boys which freed up Dana and Graham to make an appearance at one of the cocktail parties for the Kentucky Derby. They sipped champagne, greeted some folks and left early. They were not in the mood to party. "I just think it's the sporty thing to do. We show up and we leave." Dana shrugged.

Graham flopped down on the large L-shaped sofa in his living room. "Now what, Dana? Do we scrap the goal of winning the Derby or accelerate our efforts?"

"You don't have to ask, Graham. Neither of us are quitters. We're both up to the challenge. We are going full speed ahead, of course. In fact, I don't even think we should take a couple days off. The faster we find a new colt and train it...well, you know the drill."

Graham was still reeling with shock. "Winning the Kentucky Derby has been my dream for ages. I've prayed fervently that we would find the winning colt. We found an amazing one. His bloodlines were impeccable. You researched it thoroughly. We were both so sure he would be the winner. You trained him rigorously, and no one is a better trainer than you. You know every nuance, every trick in the book. Still, with all that, we didn't win." Graham shook his head. "It just wasn't meant to be."

"We both know there was foul play, Graham." They sat in the family room drinking cinnamon apple tea. He reached over and took her hand. "The only thing I can think of is that God has a much better plan for us. That has to be it. There is a reason why we didn't win. It doesn't make any sense now...it may not for some time. But sooner or later...it will make a whole lot of sense." Graham peered over at Dana. He was trying to comfort her despite his own acute disappointment.

"I'm glad you can philosophize about it, Graham. We need to head out early tomorrow and pump the Vet. He might have something by now."

"Yes. So...what it the most common way of tampering with a racehorse?" Graham peered at Dana, looking for answers.

"Well, you drug them just enough so that they can perform well but not at optimum. It's a fine art, actually...and not something you learn overnight. It takes the hand of a real expert. That's why I think Tanner might be behind it." Dana sighed.

"When and how is it done? Flaming Bullet was watched very closely. When would Tanner or his boys have had a chance to tamper with him?" Graham had an analytical mind. He was going to get to the bottom of this. And fast.

"I don't know. In the case of Flaming Bullet, I suspect Tanner may have gotten into his paddock and slipped him something. Something slowed him down. He was off. Only slightly. Just enough to give another colt the edge. This was a professional job. No question about it. Subtle but effective."

"Slipped him something...like what?" Graham raised his eyebrows, his mind racing.

"Arsenic. The vet is giving him a series of tests. He might have been given small doses of strychnine, belladonna, cocaine and/or coffee, also."

Graham was impressed by Dana's knowledge. "How do you know all this stuff?" He took a sip of his tea.

"Are you kidding? I've been in the business since I was a teenager hanging around horses. I could probably write a book..." Dana laughed.

The magical sound of her laughter was music to his ears. He was crazy about her. He'd thought it was great when she had started cooking for him and the boys. Now he found himself looking forward to some candle light dinners in his formal dining room with just the two of them.

"I want to make something special and memorable for our engagement dinner. I have something in mind. It will be a surprise." She laughed, playfully.

The sound of her laughter rang in his ears like a symphony. Something really weird was going on in his brain. He had begun thinking of her the moment he awakened in the morning. He usually saw her during the day. And at night she was the last thing he thought about before drifting off to sleep. He finally admitted to himself that their connection was not just about the horses and winning the Derby. Maybe God wanted them to be together. Maybe he deemed their relationship more important than the winning the purse and the heady experience of winning the Derby. The strange thing is, he hadn't planned to propose to her. Hadn't planned to buy the ring, either. He'd spotted it in a jewelry store when he'd gone in to fix his watch. The pear-shaped diamond with the antique baguettes trimming the edges was stunning and just seemed to jump off the rack. The owner of the small jewelry store, a mature woman, had told him she'd just purchased it from an estate sale. "Stunning, isn't it? I can give you a good deal on it, because I got a really good deal..."

Graham found himself buying the ring, despite the fact that he'd had no intentions of buying one. Had God nudged him? God was always ten steps ahead of him. In retrospect, he was sure of it.

Graham chuckled. "Dana, you are too much. The way to a man's heart may not be through his stomach...but it's a darn good start." He smirked.

"Tell you the truth, Graham. I was afraid to make you my Southern fried chicken, because I'd never get rid of you..." She laughed. Her eyes were lit with tenderness and joy.

"You know, for a gal who doesn't cook much, you sure are full of surprises." He chuckled.

Dana peered over at him, her eyes twinkling in amusement. The man didn't miss a beat. "Well, the pressure of training is off... maybe I'll get into shopping and cooking for a while."

"I'll give you some money to go grocery shopping...and don't even think about turning it down. I can get downright nasty, if I have to...because I know how proud you are, Dana...but you *are* taking the cash I give you." He pulled out a money clip, stacked with large bills and pressed several of them into her hand.

"Sure, fine. Who am I to argue with a bank robber?" She smiled at her own joke. It broke the ice. She knew when she was beat. Graham liked calling the shots and she hated to admit it, but she actually enjoyed following his dictates. "I hope I'm not putting Violet out of a job. But with the size of the house, she has her hands full."

"It's an ideal arrangement. The two of you can share the cooking. If you get really bored, you can help Violet with the housecleaning, too. I'm sure she could use the moral support. You know she doesn't have any family, right?"

"I...I didn't know that, actually. I confess I've been so preoccupied with training that I haven't really gotten to know her. I will, though. She's a grand character."

"You don't know the half of it."

"Really?"

"Yes, really."

Dana served her special fried chicken, with black eyed peas and Southern cornbread, which she made with buttermilk, jalapeno, sweet onion, eggs, sugar, etc. She served those two items with a crisp Caesar salad. Graham lit the candelabra that graced the formal table. He'd been fortunate to purchase the old mansion turnkey, including silverware. The aging owners were scaling down. It was a property match made in heaven.

Dana had set up the boys in the family room and made sure they had plenty to eat.

They dined to Tchaikovsky, symphony #5. Dana was in heaven, fast recovering from her disappointment. It was the best night of her life. She'd just been proposed to by the man of her dreams. She'd cooked up a formal dinner for the two of them, dined by candlelight and classical music and the wonderful company of her fiancé.

Violet had made Lasagne for the boys. They ate it at the kitchen table.

Graham waited until they were on dessert. Dana had bought Key Lime Pie and she served it to them. "You know what? There is a new, relaxed, harmonious atmosphere around here. I don't know that any of us realized how much pressure we were under. Honestly, Dana. With everything we've gone through, maybe we should just give up the idea of winning. Scrap looking for a new colt to train...I'll tell you what's really bothering me. I have a strong hunch that there *was* foul play. The tests will come back tomorrow as you know...if *Flaming Bullet* is found to have any kind of substance in his system that appears questionable...well, what's to stop the perpetrator from repeating the process with our next colt? Tanner will be in prison but it actually could have been someone else. We may never know for sure.

Dana set down her fork. "Graham...I can't believe you're going to roll over and play dead. Where is your...spunk? Your determination? Your goal of winning and donating the money to Israel? You must not walk away from this noble quest. I believe God wants to bless Israel through the generous donation you intend to give them when you win the purse. It's spiritual warfare. Because you *do* have a mission and a purpose, Satan wants to destroy your good deeds and thwart your purpose. But God is on our side. Having the Lord on your side is a majority, don't forget..."

Graham leaned back onto the comfortable, Jacobean chair and took a sip of the fine, red wine. He rarely drank. But tonight was a dinner just for the two of them to celebrate their engagement. "Honey, let's just have a peaceful, harmonious, enjoyable dinner. We'll talk business...tomorrow, if that's okay. Tonight, I just want to enjoy you, look at you, savor this amazing venture we've entered into...it is far more important that talking business." He peered into her eyes.

His gaze held her spellbound. "Oh Graham... I love you... I love you so much. I don't know how I managed to live this long without...without knowing that we would be together...forever." Tears filled her eyes. "Oh Graham. I'm so ecstatically, amazingly happy. I can't believe this is really happening. You're everything I've ever dreamed of and more..." She fought back sentimental tears laced with euphoric, heady joy. I guess if God wants us to have a winning colt...if he wants us to win the Kentucky Derby...he will cause it to happen. We just need to be sensitive to his leading." She took a long sip of the fine wine and set it down, admiring the fine crystal glass.

Graham lifted his glass in a toast. "To...us. To joy unspeakable. To a glorious, ecstatically happy life together." They toasted and clinked glasses. Graham looked heavenward. "Lord, thank you for this wonderful woman. Thank you for bringing her into my life even when I didn't think I needed or wanted anyone..." He was overcome with emotion and fought back the start of a few tears that were threatening to tumble down his cheeks.

"The horse training...maybe it was an exercise we needed to go through... maybe there was a lesson we needed to learn. Maybe God was more interested in us finding each other. Maybe the colt is a project we can work on together in the future..." Graham grinned and took her hand.

"Maybe you're right, darling. Maybe you're right." She smiled, peering into his eyes. He made her feel like she had been in a deep sleep all these years and had suddenly been awakened, suddenly knew what love and real living was all about. God was smiling down at them, and it felt just incredibly glorious.

"*Unless the Lord build the house, they labor in vain that build it.*" "Maybe we ran ahead of God. Maybe we just set our sights on winning without really seeking Him. I have found in my walk with the Lord, that much of it is about timing. *His timing...not ours.* He knows our life from beginning to end. We may not be ready for something he has for us. But if he opens a door for us, we need to walk through it whether we're ready or not...I don't think either of us was ready for this commitment we've made. It would be so much easier to just float along, fighting or ignoring the attraction. But you know what? Maybe one day God would wake up and say something like. "I've given these kids a great love for each other. They want to keep fighting the attraction? They want to busy themselves with everything but the great love for each other that I've placed in their hearts? Fine. They can do that. I've tried everything but clobbering them over the head with this powerful attraction, and they just didn't want to give in to it. Well, I'm glad they finally saw the light, because I was really thinking about pulling the plug." Graham's voice held a serious tone.

"Wow. That's quite a speech, Graham. Quite a speech, indeed. I...guess we were both so busy running from each other and using up all our energy doing it, maybe we didn't have enough left to focus on the colt. Maybe if we'd prayed diligently..."

"It's over, Dana. The race is over. We need to move on. When God closes one door, he opens another. We need to walk through this door called *Love* that God Almighty has opened for us. He gives favor to whomever he chooses... folks tend to forget that. They think *they* are calling the shots. Then they wake up one day and realize that God was in control the whole time..."

It was the most magnificent dinner and conversation and company she had ever experienced. She couldn't wait to spend the rest of her life with Graham and his sons. God had blessed her above and beyond her wildest dreams. *Praise his Holy Name!*

Dana was over the moon. She had prayed that she and Graham would get together, though at times she doubted they ever would. *Forgive me, Lord, for not trusting you.* She wanted to leap and dance and jump up and down with joy. Instead, she took a deep breath, grinned and said. "Well, it's about time you saw the light, Graham; it's been shining in your face for quite some time now."

He chuckled and it broke the ice. He picked her up right there in the formal dining room, which was closed off by the smoky, leaded glass door. It was totally private. He twirled her around and then took her in his arms and kissed her over and over and over again.

She was his. Forever. It had to be that way. This was from heaven and God had pre-ordained it. They were mere mortals following their destiny. This was what the songs were all about...and the plays and movies... She instinctively knew that this was the kind of rare, true love that got deeper, richer; the kind of love that just kept growing, the sort of joy that just kept moving upward to higher more magnificent, joyful and heavenly levels as the days went by.

~

They were married three weeks later with a small ceremony at the quaint, ancient white church that stood on the nearby hillside in town. The locals said it had been there over a hundred years. Dana was elegant in a simple, white gown. Graham, dashingly handsome in a tuxedo. Danielle wore soft blue. She sobbed throughout the short ceremony.

When it had concluded, Danielle handed Dana a note. She felt better knowing that she had fully confessed the rivalry she'd felt with Dana. She knew that God had forgiven her, because she asked him to. And she had finally come to terms with the sin and forsaken it. Dan quickly forgave her. She believed now, that she would be next in line for true love to sweep her away, the way it had swept her only daughter away.

THE END

BOOK TWO (COMING SOON)
KENTUCKY DREAMS

Chapter One.

Dana moved into the mansion as Graham's bride. Love was in the air.

The next morning Dana and Graham hand-in-hand strolled to the barn to do the chores. Will and Jay milled around, doing their chores. They were becoming surprisingly good at the job.

Dana smiled, raised her eyebrows and peered right into Graham's eyes. Her voice was soft, mellow. "Good morning, handsome." She whispered it so his sons could not hear.

Graham grinned. "Hey, good lookin'" He grinned over at her while he watered the horses.

Dana knew his sons were out of earshot, allowing him to say whatever he wanted to. He did. He strode toward her. "Are you free for lunch, gorgeous?"

"I...I don't know...I'd have to check my calendar." She wasn't being facetious, she had a lot going on. The man looked so remarkably handsome, he threw her off balance and that made it harder to recall her schedule.

She flirted with him. But now, knowing it was not a one-way street and he was now her husband, upped her confidence. "Where are you taking me?" She batted her eyelashes just for the fun of it.

"Anywhere you want to go, Princess." His tone was edged with seriousness.

She took it as a double entondre. *Was the man actually saying that she could call the shots?* She was on cloud nine. He looked so handsome and appealing in the blue fringed shirt, jeans and his well-worn cowboy boots. She suddenly had an impulse to throw her arms around him and kiss him. Would he scoop her up in his arms like she was a rag doll? Only one way to find out.

I must get out of the fantasy world. His sons are in the barn. Just then, something close to a miracle happened. They finished their chores and went hopping out of the barn in high spirits. "We're done, Dad. We're outta here." Their youthful voices rang with joy and mischief.

They were alone. Well, expect for the horses. He moved closer to her.

She took a heady whiff of some incredible masculine cologne. Her spirit soared with joy. He peered deeply into her eyes. They looked at each other, spellbound. This heady, unearthly wave of powerful emotions soared through her. A song ran through her mind. *I'm in love, I'm in love, I'm in love with a wonderful guy!* She wanted to dance with him, right here in the barn. Another part of her wanted to shout praise and thanksgiving to God Almighty for bringing this wonderful man into her life. Maybe she could do both at the same time.

A gunshot pierced the air. They stared at each in shock for a split second. Graham pushed her behind him. The sound startled the horses and several of them reared up neighing. One of them, the wild one, *Prince*, became totally spooked, rearing up, neighing. His powerfully muscular, shiny body seemed to fill the room. Graham locked the barn door, speed-dialed Will and Jay and then phoned the sheriff.

Dana was in shock. "What's goin' on?" She whispered nervously to Graham. "It's a...probably a warning from Tanner. Maybe he asked one of his boys to rattle us. He figures we are probably going to get back in the race for next season...maybe he just wants to spook us...he's a weird dude...a lot of stuff he does doesn't make a whole lot of sense."

"Jay. Stay in the house. Lock the doors. We heard a gunshot. The sheriff is on his way. Take the rifle from the hall closet. If anyone tries to enter the house, smoke them out. Holler *Freeze!* That outta stop the perpetrator in his tracks."

The dogs outside the barn were going nuts, barking up a storm. "So, looks like Tanner is trying to rattle us to get us to give up competing for the next Kentucky Derby. Doesn't know us very well, does he? All this does is make me more determined." Dana smiled. "Besides, they can only kill us once...and then we get to see Jesus sooner. Anyway, we're going to find an amazing colt and win the Derby. I really believe that, don't you?" Dana smiled at Graham. The dark bay Thoroughbred was unsettled and began whinnying again.

Suddenly the door burst open with a loud crack. Troy entered, aiming a shotgun at them. "Think you're gonna fool with my twin brother and live to tell about it, do ya?"

Dana could feel her eyes widen like saucers. She sensed Graham's mind racing a mile a minute. Dana signalled to the dark Bay and managed to get his paddock door open. The dark Bay Thoroughbred moved toward the gunman to protect her and shield Graham and Dana. He reared up. The surprise caught Troy off guard. Graham managed to grab his gun.

The sheriff and deputy sheriff burst inside."What took you so long?" Graham joked.

"We were tipped off. We were just driving into Sugarbush when you phoned." The sheriff said.

They handcuffed Troy. The sheriff smirked. "Hey, thanks for turning yourself in. It's going to be really easy from here on in. You're probably going to be able to keep your twin brother company."

"Maybe I'm Tanner. You can't tell the difference." He smirked.

"You're brother's in prison. Don't get cute. I'll look at your I.D. anyway" The sheriff nodded.

"Don't have any with me." Tory smirked again.

"All right, let's go Buddy. You'll fess up soon enough, if you want us to go easy on you. You want to play hardball? We'll throw the book at you. You're not gonna win." The sheriff's voice was cold steel.

"Let's go somewhere nice for lunch, Graham. We have a lot to talk about." Dana was shaking from the ordeal.

"I know just the place. It will be a surprise. He grinned at her.

"Perfect."

Dana realized she was shaking as she dressed for lunch. Neither Tanner nor Troy was going to stop her and Graham from pursuing their dream of winning the Derby. Dana went online to look for horse auctions and checked with the top horse farms in Kentucky. Suddenly, she stopped her frantic search. *Lord, I need to seek you first.* A scripture popped into her mind. *"In all your ways acknowledge Him, and he shall direct your paths."*

She went into prayer. Spiritual warfare was being waged over her, Graham and their dream. She prayed *Ephesians 6* over the situation. God wanted them to win, he wanted to bless them, bring them joy and bless his beloved Israel. Satan wanted to dampen their spirits, destroy their hard work and dedication to the pursuit of winning the purse. Dana would stand on God's promises. *"Greater is he that is in you than he that is in the world."* It wouldn't be easy. It would be a great challenge. But she was up to it and so was Graham and his sons. Yes, Will and Jay were growing up fast, and the insights, courage and humor and all the youthful stuff their spirits flourished with, sparred Dana on. Good things were about to happen. Great things even. She was deeply, passionately, crazily in love with Graham. And finally, it seemed he was coming to his senses and admitting it was not a one-way street. Would their love last? *Please God, make it last.*

"Hey gorgeous," He grinned over at her.

He had changed to a blue, tropical, short-sleeved shirt and actually wore a pair of crème slacks and topsiders. He smelled of some, probably pricey, masculine cologne and doubtless just stepped out of the shower.

She wanted to beckon him inside and kiss him and hold him and never let him go. *Get a grip, girl. It's a lunch date.*

The long, leisurely drive in the country was just what she needed. Finally, he stopped at beautiful restaurant Dana had never been to or heard of. *He sure is resourceful. It was called Villa De Vinci.* The terra cotta Villa featured a Mermaid waterfall at the entrance with water sprouting out of her belly. Twin Palm Trees flanked the stately entrance.

A Spanish man in his thirties greeted them with a warm smile. "Welcome. Lunch is served at 1:00. You are just in time. Please... let me show you to a seat." Grinning his welcome, he escorted them to an outdoor seating area. It was a virtual, tropical garden. Dozens of flourishing, huge Aloe Vera plants, Cacti and Palm tree varieties filled the area. Classical music wafted throughout the Villa. A strumming musician with a violin entertained with romantic tunes.

"Graham, I've lived in Lexington, Kentucky all my life and I never knew this place existed. Unless we're in heaven, this is all very strange..."

"We are...in a kind of heaven, my darling. I resisted you for such a long time, even knowing I was deeply in love with you...even knowing...that you are irresistible..." His tone was husky, tender. He peered deeply into her eyes.

"Graham. When did this place open? Why didn't I read about it?" Dana was stunned.

He laughed. "Because it is not officially open. I

contracted the place twenty years ago, that's when construction first began. It was never quite finished. When Myrna became ill, I shut down construction. When I knew I was planning to move to this state, I contracted the trades, hired a foreman and proceeded to finish the project. The concept would be something like Palm Beach's Mar-a-Lago. It would be a club with lunch served on Thursday, Friday, Saturday and Sunday. Guests would be given three delectible choices. And of course, there is an impressive wine cellar. The Villa has guest rooms making it a destination point for travellers and folks making the drive to the Derby and want to stay a few nights. There is also a screening room, Olympic-sized pool and tennis courts. The property sits on ten acres. And yes, it is a well kept secret. I opened up membership six months ago, and already we are close to capacity. It is mostly the horsey set and folks driving from other cities for the Kentucky Derby. You'll see a row of limos out front in the future. I had a strange hunch that something was going to go amiss—that's why I didn't open the club officially, this season and plan to have our celebration Derby party here. It will be opened next season. "

"When we win the Kentucky Derby?"

"Exactly. I'm a great believer in calling things that are not as though they are." Graham peered into her eyes.

Dana glanced around at the other guests. The horsey set...yes, of course. What a brilliant concept, Graham." Dana laughed.

A waiter set down two elegant, crystal flutes and bottle of cold champagne. "May I?" The young, Latino asked.

"Please." Graham grinned.

The waiter poured the champagne into flutes.

"Fine champagne for my beautiful wife. I shall call you Countess. Do you like the nick-name? " Graham grinned.

"Countess. I like it very much, Count Graham."

"To life together. May we live in joy, love and peace."

They clinked glasses in heady celebration.

Just as they were finishing lunch, they turned simultaneously as Troy walked in with a cute redhead. She had freckles and wore a pink floral, halter top dress and pink pumps with a matching purse.

Graham couldn't resist. "Join us Troy? Or is it your twin brother, Tanner? Oh no, I forgot, he's in jail."

Troy didn't skip a beat. He glanced over at his date. "We'll join some friends, Carol. You'll like them, I'm sure." He flashed an odd smile at Dana and Graham.

Graham pulled out two chairs and let Troy finish the honors while his date took a seat. "I'm Troy and this is my fiancé, Carol Dancer."

"*Are* you a dancer, Carol? You look like one." Graham peered at her, amused.

"I wear many hats." Her voice was velvety steel.

His accomplice, I bet. And I think this is Tanner. The game will be to discover whether it's Tanner or Troy. Could Troy have taken the rap for Tanner? Could they have switched I.D.'s? Graham loved games like crossword puzzles. Actually, challenges of any kind. "Champagne, Tanner? I'm guessing you already know the menu."

"You guessed correctly. I'm going with the Lobster Bisque and Cornish Hen with wild rice and shitake mushrooms."

"To..." Dana peered directly into Tanner's eyes. "Honesty, integrity and nobility" Everyone raised their glass in a toast."As long as we have chosen the noble sport of horse racing, it would seem appropriate that we conduct ourselves like nobility."

"Splendid concept." Tanner grinned.

"We shall win next year." Carol morphed from sweet to ice cold in seconds.

Dana glanced over at her. Her eyes were cold, lifeless, a dull grey. She sensed that behind the freckles, red hair and coy smile, lurked a Cobra; the most dangerous kind. She actually shivered. They'd clearly been followed here. What would happen next? Had Tanner paid someone to poison the food? Suddenly, she was very angry. *How dare he interrupt our romantic lunch? I'll let Graham handle this one. I'm out of my depth. Besides, Tanner is bigger than me and I wouldn't put anything past Freckle Face.*

Lunch was served. Graham was remarkably relaxed. Suddenly, it hit her. Graham set this whole thing up. He managed to lure Tanner into his web. It would be very civil. After lunch, the sheriff would appear and handcuff Tanner—maybe Freckle Face, too. Dana knew a Cobra when she saw one.

They were just finishing Zagblioni when the Sheriff and Deputy Sherriff walked it. "Good afternoon, Tanner and Carol. How very nice to see you. They grinned as they simultaneously and quickly handcuffed the pair.

"You creep." Carol's eyes were slits, her face a viscious mask of hatred.. She kicked at the Deputy Sheriff and hit his knee.

"Real smart, Carol Chalmers. Assaulting a police officer. Of course, it won't make much difference. You've been on the run for quite some time. And you have a lengthy list of charges. You've made a few smart moves in the past. This was a dumb move. You walked right into a trap."

Carol kicked furiously, to no avail. Dana thought she could see smoke coming out of her nostrils and ears. The woman was livid. "You idiot!" She spat at Tanner.

"No, you're the idiot. Freckles." He sneered. "I give them you and I get a reward for it...a little time off my sentence." He shot her a sarcastic sneer and then chuckled, cruelly.

Carol went nuts. She screamed.

The other guests in the restaurant were appalled, some folks began leaving the premises.

The sheriff spoke up. "Ladies and Gentlemen. My apologies. But as long as these two were on the loose, nobody was safe. We've got them now. And they've got charges as long as your arm..." The sheriff nodded to the Deputy Sheriff. He hustled the angry pair out of the Villa.

"Back to you, Dana. Where was I?"

Dana took a sip of champagne. " I need to sit back and figure out exactly what happened here..."

Graham peered over at her. "Do you want to have the reception here?" He grinned at Dana.

She was hearing things. How weird was that?

"P...Pardon?"

He grinned mischievously. "I asked you if you would like to have the reception here? The wedding reception, that is."

Dana's eyes grew as big as saucers. "W...What could you possibly mean by that statement, Graham?"

"What do you think I mean?"

"This is...a proposal?"

"Smart girl. Yes, Dana, darling, it is. I want you to be my wife. I love you...I've loved you from the moment I laid eyes on you. I fought it tooth and nail...but nothing worked. God ordained it. We need each other, darling. We're good for each other. We can walk hand-in-hand through life as God leads us..." He stood and took her in his arms.

In a few minutes, Dana moved apart. "Your sons...what about your sons?"

He grinned, mischievously. "Actually, it was Jay's idea. Both my sons kept badgering me to ask you to be my wife..."

"You're kidding right?" She laughed uproariously.

"Yes, I'm kidding, Dana. But they are good with it. They asked me if they thought you would mind cooking for them as well as me..." Graham smirked. "I told them that I thought you would love it. Am I right?"

"Ya, you are. I'm crazy about Will and Jay." She reached her arms up and circled his neck. "And...I'm crazy about you, too. What about the Kentucky Derby?"

"Our goals remain the same, Dana. And I have a strong hunch that we will be much more focused, now that we are a team. We'll be unstoppable. Quite honestly, I couldn't get you off my mind..." He kissed her again with intensity and fervor.

She had never before known this kind of magic. A heavenly, euphoric kind of heady joy soared through her entire being. This was somewhere close to heaven. She glanced heavenward. *"Thank-you, Lord, for hearing and answering my prayer."* The words were a soft whisper. No one but God could hear her.

Footnote.

Graham and Dana bought another three-year colt. They named him Soaring Liberty. Dana trained him with a fervor and lazer-like focus she had never before known. Graham took care of the myriad of challenges and details training a colt to win the Kentucky Derby entailed. They won the million dollar purse the following year and donated the winnings to Israel, fulfilling the promise they had made to God and each other.

The Kentucky Derby Winner's party was held at the private Palazzo just like Graham had always envisioned it would be.

They learned than Tanner had escaped from prison by hiding in a service truck. He had taunted authorities. Graham had laid a trap for him at his Palazzo. He was charged with horse theft. Bail, was of course denied, given that he'd jumped bail in the past. The sentence was twenty-five years with no chance of parole. Finally, they could breathe easy and enjoy their life.

You may enjoy these other books by Marlene

MARLENE WORRALL

Worrall

Angel in Shining Armor
Love Found in Manhattan

Made in the USA
Columbia, SC
03 May 2019